OLIVAY

Also by Deborah Reed

Things We Set on Fire
Carry Yourself Back to Me

As Audrey Braun:
A Small Fortune
Fortune's Deadly Descent

OLIVAY

DEBORAH REED

LAKE UNION
PUBLISHING

Published by Lake Union Publishing, Seattle

www.apub.com

Amazon, the Amazon logo, and Lake Union Publishing are trademarks of Amazon.com, Inc., or its affiliates.

ISBN-13: 9781477821411
ISBN-10: 1477821414

Cover concept by Andrew Reed
Cover design by Kerrie Robertson

Library of Congress Control Number: 2014921693

Printed in the United States of America

For my Westside students

We always imagine eternity as something beyond our conception, something vast, vast! But why must it be vast? Instead of all that, what if it's one little room, like a bath house in the country, black and grimy and spiders in every corner, and that's all eternity is? I sometimes fancy it like that.

—Fyodor Dostoevsky, *Crime and Punishment*

PART ONE

ONE

THOSE WHO SAW WHAT HAPPENED THAT MORNING never said a word about Will's long stride when he walked down the sidewalk, or the way his legs bowed slightly with every step. There was nothing in the police report about his hair flitting around his ears in the Santa Ana winds, or the dimple carved near the corner of his grin, but Olivay knew exactly how Will moved through the world, exactly how happy he would have appeared before he died.

According to witnesses, Will stepped out of the apartment building shortly before nine a.m., wearing a light gray T-shirt, dark jeans, and aviator sunglasses. He seemed to be texting with both hands, eyes on his phone while heading west. His leather messenger bag contained a laptop, wallet, two small notebooks, three black pens, and ATM receipts. Everything was later picked through in search of his I.D.

Olivay had been about to shower and run to work herself when the doorbell rang. Then her neighbor Mrs. Hightower was pounding on the door, screaming *"Olivay, Olivay!"* like a rising, frantic chorus, pulling Olivay into the hall, rushing her barefooted down four flights of stairs, wearing only a sheer nightgown, and out the front door where the wind charged her skin with a panic-stricken buzz. She'd understood before she'd even seen him, before she'd even slipped in her husband's blood that whatever had happened was worse than anything she could allow herself to believe.

She didn't know that a motorcycle had jumped the curb, collided with Will's chest, and crushed his skull against the ground, or that the driver had managed to scramble back onto the bike and speed off before anyone could catch the number on his plate. When a woman shouted, "The son of a bitch is gone!" Olivay thought she was talking about Will, splayed out inexplicably on the sidewalk.

She slumped down where he lay and cradled his head between her thighs. She pressed the sides of his face to stop the oozing, to stop his eyes from rolling back where she could only see the whites. "No, no, no," she said, and four different cell phone cameras captured her pleading. No one understood what she'd meant. Not the millions who would view the videos in the weeks to come, nor the bystanders aiming their phones. "Don't do that," Olivay said, not wanting Will to look up, to be frightened when he saw inside his own head.

The stench of burnt rubber, of warm blood on hot concrete would remain in her nose for weeks.

TWO

OLIVAY HAD TROUBLE CRAWLING OUT FROM UNDER THE duvet, its downy weight like arms, this quilt they had shared, this bed, everything familiar, everything as it was until her dreams severed into the bright white walls of noon.

Snow White.

"Not *Disney*," Olivay had said when she reached for the paint swatch.

"It's really Brothers Grimm," Will said.

"Either way, this *is* the perfect tone for the apartment. Clean and pure."

"Just like you," he said.

"Hilarious," she'd said, walking to the counter with the paper swatch. "The funniest man alive."

Snow White, like a premonition, like a joke that Will would never get about her dark hair and endless days of sleep.

When she opened her eyes, scenes flared across the white walls like starbursts—a kiss in London rain, sweaty hands and salty lips entwined in Sayulita, the first *I love you* whispered in this room in this bed—and Olivay would scramble to the floor, panting and sweating in the air-conditioned room. She never knew if the concrete walls prevented the neighbors from hearing her weep. If they were listening, they never said, and anyway, there was nothing left to do but press the heels of her hands into her eyes, catch her breath, and crawl back beneath the duvet. After that she didn't make a sound.

The first months were like this.

Impossible to stop herself from inventorying things Will would have held or seen or done for the very last time, and still others he would never come to know. It was three weeks before Olivay touched the coffee mug he'd used that final morning, and when she pressed her lips against the weak stain on the rim, she didn't feel him there, didn't taste him or smell him. The stoneware was cold and hard on her mouth, and she dropped it into the trash beneath the sink.

On his birthday, she watched Alfred Hitchcock and Ingmar Bergman films in bed because they were made before she and Will were born, and no connections could be drawn, no references to a time when Will existed. And then she couldn't stop thinking how he would never get a chance to see them, that she could never tell him how the female characters in Hitchcock's films were dangerously sexy women in peril, while Bergman's were cerebral and far more in touch with their own sexuality than the men were with theirs, and how different each story might have been had they been switched. Then she considered the possibility that Will *had* seen these films before he'd ever met her and had never mentioned them. It was impossible to fully know another human being. This thought disturbed her as much as any coiling through her brain.

She didn't answer when Will's mother called. Her own grief had become something of a simmering, personal burn, while Will's mother's remained fluid, massive, and unwieldy. "My only son," she'd cried to no one in particular at the funeral, and Olivay had hated herself for feeling irritated by the theatrics, the melodrama, thinking that at least his mother had *had* a son, two children in fact. As Will's sister had comforted this woman on one side, and her husband had shuffled over with open arms to *shush, shush, shush* her with his love on the other, Olivay had stood alone and childless and ten pounds too light in her sweltering black dress. The sun had beaten the sweat from her body that day, making her dizzy, forcing terrible thoughts into her head. She hated self-pity. She hated being around people who brought it out in her, and more than anything, she wanted to turn that shadeless expanse of lawn into her bed, just lie down and *sleep, sleep, sleep* until someone dug her a nice cool hole next to Will.

"What's the worst that could happen?" Will used to say, kissing her forehead whenever Olivay fell into a bout of anxiety, insomnia sharpening her vision in the dark. "And if the worst were to happen, could you live with the consequences?"

The answer was no, she could not.

It became harder to recall Will's face, this face she had seen from every angle for three years began coming to her in pieces— Nordic nose with pale freckles, blue-green eyes, and wisps of deep brown hair. His face turned into a *sense* of a face, his body into a sense of a man. Olivay didn't know if this happened to others left behind by the ones they loved. She was afraid to ask. Afraid to discover that she alone was to blame for allowing him to disappear.

Two years of dating. One year of marriage, until death did they part. A tiny little marriage, like a prologue before their real story began.

And what a story it was. *Widow* written on all the paperwork in her desk drawers. A widow with a life insurance policy that paid all of her bills.

A widow who began ducking out the back door to avoid the makeshift memorial—plastic flowers and candles and strangely intimate love letters addressed to Olivay, to Will, to Mr. and Mrs. Chilton (she had not taken his name so there was no Mrs. Chilton), appearing again and again during those first two months no matter how many times the super threw them away.

Will had been a journalist who'd covered homicides, a serial killer, corrupt politicians, and child rapists, but Olivay was sure he could never have imagined that the biggest story of his career would be his own mysterious death, complete with a viral video of his crushed head in Olivay's lap.

No, no, no. Don't do that.

A widow whose tragedy turned into a commodity, sponsored by the Industry of Grief.

Internet, newspapers, CNN. "We want to warn our viewers that the video we are about to show contains graphic content that may not be suitable for everyone."

Oh go fuck yourselves, Olivay whispered and wailed. She never saw this coming, never could have imagined how impossible it was to control.

"One can't help the comparisons to Jackie O," a morning show host chirped.

"You mean Jackie *Kennedy*," her cohost said. "She was still a Kennedy then."

"Right."

"Her dark hair, his head in her lap."

"The love between them. Like Camelot."

"Yes, Camelot."

Who had killed her husband? This was the mystery that kept the media interested in their story, along with the video of Olivay crying on the sidewalk. She had no memory of her reaction at first, not until hearing others speak and write of it recalled in her the sudden disassociation, the bleached silence in her head, the magnolia leaves twisting and flailing from the fierce winds; yet somehow in her mind they drifted slowly as if having all the time in the world, like sea grass deep beneath lazy blue waves. She remembered her head thrown back and the ugly animal anguish that escaped her throat. Those who were there said they could never forget the sound, never get it out of their minds, and those who watched it on video said it made them feel more human, more in love with the ones they loved. Horror and grief bulged the veins in Olivay's throat, the flash of her breasts through the nightgown sent an instinctual, carnal message to the brain, or so an expert on trauma explained on the six o'clock news—and it struck a chord, this essence of Woman, the beginning of us all, what it was to be human and love in the face of death. *An agonizing, yet beautiful form of artistic expression,* an abstract painter tweeted to his one million plus followers and was immediately told by hundreds of people to take it back, but instead he added, *Other primates have been known to grieve themselves to death,* and 856 people retweeted it like an act of forgiveness.

An open skull makes a licking, creaking sound. No one talked about that. No one knew that, for months afterward, a similar raspy groan could churn inside Olivay's own head for the better part of an afternoon.

THREE

THE TV. THERE WAS NO ONE TO SAY, *TURN IT OFF, OLIVAY.*

"And now, more on that story about the unsolved killing of William Chilton, journalist for *The Tribune*. The autopsy stated that his heart, gunned by the impact, jolted into cardiac arrest. The sad fact here, Miranda, is that according to the coroner, a defibrillator might have saved him if the motorcycle hadn't damaged his brain when the front tire struck his skull."

"Oh, that is just *so* sad. His poor wife."

"Sad indeed. Reporting to you live, I'm Ricardo Ortiz for *News at Six on 7.*"

"Thank you, Ricardo."

The Internet. There was no one to change the password and hide her from this soapbox of trolls, religious fanatics, lawn chair philosophers, amateur psychologists—all the message boards and chat rooms like some kind of casting call for the deranged.

Talk radio. There was no one to stop her from listening to the vulgar things they said, to the questions posed about why Olivay still lived in the building. "Seriously, why move? I heard it was a nice apartment. Now it's roomier." They laughed while telling each other it wasn't funny. They considered it hilarious when they said she probably wanted him dead. "Didn't you ever get so mad at your wife that you wanted her dead? You look around the place, picturing what it would be like to have it all to yourself. Come on! You know you have!"

There were times when Olivay wished for a gun. A revolver. She liked the sound of *revolver*. A *silver revolver* she could tuck inside a cedar box lined with blue velvet on the mantelpiece. A revolver to take out every now and then and point at the TV like Elvis Presley had, only she wouldn't shoot the screen. She didn't think she would.

Everyone knew major life decisions should not be made in the first year of grief. This seemed the only advice she could follow without trying.

The man on the motorcycle. Who was he? Where was he? *Let's talk about that.* Everyone wanted to break that story. Break it right in half. "We are counting on the public for leads," the police kept saying. The rider's face had remained hidden inside the bulk and glare of his helmet. "Someone out there knows something, and we're hoping that the fifty thousand dollar reward will encourage him or her to come forward."

No one came forward. Everyone came forward, mostly to each other. *I wouldn't be surprised if it was my neighbor, the reckless guy with the motorcycle. My brother. My stepfather. My ex-boyfriend. It was not my son! Could it have been a woman?* The hotline lit for days, slowed after weeks, until the calls trickled to several a month. The tire tracks matched nearly every bike in town. Who was he? *US Weekly* posed the question in grocery store aisles. *LA Couple's Tragic End. Who Killed William Chilton?* Maybe Motorcycle Man was one of the trolls making fun of Olivay's life on the Internet. Maybe he was the sharp-tongued troll lashing out at the troll. Or the woman leaving plastic flowers on the sidewalk, or the twenty-year old who processed her electric bill, or the man offering Sunday mass behind a priestly robe. Maybe he was the doctor who prescribed her Xanax.

Several weeks after his death she was standing in line at Von's buying cereal, milk, and bananas, when she overhead a woman in the line next to her say, "Don't look now, but it's that *Olivay* woman. That widow whose husband's head . . ."

What the hell do they want? she said into the dark that night, but it was Will she was asking. Will, she was sure, knew the answer.

They have mundane lives, he whispered at the edge of her ear. *They love it when something finally happens.*

But why?

It makes them feel fortunate.

Because they aren't me?

Yes. Or me.

Why, why, why? She begged for someone to tell her that everything happened for a reason.

Of course not, her mother would have said if she, too, hadn't passed years before. *No. No. Look at me, Olivay. Look at my own life. There is no sense to be made in this world. No answer that is going to make it all right, so please stop taking everything so hard to heart.*

Like those long days in bed, waiting for twilight to settle around her, so weary she could not reach for the lamp. She often dreamed she was in the hospital again, everything playing out as it had in real life—a doctor stalling to explain how Will was already dead. *DOA.* The hissing, staticky shot of white light around her eyes, the pale blue chairs spinning as she cried out, a social worker pulling her by the elbow to a cold green room where she shut the door and told Olivay that people in shock behave in ways very different from what the situation calls for. She said Olivay should stop, just stop, and try really hard to *think.* Olivay had demanded they sew Will's head back together. "He's got to get to work," she said, and insisted they help him before he really *was* dead. She called them obscenities she'd never used in her life—*cocksuckers* and *pigfuckers*—until they held her down, until they got in her face and made her understand what she refused to see.

FOUR

SOMETHING FINALLY HAPPENED.

It was early spring, and the Santa Ana winds had returned to Los Angeles, threatening fire along the dry, windswept canyons. Will had been gone for just over a year, and for the third time that week Olivay needed to get out of the apartment. She'd twice gone to Levine's Coffee Shop down the block, and even though she hadn't stayed longer than it took to drink a small coffee, it was still something, her going out like that, sitting in public, less afraid of the world than she'd been in the months before.

She began to reclaim things she'd long since put away, like linen blouses and summer skirts and the turquoise necklace in the bottom of her jewelry box. *Can you clasp this for me, honey?* She clasped it herself, and now it hung around her throat between the two points of the collar of the white blouse Will had always loved on her.

Today, already late afternoon, she needed to get out and stay out, and she pulled on her summer sandals, picked up the novel she'd abandoned six months ago, and—with the exception of habitually slipping out the back of the building—she began to feel like someone, anyone, other than herself.

Levine's still resembled the bar it used to be. Paneling, neon jukebox, red vinyl booths and rickety wooden tables along the wall where Olivay wedged between the steampunk coffee machine and a sign that read CHEAPER THAN YOU THINK. It was easy to imagine poker and beer, dirty ashtrays and funnels of tobacco smoke. Patsy Cline came over the jukebox and Olivay remembered what it was to feel lighthearted, to be content with coffee and a book.

She was thinner than she used to be, her hair longer with flyaway ends she'd trimmed herself, but she was likely still recognizable, maybe she was, and a barista with a myrtle leaf tattoo on her arm whom Olivay hadn't seen this week smiled knowingly when she ordered coffee. "Enough room for cream, right?" the woman said, and Olivay lifted a hand in the air, unsure of what she'd meant to do until she realized she wanted to touch the barista's shoulder and thank her for knowing her from before, from the time when Olivay was just another architect with an office down the street, a married young woman who lived and worked on the block, stopping in once a day to say, "Enough room for cream, please."

"Yes, thank you," Olivay said with more sincerity than was called for, while outside the winds marked the season, spinning clouds of yellow pollen through dry desert air, sweeping cups and straws from overflowing trash bins on the streets. The swift charge of positive ions made Angelenos even more uneasy than they already were (droughts, earthquakes, traffic, impossible odds of "making it"), but Levine's had offered up a reprieve, a hidden little pocket of peace.

Within minutes she was lost inside her novel about a woman who rode an Italian motorcycle (yes, she could read it now—slowly) through the salt flats of Nevada as a way of making art, which was the part that really interested Olivay, even if it was clear that the story would come to no good end. That was fine. She could handle it. Let these things happen to other people, she thought, and remained consciously undisturbed by the woman's mode of transportation, which was, along with the writing, handled with impressive expertise. This was progress. *The Two Ps,* Olivay's therapist used to say during the weeks Olivay saw her after Will's death. *Progress through Process,* the woman repeated as Olivay struggled to articulate the murk she waded through each morning just to sit down and take a piss. More than once Olivay had to stop herself from saying *Pain and piss and pox also start with P,* until ten weeks into things when she shouted that very sentence on her way out of the windowless, lemon-colored room. It was only then that the first wave of relief from Will's death billowed up inside her. She stood at the door with a vague certainty that a slightly improved life was waiting on the other side, and she would never again have to lay eyes on rubbery, artificial plants and mass-produced furniture with royal blue upholstery, or feel the dreariness of the therapist's office that depressed her in ways she could not explain without sounding self-indulgent, without launching into a lecture on the role environments played on moods, not to mention mental health. All along the generic milieu in that office had made her feel like a common customer being offered the same facile answers as the next damaged person, who was certain to be damaged in her own particular way. Oh, how glad Olivay was in that moment to think that she would never again have to hear the relentless whir of the white-noise machine that kept the patients in the waiting room from hearing sobs and cries and stutters and shouts that began with *P.*

"Mind if I share this table?" a man said.

Olivay looked up from her novel to see a tall, tousled-haired blond dressed in faded Levi's, a white T-shirt, and well-worn Chukka boots. The tips of his long fingers rested on the table.

She snapped the book shut and peered around the room, surprised to find it so full.

Normally she *would* mind sharing her table. She would mind it very much. But the easy way this guy's shoulders fell to one side as if he were aloof to the world, aloof to *her*, made his smile more attractive, and sincere. He was already attractive without that smile. She leaned back and crossed her freshly shaven legs, tugged the hem of her skirt over her knee, though, really, who was looking under there? "Feel free," she said. "I don't need the entire table."

"Thank you. I'm Henry Wilkins, by the way." He settled across from her. His mix of fair hair and dark eyes was striking, his name more suited to an old man, though he appeared her age—mid-thirties at most—and Olivay caught herself staring, struggling to piece it all together.

"But you can call me Jack," he said.

"Okay, Henry," Olivay said, surprised by the bold familiarity she felt toward him. "I bet your mother called you Henry."

"She did. Still does."

"Have we ever met?" she asked.

"Maybe you've seen me here this week. I finally got the nerve to come over and introduce myself."

You call that nerve? she wanted to say. She wanted to laugh. "I'm Olivay," she said, wondering if he already knew.

"Olivay," he said, and his coffee-colored eyes, black as her own, held her steady.

Within minutes she could see how his name seemed to suit him—a little old-fashioned, recalling another time, another place, the way he counted to three, beginning with his thumb. Who did that? Her mother, born in Europe during World War II, had done that. In the States, it was always the pointer, middle, and ring finger, in that order. But when the conversation turned to dogs, Henry used his thumb to begin counting the breeds he'd had as a kid. "Springer, Cocker, Irish Water."

"All Spaniels," she said.

"Gun dogs," he said, and got her to tell about a cat she'd had growing up. She hadn't thought of Oskar in ages and here she was explaining to him her fondness for the cat's pointy ears, how the white tips appeared to have been dipped in turpentine, erasing the solid gray of his body. "Oskar fetched little felt balls like a dog," she said, "which did not make him a better cat."

Their smiles lasted too long. Olivay was first to look away.

"I just noticed the tea they serve is the same I had years ago in London," Henry said, as if searching for something to fill the silence that had risen between them. He sipped his coffee. "I haven't seen it anywhere since."

Olivay couldn't stop the memories from rushing forward, the Georgian architecture, her fingers running along porous London Stock bricks, the laughter as she and Will cut their sightseeing short for the small hotel with florid sheets, a camouflage of prickly, sprawling roses across the quilt, wallpaper, and drapes. *Making love in The Briar Patch with my baby,* Will sang as Olivay pulled him toward her on the bed.

"Did you spend much time over there?" Olivay asked, feeling a strain in her left eye, a twitchy, nervy kind of squint, which she rubbed until it quit.

"Not really. Just that one time. I was taking a break from all the stuff I'd done right after college—working for the Peace Corps, and then woofing in Germany—"

"*Woofing?*"

"Oh. Sorry. It's an acronym for working on organic farms. I picked turnips and carrots. The farmer basically paid me in turnips and carrots."

"What a deal," she said.

"Yeah. The Peter Rabbit package."

Olivay had not smiled this much in nearly a year. "And what, if you don't mind me asking, inspired you to woof?"

Henry glanced at the floor and scratched behind his ear. "I don't know. Just being young, I guess." He massaged his wrist, pressing his thumb down unusually hard over the tendons, or so it seemed to Olivay. *Body language*, her mother used to say. *Sum up a person within seconds by studying the body.* Her mother, California Bohemian by way of Warsaw, Poland. *It's metaphorical. Don't look at me like that. The CIA uses it, for God's sake.*

"I was actually staying in Windsor Safari Park just outside of London," Henry explained, "with a friend who worked in the water show. I spent a few weeks checking out the city, reading in coffee shops. Not much else."

"You stayed *inside* the Safari Park?"

"I was broke." He continued to knead his thumb up and down the artery, and the only metaphor Olivay could think of was that he wanted to slit his wrist.

"The guys in the water show had an extra trailer where they let me sleep for free. It was pink inside and out. The 'tin confectionery' we called it. Well, one guy called it something else, which I won't repeat in mixed company."

"Ha," Olivay said, thinking of a group of guys joking about Henry climbing in and out of the pink day and night.

"I know," he said. "Anyway, there was no running water, the only bathroom was in a small house next door, and the weather was a steady dose of miserably cold rain."

An accent trailed on *miserably*, as if Henry had once been British himself.

"I'd wake up to the sound of elephants' trumpeting, or these long mournful cries of peacocks. It was crazy. Every now and then a lion roared so loud it was like a cyclone had hit. Then complete silence, except for the rain."

Olivay felt a peculiar awareness in her body, airy and anchored to the chair at once.

"How strange," she said.

"You mean incredibly weird."

"I mean beautiful."

Henry let go of his wrist. "Well. No. Yes, I mean. I thought so, too."

Olivay wasn't sure she'd ever heard a peacock cry, but she knew they sounded like babies in distress, and she thought of her once-imagined future with Will. *A daughter who inherits your eyes and my temper,* she'd said.

And a boy with your brains and my stupendous schlong, Will had responded.

You are horrible! She'd laughed, swaying in their embrace like a tiny slow dance in front of the kitchen sink.

"I don't know why," Henry said, "but I was especially happy after one of those roars. All that quiet before the noise started up again. Like the world reset."

Olivay glanced at her hands, at the shredded napkin she'd torn without realizing.

Will's death had robbed her of so many things, not least of which was conversation. No one sat easy with her now. To be young and widowed was an aberration, a darkly curious digression, a reminder of how cruel life could be, and it lifted off her skin like fine, toxic fumes. No matter what she spoke of—design, the weather, her lunch—others heard the undertow, the story beneath the story, The Obvious Monstrous Thing. Her loss had turned her into an embarrassment of sorts to everyone she met. At night, she lay in bed replaying all the weary mouths too careful with words, hands in pockets, eyes searching for anything other than Olivay to settle upon. More than once she'd tried distracting others from the mood she'd caged them in. *So, tell me about you. What are you up to, how are the kids, where are you working these days?* But people didn't seem to want her voice in their ears, her eyes catching a glimpse of all they did not say. One after the other they scurried in the opposite direction, and Olivay watched as the burden was tossed from their shoulders, like a blanket so thick she could nearly catch it in her hands.

"And the Peace Corps, too?" she slipped in as a way of staying with the conversation. "Which country were you in?"

"The Central African Republic," he said, "or CAR, for short." He turned his face toward the line of people waiting for coffee.

"Oh." She nodded, knowing nothing at all about the CAR, quite sure she couldn't even locate it on a map.

"Sorry," Henry said. "I thought I recognized someone." He was looking at her again, and they were on to the next thing—traveling by train—Henry saying how much he loved the rhythmic chug, the hypnotic escape. Olivay couldn't recall the last time she'd been on a train. Was it London? She couldn't recall the last time she'd traveled anywhere beyond her own block, other than Christmas, when she'd forced herself to attend a former coworker's holiday party on the Eastside—so she ended up telling Henry about the mistletoe in every doorway of the small, mid-century home where fifty people shuffled through the rooms with peppermint cocktails, telling client jokes, and reaching for one another to exchange too many hugs and flirty kisses while their partners pretended to approve. And how all of that laughter was just too loud for Olivay's ears, and she'd crawled into the Womb Chair in the back corner along the glass wall of the living room. The only way to speak to her was to cross the open space, come close, and lean in, and no one wanted to do that, but she didn't tell him no one wanted to do that.

She couldn't quite read the look on Henry's face.

"I'm sorry." Olivay looked down. "I don't know why I told you all that."

"No, no," he said, "I'm glad you did." She glanced up again and his eyes tunneled straight into the back of her mind, where her thoughts scattered and slipped and groped for something solid to hold on to, and it was no use at all because she could see him look-ing into The Obvious Monstrous Thing as if it were a dollhouse, all its rooms neatly set on display.

She didn't ask if he knew who she was. She didn't want to know the full truth, not yet. And so she didn't tell him that the only per-son to speak to her at the party was Eileen, the receptionist at the office, who'd crossed the room to tell Olivay how the Robinsons and Zieglers—owners of homes Olivay had designed—had received phone calls from a tabloid, because that was the other story cov-ered in *Architect Today* e-newsletters—*Promising Architect's Career Set Back By Tragedy*, or something like that—and then Eileen had walked away, allowing the tawdry scene to resonate in the space that grew between them. After that, Olivay had drunk too many Evergreen Swizzles until someone toted her off to the guest room from which she'd snuck away during the night.

"Do you like these people you work with?" Henry asked.

"I quit," she said.

"Oh."

"But no," she said, understanding the truth of it only now. "I guess I never did." This made her laugh, and she was still laughing when she told him how, the morning after the party, she'd discov-ered a black wooden Eames crow in her purse that she must have stolen on her way out. She'd barked the same kind of laugh then, too, standing alone in her spacious loft apartment with a hangover and a smooth, weighty bird in her hands. This person was who she'd become, but she didn't say that part to Henry. She didn't say that denying this truth exhausted her more than the prospect of liv-ing with herself. Phone calls from her coworkers trickled and faded away, and this came as a relief that also hurt her shabby little feel-ings, even though she rarely picked up, so who could blame them? Still, to be rid of them was a welcomed freedom that shamed and grieved her at the same time. She was fond of the eyeless, black bird lurking like Poe's Raven on her balcony windowsill and sometimes found herself standing next to it, idly caressing its hard, bald head.

But now? *Something happened.* Here was Henry, breezing his way into her life without warning, never casting his eyes to the floor, not once speaking down to her as if she were a lost and frightened child. Even as she'd stashed herself against the back wall, he'd found his way to where she was and offered her gun dogs and lions and reached down to pull up memories of Oskar, and she suddenly recalled something she'd once read about how the most beautiful things in the world were the most useless. *Peacocks and lilies, for instance.*

"And, I don't know," Henry said, the conversation somehow continuing on, going everywhere at once, like chatter between old friends. "It was always so much easier to know what I *didn't* want than what I did," he said. "How about you? What don't you want?"

"To feel helpless," she said, jumping back in, not caring if it was too personal or irrational or completely unsuitable for a stranger to hear. "I never want to feel helpless again."

He eyed her mouth, her throat, her chest. *What might have happened if they hadn't been sitting in a crowded room?* She'd never been filled with so much desire within minutes of meeting someone. *What exactly was this?*

A first step through a doorway where Will had never gone, could never go, could never imagine what she was thinking, could never see what she was about to do.

What's the worst that could happen? And could she live with the consequences?

Maybe Henry knew exactly who she was. Maybe he had no idea.

"What do you say we go for a walk?" Olivay said.

Henry was quick to his feet.

FIVE

FIRST THING IN THE MORNING, A GARBAGE TRUCK EMPTIED the large bin in the alleyway behind Olivay's apartment. Metal clobbered against metal, and the enormous racket rattled through the open window above the bed. She was used to this. It wasn't the thing that woke her. She was startled instead by the touch of warm fingers on her shoulder, by the fact that she was sharing the same quilt, the same pillow with a stranger. And what they'd done to each other with alarming urgency—the buttons on her blouse torn loose, hands clenching so fiercely that Olivay closed her eyes now, remembering, tracing her arm for bruises, smiling to herself, wondering about his arms, too. Her lips felt raw and dry to the touch.

She was naked except for the turquoise necklace she'd clasped herself the day before, and she fumbled and squeezed the stones between her fingers—her body language revealing who knew what; all she could think about was how nice and cool the silver felt against her skin and how nice it was to have something to clutch, like a crucifix in her fist.

"Good morning," whispered a man who was not her husband.

"Good morning," Olivay answered, lying stiff on what used to be Will's side of the bed.

It was barely seven a.m., but the sun was already hot against the east-facing windows, and if it weren't for the clamor of the truck, they would have heard the wood and metal panes crackling and pinging as the dry heat sucked what little moisture had formed overnight. She'd once said to Will that the noise was like a tiny, abstract orchestra, and he looked at her the way parents look at children—amused by this adorable little thing. She hated when he did that. She could never get him to stop.

The truck's engine continued to grind so loudly that Olivay and Henry couldn't have had a conversation even if they'd wanted, and anyway she didn't feel like mentioning the mini music hidden above their heads.

She remembered the LA Marathon was today, and runners would soon be passing by her apartment at the front where the balcony was.

It grew quiet and Olivay lay on her back, stretching her arms above her head, listening as some other man zipped his jeans, buckled his belt, and *ship-shipped* his socked feet all the way across the glossy concrete of the open apartment to the front door, to his shoes.

"I'm sorry," he said. "I need to leave."

"I see that," she said, her head still on the pillow but watching now.

His hand rested on the oversized deadbolt, his backpack hung from his shoulder. "I wish I could stay."

No one has asked you to stay.

He appeared awkward, nervous in a way he hadn't been before.

The light of a new day had arrived with a cool detachment, a distant, neutral gaze. Olivay couldn't quite believe what she'd done, and even though she never asked him, she wasn't actually convinced that Henry hadn't already known her name before she told him, and yet, how relaxed he'd been, how comfortable with her body, her bed, the bed she had shared with Will, and never once saying it, never once mentioning The Obvious Monstrous Thing.

"So. Yeah," he offered. "I've got to get going."

"Okay," she said.

The dim light in Levine's and the dull yellow glow of her bedside lamp hadn't done justice to his wavy sun-streaked hair, or the warm golden tan on his cheeks and arms. A surfer? A gardener? He hadn't mentioned either of those, just the woofing from years ago. *KAPOW* she used to say when Will dressed for a wedding or his niece's graduation or a dinner date, including evenings spent at *Fortuito*, an Italian restaurant they'd affectionately renamed *Casa del Perdono*—House of Pardon—because it was where they often made up after a fight. Crab cakes, pasta, and wine. Soothing hackles, stitching holes. She loved Will's clean, citrusy cologne, even though it was nothing more than pheromones engineered to manipulate her urges, but so what. Sometimes a husband and wife could use a little help. *KAPOW*, hot husband in the house, ladies. Mine, mine, mine, and he was, all hers, even when she didn't want to go to *Casa del Perdono*, even when she refused to acknowledge the nice shirt, when all she saw was the bright, silent room swelling with a million dust motes that seemed to add weight to the air, making it harder to speak, to say *I'm sorry*.

KAPOW. She liked the shadow of whiskers on Henry's cheeks, and she wondered what he thought of her in the light of day, a bit spindly and pale, eyes sunken and bigger than they used to be, as if she were strung out, or pretending to be, like the young women with knobby knees cast in magazine shoots for shoes.

"I understand you need to leave," she said. "It's not a problem. Really. Listen. Have a great day."

Gusts smacked the windows and startled them both.

"The winds again," Olivay said.

Henry nodded as if he were about to say more but changed his mind, and she thought of his open-eyed kiss from last night, that wistful need unmistakable, like young-love longing, the same look Olivay had feared she may have had on her own face until she'd thrown him off and taken him in her mouth to set things straight.

"Okay," Henry said, relieved. "You have a great day, too." He continued standing with the door towering behind him. "By the way, your place is awesome." He drew a long breath and Olivay noticed how stale the air was, as if breathed too many times. She would open the windows all the way, regardless of the heat, as soon as he was gone. "The furniture," he said. "That Egg Chair. I've always loved those."

"Thank you." Was he trying to impress her? If so, he had. She'd traveled all over Southern California on a moment's notice to find the mid-century pieces, and across to Palm Springs for the original Eames lounger in mint condition. The Henning Norgaard coffee table was the exception, a surprise from Will on her birthday, its glass top so solidly built that when she beat it with her fists one night—long before Will was dead—it appeared to be indestructible.

That temper of yours.

As if I have no reason to be angry.

You don't, Olivay.

So you say.

"We planned to sell the place once the renovations were finished," Olivay said, the *we* somehow mentioned on purpose, though she didn't know what she was trying to prove. "And look, the renovations are finished."

"Oh," he said.

"You want to buy it?" she asked.

"Are you serious?"

"No. I don't think I am. Maybe I am."

"What's that?"

"Never mind."

She flung her arm across her mouth to stop herself from telling him how she'd already sketched the build-out for their new house in Silver Lake. That the place was in escrow when Will died, but his death made no difference to the owners who refused to return the deposit. She wanted to say that people could be so cruel. And to say, too, that she couldn't help wondering what it might have been like to live in a house where *bad vibes*—as her mother would have said—lingered in the rooms and speculating if she and Will would have been happy there after all.

"Did you say something?" Henry asked.

"No," she said, but wasn't even sure. Sometimes it was hard to keep track of what came from which direction in her mind, as if she were missing a compass. She didn't quite remember how to spend this much time with another person.

Henry thumbed a text into his phone. Their conversations had never circled back to the kind of work he was doing now, and she kept thinking of him as a farmhand. All that white-eared cat talk, crying peacocks, and turnips. They'd talked about books and films (Hitchcock and Bergman, which he'd seen), and all the places they'd traveled. Henry had lived all over the world it seemed, and she'd wanted to know more, but then they'd gone off on food and coffee and what kind of pizza they should order, and after it was delivered they laughed like pot-smoking teenagers over how incredibly good it tasted—"My god, my god," they said, like the sex itself, so ridiculously good—and then they reached for one another a second time, their breath spiced with dough and sauce, and went at it like the first, with the same fierce greed.

Where exactly did he live? The Eastside, he'd said, Echo Park or Los Feliz, or maybe he had a house, a wife, a baby in Silver Lake. It was as good as any truth he could be hiding from her. Maybe he was a serial killer. Or a prostitute waiting at the door for her to pay.

"I guess I need to use the bathroom," Henry said.

"Of course. Feel free."

He went into the small room with its warehouse-size door. Once closed, no sounds could be heard either way. It was like he was gone. She could hear herself breathe.

He came out moments later and stalled again with his hand on the deadbolt. The quilt was draped to her waist, the morning sun like a spotlight on her breasts, and the silver in her necklace sparked at the corner of her eye. Henry shifted his feet as if wanting to speak but couldn't seem to look directly at her. They had bared something raw before its time. Not just sex, more than sex—an intimacy gleaned from all the words she said and didn't say when she came, the deep whisper of her breath in his ear, a grief she was sure still hung in the room. She had allowed this stranger to witness her pleasure, and then glance around her home and absorb the quiet residue of her pain.

"I might stop at Levine's," Henry said.

"Hm." She tapped her lip. Her crooked smile was innocent and criminal at once, according to her late husband. *Late*, as if he hadn't yet arrived home from work. *Late*, as if she were still expecting him to show up any minute now and let loose about his grueling day.

Tap, tap, tap on her lips and she could hear her mother saying, *Don't lock your words inside your mouth.*

"So . . ." Henry opened the door slightly to the outside hallway, putting Olivay in full view of the neighbors should they walk out, but it was Henry she wanted to save from embarrassment. She pulled the quilt over her chest.

"The sticky buns are pretty tasty," she said.

Will would have laughed.

"Sounds good," Henry said.

"I was lying in bed just like this right before he died," she said, and quickly bartered with her own mind not to tell about the way she'd been laughing when Will kissed her entire face. How she now thought of him every time she applied moisturizer and makeup from her blue bottles, every time she brushed her hair, picturing the human head as nothing more than a tiny walnut under the right circumstances. *Don't mention how Will had peeked beneath the quilt and into my nightgown at my breasts.* How his eyebrows raised in a tease as if he didn't know what he might find under there. How he slid her straps to the side and kissed each nipple with a tiny suck, and said, "I love you, ladies," and then he kissed her face, her closed eyelids. *Don't mention the thing I never told anyone, not even the therapist, about how I said there wasn't enough time, that he had to get to work, and forced him out the door and onto the sidewalk to meet his death with precision timing.*

"I'm really sorry." Henry peered into the hall as if he couldn't take her any more, and then he looked right through her again, and she was certain he had known all along about Will.

She was so damn sick of herself.

She lifted the quilt to her collarbone.

"So. Right. Sticky buns," Henry said.

Why didn't he just leave? Who was he texting? Maybe he was just pretending to send a message.

"Yeah," she said. "If you like that sort of thing."

Henry didn't smile, and in that moment she didn't care to know what he liked and what he didn't.

He slipped a hand in the front pocket of his jeans. "Better than turnips and carrots," he said with a swift, warm smile, and the distant spell Olivay had fallen under began to break.

"Well." He pulled his hand out and eyed his phone. "Can I bring you something back?"

Oh. She was not expecting that.

"That's very sweet," she said. "But I'm going to shower and get some stuff done today." It wasn't a lie. The early morning liveliness that had once been a part of her personality—a part that used to drive Will crazy as he watched her from behind his a.m. fog—kicked through her bones. The upshot of finally getting a good night's sleep after a year of fitful dreams. Or the winds. Or the sex. Or all of it at once. "Thank you, though," she said, feeling changed, feeling as if something other than this was still about to happen. "For everything."

The room seemed to shrink when she looked away.

"Last night is still with me," he said.

A tender heat traveled between her thighs and up into her chest where it settled into a strange and not unpleasant grief. His voice in her apartment was foreign, eerily misplaced, like a television running in an empty room. Turn it off. Look away. He did not belong here. It wasn't meant to go any further than this. She'd imagined him having the same thought earlier, perhaps worrying that their sleeping together meant that she would need him long afterward, that he might be stuck with someone mental. If he had felt that way, he didn't seem to now.

She was nodding at the quilt when the door closed, and even though she didn't expect him to be standing there, she was still surprised to look up and find him gone.

SIX

SHE MOVED AROUND IN A STARTLED KIND OF DAZE, thinking of her face in his hands, his fingers weaving down her body, soft and warm, his mouth on her neck and then the shock waves beneath her skin, shuddering her back among the living. The way she'd fallen asleep so easily against his shoulder, so deeply gone it was as if she'd been drugged, forgetting he was there when she woke, and then the inescapable past tugging with that sly, encroaching guilt when she remembered.

It had been nearly an hour since Henry walked out the door, and in his absence, Olivay felt an energetic rustling, an unfurling all around her like a flag snapping in the wind. Her body moved through the apartment as if grasping it for the first time, the smooth hard feel of a glass in her hand, ice water slipping down her throat, plush throw rugs combing the soles of her bare feet. And when she opened her old tackle box full of supplies, it felt like spring, the familiar scent of lead and ink as potent as cherry blossoms, transporting her back to the years before Will, before software did everything on a screen, back to when her designs began with the smell and sound of a sharpened pencil on crispy trace paper. She caressed the thin-tipped markers and triangles, the dirty, white eraser and glue, all pieces of the person she used to be.

There were so many things she'd forgotten, things she'd missed without realizing, and now the realization, surprisingly, didn't come with a sting. *Tell me your three favorite things*—a game she and Will used to play, and how quickly the answers could change over time—favorite foods, favorite books, favorite places to visit in the world. It was a way of assessing their lives, each other, the future they would share. *Tell me your three favorite answers*, Will once asked. *You, you, and you*, she'd answered, and now her heart made a queasy little leap when she wondered if this were still true.

Favorite things she'd missed? She was surprised at how simple they were. The pleasure of gliding the heavy, clear-paned windows sideways with their hefty suck and seal, as tight as a submarine's when they closed. How she loved the sound as much as the solid engineering, the conceptual, contemplative design.

What else had she missed? Standing in the middle of a room, rearranging its contents, as simple as tossing a soft lambswool throw across the dark leather lounger, stepping back to have a look, the satisfaction so completely uncomplicated. Will once took a photo of her on his phone doing this very thing, and then he'd kissed her on the temple and showed her how the light made her look more beautiful than she already was. *If that is even possible,* he'd said.

She'd missed the awareness of light. It had been her job to understand what a blazing sun or cast of moonlight could do to walls and windows and views at different times of the day and year, the way the color of a floor could vary by the hour, and all of this alchemy rooted out and conceived long before a house was even built.

Weeks before Will died she had raised a vintage cocktail glass toward him, toasting the setting sun on a Saturday evening, and the happiness he saw in her face came from the honey-brown glow of bourbon tinting her fingers through the glass, a light that filled her with an inexplicable joy.

She had let go of so much for so long, and yet she was starting to see that everything had been waiting for her, as if on the other side of a door. All she had to do was push through. Will was never coming back. But dancing and sketching and the peculiar meditation that collected inside her when she cleaned the apartment had never really gone away. Will used to tease her about finding solitude in a vacuum. From *a vacuum,* she'd say, and the shtick barely ever got old.

And so she began by putting in her earbuds and turning up what had once been her and Will's favorite artists at one time or another— Van Morrison, Lloyd Cole, and Richie Havens—*Ooh-oo child, things are gonna be easier.* She had forgotten that music hadn't always stirred a gloomy, forlorn ache in her chest. It shimmied lightly across her skin as she spun across the floor. Adrenaline pumping, her dust rag sweeping, pausing long enough for her pencil to stream across the paper on the table until beams and stairwells took shape— *we'll walk in the rays of a beautiful sun*—floor to ceiling windows appeared, an entire house began spilling with light—*someday when the world is much brighter.*

She cleaned and sketched and danced, and why not listen to a symphony now? Classical music had been a thread that bound Will and her mother to each other, and now that neither of them was alive, Olivay's disinterest in it seemed irreverent. She chose a compilation Will had given her before they were married. *Just give it a try,* he'd said, which was what he'd said about a myriad of things, some of which she regretted giving into (oysters and absinthe), and others she regretted never going for (skinny dipping in Santa Monica on a moonless night). Anyway, she didn't care about the difference between Beethoven and Mozart, but she was starting to see, starting to get at something new—this rise, this fall, this crash like a trap door unbolting beneath her.

SEVEN

NEARLY TWO HOURS AFTER HENRY HAD LEFT, OLIVAY
sat down to catch her breath in the Egg Chair. She was smiling to
herself. How loosened up she was! A hard layer of leaden weight
chiseled off her shoulders just like that.

Then the doorbell rang.

"I need to talk to you," Henry explained through the intercom.
"Can I come back up?" His tone was flat, a little strained.

"Sounds serious," she said.

"I'm sorry. Do you mind buzzing me in?"

A tiny switch flipped inside Olivay's brain and the circuitry
fired in all directions at once.

What had she done?

*A complete stranger. Could be anyone. Texting on his way out the
door. What did he send and to whom? Photos? Videos of them doing
who knew what with each other?*

"Say it now." Her hands shook, her insides spiked with dread.
"And we'll see about letting you in."

A long pause filled with the rumble of background noise—a

crowd, a whistle, a horn. The LA Marathon. The Finish Line was just up the street.

"I'm a journalist," Henry said. "I was hired after Will . . . I work for the *Tribune*."

Did she hear that right?

Henry didn't say it again.

Olivay slid her hand to her throat, stepped back, and sat on the bench near the door.

Oh, go fuck yourself! she'd said just a week before Will died, sitting on the same bench, tying her running shoes, needing to sprint the hilly streets to burn off some steam.

I don't even know who you are anymore, Will had replied.

Well, that makes two of us, Olivay'd said, the whole of her emptied out, all that caramelized glaze of warm love stripped away during their fights. *Where did it go? Because it always came back.* Watch this trick! Peek-a-boo love. Now-you-see-it, now-you-don't love. Fill-your-heart, oh-shove-it-up-your-ass love.

"Olivay?" Henry asked. "*Olivay?* Can you still hear me?" A tinny string of declarations funneled from a square in the wall. "I thought when I told you my name you would know—*Jack*, I mean. When I told you to call me Jack. But you didn't seem to, maybe you don't even read the paper, and—I, after a while it just wasn't right to mention it. I'm so sorry. Can I please come up and explain?"

Jack Wilkins. Did she know this name? *Should* she know this name?

"Oh, go fuck yourself," Olivay tried to say, but the force of Henry's words smacked her all at once with the full weight of The Obvious Monstrous Thing.

She punched the intercom off with the side of her fist and Henry disappeared.

"Today's Jackie O" they'd begun calling her not long after Will died. And the thing they loved about that was this: No one would ever be sure whether Jackie Kennedy had crawled onto the back of the convertible to collect her husband's brains or whether she was trying to get away from the line of fire. But Olivay had left no doubt about her intentions, *cradling the man she'd loved*, trying to put him back together, this selfless hero, this love that knew no bounds. One video alone registered 21,354,472 views on YouTube. *No, no, no.* She hadn't wanted him to look in there. To be frightened of what he might see.

Olivay gripped her hair so tightly it burned.

The son of a bitch is gone.

Camelot.

Yes, Camelot.

What she wouldn't give to have Will return for one minute, just long enough to shove him in the chest and call him an asshole for looking at his phone instead of jumping out of the way. Just long enough to tell him how she would never, *ever* forgive him for taking away the person she used to be, for taking everything she had ever hoped to be, with him to his grave.

She dropped her head and rocked against her knees. Harder and harder, that stupid ball of agony in her throat that she had not felt in some time, not like this, the way it made her cry, like this.

EIGHT

FIVE MINUTES LATER HER TEARS HAD BEEN USED UP.
She'd stopped shriveling, stopped feeling sorry for herself, wasn't
any more lost than she'd been the past year. She was fine, or would
be fine within the hour. No more self-pity. Henry had simply made
a fool of her, and feeling foolish was nothing at all.

Getting up and out of the chair was the only thing she needed
to do. Getting that movement back, that feel beneath her feet.

She was still in the chair when the doorbell rang again, and it
was fury that propelled her across the room to the balcony window,
where she could easily see down the sidewalk to the front door of
the building, where the top of Henry's messy hair was unmistakable even from four flights up. But the warbling sway of the crowd
on the sidewalks was the thing that caught her full attention among
the banners and beach chairs, signs whipping above headbands and
baseball caps, everyone holding on against the wind. A fluid rain-
bow of activewear filled the neighborhood. The sight of so many
people gathered on the street unnerved her, and suddenly her breath
was too thin, too high against her ribs.

She gripped the neck of the wooden crow on the sill like the handle of an ax.

The air in the room didn't seem enough. She opened the balcony door just a crack and a burst of dry wind blew in the scent of honeysuckle from the clay pot several feet away, and still her breath wouldn't reach all the places it needed to go. Her eyes felt too heavy for the space inside her light and flimsy head.

She and Will had planted the honeysuckle to attract hummingbirds. He never lived to see how often they darted back and forth, common as flies, and how Olivay had come to ignore them. She breathed and breathed and still there was not enough air in the whole outdoors to fill her.

What does Post-traumatic stress disorder have to do with me?

The therapist had said it wasn't just for war vets, and handed Olivay the information, made her read it right there in her presence, but Olivay hadn't adopted any peculiar behaviors. Strange thoughts sometimes, sure, even violent ones had crossed her mind, but it seemed natural to want to hurt someone under the circumstances. She'd never acted on such thoughts, never believed she could. And the deep sense of sorrow she felt, along with not wanting to leave the house, seemed like reasonable and healthy reactions, too, in the flush of her fame, or infamy, or whatever it had been. She wasn't overcome with tremors or panic attacks. No hording or avoidance of certain foods. But then there was the part about the insidiousness of PTSD, the crafty way it snuck up when one least expected, taking one's breath away, clouding one's thoughts, rendering one suddenly and inexplicably helpless.

It was only honeysuckle.

The crowd in the street was just part of the marathon.

But being lied to? Was that it? Was it stirring something she wasn't fully aware of, some dormant little creature now shaken awake?

What had the therapist told her about situations unexpectedly triggering the nervous system? A smell, a sight, a noise that unlocks a place where the trauma is stored and categorized, a place that exists without the clear knowledge of the traumatized individual? It had all sounded like nonsense at the time.

Her cell phone rang. A number she didn't recognize. She looked down to see Henry with his phone to his ear, and no more than ten feet beyond him a freshly laid memorial, something she hadn't seen in some time. White, spray-painted flowers and a tall glass candle, the prayer kind with Jesus or Mary on the side. It was too far away to see.

The doorbell rang again.

Her heart banged against her ribcage, trembling, her breath came up short.

The bystanders erupted into a round of applause, and even though she didn't think they saw her there, it felt as if she had stepped onto a stage to star in her own emotionally damaged play, and all the whistles were for the seamless way she carried the role. There would be cheering throughout the morning, *Clap, clap, clap, go, go, go* breaching the stone walls of her apartment.

She slammed the crow back onto the sill, closed the balcony door, and buzzed Henry upstairs. She let the front door stand open while she sat in the Egg Chair across the room, recalling something Will once said, half-jokingly, about her ending up in a bar brawl someday with that temper of hers.

Olivay laughed out loud, waiting for Henry to appear.

Breathe from your belly. Progress through Process.

After the morning show host had said she looked like Jackie Kennedy, a reporter for *LA Daily* coined "Today's Jackie O," and off they ran for weeks with the *Post* picking it up, and *Daytime Talk*, and after an updated non-story on the evening news about having never found Motorcycle Man, Olivay had received two apparently serious offers for porn. O for Olivay had been the tweeted sales pitch.

Would Henry start out by reminding readers of all this? Or would he dive straight into the lurid details of their night? Just exactly how would this story be told?

Moments later he appeared in the doorway, and his sexy, scruffy look had given way to something tattered, to the look of a man who might have slept in his car. He stepped inside with one hand out as if readying to explain. In the other was a white paper bag from Levine's. Sticky buns, she guessed. He closed the door.

The urge to slap his face skittered through her fingers and she reminded herself that Henry was a journalist with a platform to tell the world whatever he liked. She would keep her recklessness in check. She would not appear on the front page of the *Tribune* for assaulting the man who (and this would surely be said in more ways than one) had taken the place of her dead husband.

"So, you're stalking me?" she said, her voice hoarse from tears. "You're some kind of paparazzo? Because I think the world has moved on from this story, at least the one that already happened. Maybe not the one you're about to tell."

His eyes had the look of pity, or was it condescension? She wouldn't stand for it, certainly not coming from him. She shoved her hair from her face to be sure he could see the heat in her eyes, to be sure he would not misunderstand when she drove the point home. "It's taking everything I have right now not to jump up and wipe that patronizing look off your face."

He slipped his backpack halfway off his arm and then held it in his hand. "I am not some kind of paparazzo. There is no story, and I don't know what you're seeing in my face, but it's got nothing to do with patronizing you."

"Do you live around here?" she demanded. "How long have you been watching me?"

"I live across town, like I said. And I have not been *watching* you."

His temples were damp with sweat. He appeared winded.

"Who gave you my cell number?"

"Jerry Woodrell."

Olivay hugged her stomach against a mounting nausea. Jerry had been Will's boss at the *Tribune*. "Jesus Christ," she said.

Henry set his backpack on the floor.

"You're not staying," she said. "Five minutes to say what you have to say. And only because I'm curious how you could possibly justify any of this. What were you *thinking*?" She didn't allow him to answer. "What could you possibly *want* from me that everyone else hasn't already taken?"

"It's not—"

She let go a small laugh. "How the hell do you people sleep at night?"

"Listen to me." Henry was about to lower himself into the Eames lounger where Will had loved to read.

"Do *not* sit there," Olivay said.

"Okay."

She realized she was biting her quivering lip and stopped.

"Do you want me to stand?" he asked.

"I don't want you here at all," she said.

"I understand that."

"Sure you do."

Henry glanced at the sketch on the table.

"That's none of your business," she said.

"Okay. Look. I'm just going to take a seat across from you. Here, on the sofa." He lugged his backpack over and sat down to face her. "You're wrong about me, Olivay."

"*Don't* say my name." She swiveled the chair away and shook her head at the bright sky through the window. She waited. He said nothing, and she turned in time to see him stand and come toward her, his face hard, eyes tightened with some kind of torment.

"Stay away from me," she warned, but he kept coming, and it frightened her to have him so close, to realize he was about to touch her, to realize how badly she needed to be touched.

He squatted at her knees and cupped her hand inside both of his.

"No," she said, and pulled away.

"I'm sorry." When he took her hand the second time she didn't move.

"I would never do anything to hurt you," he said.

"Too late for that, Jack Wilkins."

He parted his lips several times before the words finally escaped his lips. "It's absolutely nothing like it seems."

"That's it? That's all you have to say?"

"It's very complicated."

"Five minutes," she repeated, but surely it had already been four.

When she looked up again, a small, mournful smile pulled at the edge of his mouth.

Los Angeles was full of actors.

"My intentions were true," he said. "Just misunderstood."

"Who talks like that? No one talks like that."

He rested his hand against her cheek, his palm damp and warm, and her urge to cry was sudden and it made her feel like a fool again. But a hard swallow, a quick belly breath, and control rushed in in a strange blend of desire and aggression as if one were feeding the other; she was caught between the urge to kiss him and slap his face, to shove him and bite him and tear his clothes from his body, to go back to being the woman who knew virtually nothing about him, rolling freely in the heat and sweat and pleasures of the night before.

She lowered his hand. "Where exactly do you live?"

"Why?"

"I need to know."

"Echo Park."

"That's all the way across town. Nowhere near Levine's. You said it wasn't the first time you'd seen me there, only the first you'd had the nerve to come over and speak."

"I wasn't stalking you, if that's where you're headed with this. It's on my way to work—"

"Why were you afraid to speak to me? What did you want? What *do* you want?"

He glanced at the floor and his face reddened as if he were embarrassed. "I was nervous. I didn't want to blow it. Then, I guess after seeing you a few times, the idea of talking to you got easier."

"A few times."

"I *wasn't* stalking you. Not *that* kind of stalking, anyway. Not *bad* stalking."

"*Bad* stalking? You mean it comes in degrees? Like murder?"

"That isn't funny."

"No one is trying to be funny."

"I wanted to go out with you. That's it. That's all I was after."

Olivay stared directly into his eyes, and this time she wasn't the first to look away. "Are you one of those people who fixates on celebrities?" she asked. "What are they called? *Starfuckers?*"

It was a funny thing to say. She got that. She allowed him his grin.

"I assure you, I am the farthest thing from it," he said.

In spite of his messy appearance, she could smell soap on his freshly scrubbed skin. It was her soap, from when he'd gone into the bathroom.

"I don't mean to imply that I'm a celebrity," she said. "Or was. I don't know what the hell I am."

They laughed, just a little, just a clumsy little release, and then took turns glancing away.

"I need to think about all of this," Olivay said, wanting to believe he was telling her the truth just as much as not wanting to be made out to be a fool.

What she needed was perspective, something to weigh against the lie he'd told her, or rather the truth he hadn't fully divulged. If he really had no intention of using her for a story, then what exactly did his crime consist of? Not telling her where he worked? Okay. All right. How bad was that? What was the worst that could happen with something like that? And could she live with the consequence that the only man she'd slept with since Will had not been honest about the fact that he, too, was a journalist for the *Tribune*?

The answer was maybe.

They looked at the floor and walls and windows, anything but each other. Some kind of impasse had risen up between them.

Then Henry squeezed her hand like a signal.

Olivay squeezed back.

"Just so you know, I wasn't expecting anything from you last night," he said. "I mean, I wasn't expecting for us to—hoping, sure, but you know, not expecting that we would . . ."

He was staring at her shoulders in her tank top, and then her thighs, her shorts riding higher because of the way she was sitting in the chair.

"You don't want to say it?" Olivay said.

Henry shrugged. "Once you call it fucking . . ."

"It becomes that," she said, feeling bold, feeling different than she'd ever felt with Will.

"The same goes for *making love*," he said. "So I wasn't sure which way to . . . You know?"

Olivay sat back just to watch him navigate out from underneath his own discomfort. When she was young, her mother told her to stay away from people who made themselves feel better by making others feel worse. Her mother had never been married.

"What would *you* call it?" she asked.

"I don't know," he said. "A range of things. *Rangy.*"

"Doesn't that mean long-legged?"

"Yes."

"You're good," she said. "You should have been a writer."

"I'm sorry," Henry said. "I didn't want to give you the wrong impression, and I was too careful about what I said. But we can see how well that worked out."

She suddenly remembered the phone call with Jerry. "Why did Jerry give you my number? Does he want some kind of exclusive out of this?"

Henry's face was stern, his eyes zeroing in with a single-minded seriousness.

"Please don't lie to me," she said.

"No. Of course not. I called him while I was standing outside. I had to. I was—I *am*, really late for work. I told him that I saw you yesterday."

Olivay raised an eyebrow.

"I said I ran into you at Levine's. I didn't tell him *everything*. Just that I needed to talk to you again, that it was urgent, that I'd explain later, and if he didn't give me your number I was going to ring your bell, which he actually forbade me to do. I said I was already at your door, and he couldn't have it both ways."

"He forbade you from ringing my bell?" she said, stifling a smirk behind her hand.

"Yes," Henry said.

"Stop," she said, and dropped her hand, but could still feel the size of her grin.

"He thought that I would be a cruel reminder," Henry said.

"He said that?" she asked.

Henry nodded.

"I guess it didn't occur to him that you might also make me forget."

Henry pulled her toward him and kissed the top of her head. He wrapped his arms around her, and Olivay's heart gave a stiff kick. She couldn't believe how good it felt to lean into him, how good it felt to allow herself to be held.

"I don't know why I didn't make it clear to you right away who I was, or where I worked." He leaned back and looked directly at her. "I got drawn in so quickly, like some spellbound boy talking about his childhood dogs."

He flashed another mournful smile.

"What is it?" she asked. "You have this look . . ."

"It's you. There's this thing you do. A kind of light pops up in your eyes every now and then. As if you're suddenly happy. A little flash of something breaks through. I saw it yesterday in Levine's. And again, just now."

"Yeah?" she said. "What's funny is that there's something in your eyes, too, when you see it."

Henry stared at her, touched his jaw, waiting, it seemed, for her to finish her thought.

"But I'm pretty sure it isn't happiness," she said.

"What do you mean?"

"It's like you're sorry about something."

"Sorry?"

"Or maybe it's sorrow, Henry. Jack. Jack Henry."

"No, come on. I feel bad about not telling you who I was. It was stupid. Especially after coming home with you."

Olivay shrugged.

"I mean, *sorrow*? Why would I feel anything like that at seeing you happy?"

NINE

A DISTANT BANG, LIKE A SMALL EARTHQUAKE, THRUMMED the windows and walls.

"Did you feel that?" Olivay said. She had lived through a lifetime of earthquakes and knew that even the smallest could sound and feel like a truck hitting a house.

"Was it a tremor?" Henry asked, rising up and crossing the room toward the sofa, where he picked up his backpack, something that wouldn't seem strange to Olivay until later that day. He slung it over his shoulders and secured it as if he were readying to walk out the door. Instead, he stood next to the armrest, facing the balcony windows.

Olivay turned her ear. The cheering in the distance seemed to have been replaced by screams. Maybe she was just imagining that. Maybe the eerie electric buzz in the air was just the Santa Anas having their way.

Henry crossed the room toward the balcony, and it was hard to say what Olivay saw in his body that made the scene feel as if it were unfolding in slow motion, in the same way the magnolia leaves had swayed above her head when Will was killed. The shadows across the walls, his backpack straightening his walk, his eyes blinking steadily, again and again.

She raised her hand to say *Henry don't go near the window*, just a feeling, just a prickling of hair on her neck, *Don't do that*, and then an earsplitting, thunderous boom shook the apartment so hard it was as if a plane had crashed into the parking lot next door.

Olivay ended up with her face on the floor, curling her legs beneath her stomach, struggling to cover her head against shattering glass and debris. Everything hanging or openly shelved seemed to have blasted across the floor. Gray smoke whipped past the windows, and a blanket of orange glowed just beyond it.

"Henry!" she called, but couldn't hear an answer.

A needling sting covered her arms and back as she peered over an elbow through the haze. Cracks like blackened vines sprouted across the empty white walls, and then disappeared as smoke continued to fill the room through holes where the kitchen windows used to be.

She had hit her head on the concrete. Hadn't she? It was a struggle to think, to move, to understand a single thing that was happening here. Why did it feel as if she were suddenly returning from some other place, as if she were waking from a deep sleep? Car alarms and sirens blared from all directions. "Henry?" she called again, but was coughing so hard it didn't sound like anything at all.

TEN

SHE CUPPED HER EARS AGAINST THE DISTANT, BOXED-IN sound of what she suddenly realized was her own voice screaming. When she let go, another noise inside her head was set loose—a pealing, clanging distortion, as if the space between her ears had been replaced by broken bells.

The smell of hot metal and charred wood filled the air.

Where was Henry? She couldn't feel him anywhere near her.

Then something jabbed her side, an arm latching around her waist with a force that jackknifed her body at the center, as if she were a child's cotton doll to be picked up and slung in a fit across the room and onto the bed, which she was.

Henry threw himself over her, and somehow along the way she struck her chin against her knee and bit her tongue, and this, more than anything, enraged her.

She roared and punched her way out from beneath him. "Get the hell off me!" she yelled, even after he was off and she had landed on the floor in a heap of mangled, razor sharp debris. She clawed at the air as if through webbing. A dense weight fastened to her chest and she clutched that, too, the pressure boring into her bones and teeth.

Henry remained on the bed, his mouth covered with the quilt, making it harder to understand what he was saying until he lurched forward and cupped the back of her head. He was asking her to *stop*. He was telling her to *listen*.

Her throat and eyes filmed with a powdery fog. She pulled back, swung her fist, and clipped his mouth. He lost his grip, and she fell further into the scattered debris where she flipped over and crawled through splintered picture frames, crying now, choking on her tears. *No, no, no.* She snatched a photo of her mother holding her as a baby, but let go when something sliced open her knee. Everywhere lay bits of papers that did not belong to her, shredded plants and grass, crumbled concrete, strings of tire tread, window glass, and there, directly in front of her, was a set of ten-speed handlebars with severed brake cables sprouting like giant antennae in the middle of her kitchen floor.

Terror, pure and blue as a gaslit flame, seared through her veins.

She hacked and struggled to reach the counter, stumbling and groping until she seized the butcher knife she was going for.

"Get down," Henry said, his voice suddenly invading her ears. "For God's sake, get away from the windows!"

She saw the room as if from above, coal-colored smoke being sucked back out by a shift in wind, and it was then she could see a sheared stop sign lodged like a giant Chinese throwing star into the back of the Egg Chair she'd been sitting in. If she hadn't been thrown onto the floor, that stop sign would have taken her head off.

The knife quivered loosely in her grip, her palms were streaked in blood and grime, a sliver of white bone peered beneath a large flap of bloody skin on her knee.

She leaned forward and puked onto a strip of pink insulation near her feet.

She could not breathe. For all the times she'd wanted to die, she now understood how badly she wanted to live.

With every passing second, a new level of chaos seemed to rise, bringing with it another layer of commotion. Every type of rescuer had a siren, every car and place of business an alarm, every person left alive had a voice with which to scream and scream and scream.

ELEVEN

COUGHING MEANT BREATHING, AND BREATHING MEANT she was not going to die, even when it felt as if she were inhaling small flames.

How long had she been standing there with the knife?

Across the room, Henry's eyes appeared huge and stupefied above the quilt covering his mouth. He held out his hand for her to come back to the bed, and when Olivay made no move to take it, he scooped the air in a fraught and desperate plea.

The room smelled like burning trash.

"Come here," Henry yelled, breaking through the din. "Please!"

The east-facing windows above the bed remained intact. The balcony windows to the west and the street had, too. But the ones above the sink had blown out, and Olivay knew it was due to the weaker cross-panes, the charming, original construction.

"You're safe," Henry shouted, but Olivay did not know what to believe. "Olivay," he said. "I don't think you understand what's happening. *Olivay.* Are you listening to me?"

People in shock behave in ways that are very different from what the situation calls for. She needed to stop, just stop, and try really hard to think.

The balcony windows were caked with dust and sludge, and beyond them nothing but smoke in every direction until the wind grabbed hold of it like mighty fists and tossed it upward, steadily higher and higher, until the street appeared out of nowhere, like some awful magic trick uncovering a world never meant to be seen.

"Come here," Henry begged.

Olivay spit her mouth clean in the sink, dropped the knife near the drain, and staggered to the balcony door.

Henry continued to plead with her as she looked through the splattered balcony windows at shredded clothing and debris hanging from trees and balconies, bodies strewn partially naked, partially intact on the sidewalk.

"You're bleeding," Henry said, as if what had happened to her mattered. Could he not see that she was still standing, still very much alive? Did he not understand what the people on the street had just been through?

"I'm sorry," she said to no one as shouts below rose from a flurry of men and women in neon vests running down the street. But when she looked closer they didn't seem to be yelling at all, and she wondered if her mind was playing tricks, if the shouting was the sounds stored inside her head from before.

A man ripped out his shoelaces and tied them around a woman's thigh with such viciousness that trying to save her was its own kind of violence. Her calf was nothing but a mangle of red and white strings, of flesh and jagged bone. She seemed to have lost consciousness, and her foot.

"Olivay?"

Police stretched their arms wide and blew whistles and pushed bystanders in one direction, then another.

The more smoke that cleared the more Olivay could see runners in the distance stumbling and coughing, covering their ears, others tripping over the metal barricades, while a sea of arms heaved the twisted fences out of the way.

Henry touched her shoulder and it was then that she returned to her body, to the trembling that had taken her over. "Your knee is in really bad shape, Olivay," he said, standing next to her now. "You need to get away from the balcony. *Now*."

She shook her head. She needed to stand there. She needed to see something through.

But then another loud bang erupted at the corner and Olivay shrieked and Henry swore and pulled her against his chest until all she could see and smell was the dust and sweat of his neck.

"Son of a bitch," Henry said, craning toward the window. "It's a water main, busted through the middle of the intersection."

Olivay closed her arms around him.

He squeezed her hair at the back of her neck. "This cannot be happening," he said. "It's a geyser now. A full-on geyser."

Olivay turned to see water bursting through the rubble that had been the street and crushing down the side street at the corner intersection like rapids, as quick as any she'd seen on the Colorado River. It rushed into the dry cleaner's, whose front windows had been blown away.

"We need to get out of here," Olivay managed to say, but she was thinking of Annabelle and May who'd owned the cleaners their entire adult lives. A telephone pole had crashed through the roof from the explosion, and she knew they were in there this time of morning, could almost see their horrified faces as it took them by surprise, as it killed them right where they stood.

Sparks jumped across the water and flashed a blazing trail along so much metal, and Olivay hated herself for thinking of Annabelle and May's husbands and daughters joining the club, how they, too,

would know what it felt like to lose a loved one in such a spectacu-
larly public way, how the world would want to watch it on replay
for months to come. These widowers and daughters were now her
kindred spirits, and Olivay felt better and so much worse in the
most terrible, unforgivable ways.

Her legs began to give out.

"Let's get out of here," she said, but closed her eyes and leaned
her forehead against the balcony window, her bloodied palms
pressed beside her face on the window.

The clang of fire truck sirens mixed with the long wails of
police cars were going to render her deaf.

"Get away from the window, Olivay," Henry said.

"If you touch me again, I'm going to hurt you," she said, and
could feel him back off.

She opened her eyes, unable to move, held in place by the horror of it all, captivated by the very thing that repulsed her. It was a
strange kind of high. *High.* That was the right word, perverse as it
was. She saw what she didn't want to see. Understood what she'd
rather not about the gaping millions who had gazed at her, latched
like sucklings onto her pain, getting off on the swelling satisfaction
of *watching.*

What she saw now must have been the coat hangers, covered
in paper, igniting into blue and orange flames inside the cleaners,
turning the twisted metal conveyor into an electric light show, setting fire to the clothes and melting their plastic covers. Then the
flames ignited what was left of the roof, and it collapsed into the
water, sending another plume of smoke into the air.

Henry was yelling something behind her. Olivay closed her
eyes again, thinking it might help right something. If not out there
in the street, then inside her own head.

"Olivay. Look at your knee." He was right next to her ear. "Goddamn it. *Look!*"

Was that her knee? Bulbous and bloody and so much bigger than it ought to be. A piece of flesh hung like a chunk of overripe tomato. And yet, how bad could it be if it didn't hurt?

"You need to sit down so we can see how bad it is. Look at your hands. You're bleeding everywhere."

She peeled her palms from the glass, leaving behind two bloody handprints.

Then she remembered Levine's. The woman with the myrtle leaf tattoo. Was she the one who had handed Henry that bag of sticky buns? Henry, who had been sitting in Levine's less than an hour ago?

Olivay reached for the balcony door.

"What are you *doing?*" Henry shouted.

"Don't touch me!" she wailed, and walked onto the balcony as if riding on the wind itself, caught inside a tornado, caught in complete chaos. The sirens blasted through her insides, long and constant and unrelenting, singeing the ends of her nerves. The air stung her eyes, making them water, and she blinked and blinked until she could finally see Levine's down the block, and a fresh wave of dread passed through her.

A corner of the brick façade was torn from the front of the building. Thin black smoke streamed in plumes where the windows used to be on the ground floor. The old neon sign was gone. There was no one she could see.

"Okay," Olivay said, suddenly aware that she was too light-headed to be standing there, four stories up. When she saw how badly her legs shook, how impossible they were to control, she swore to God and closed her eyes and groaned.

"I've got you," Henry said, but she didn't want him to have her. She didn't want anyone to have her.

"Shit," Henry said. "You smell that?"

A gas line.

"I hope they kill whoever did this," she said, expecting to be blown to pieces any second. "Torture them first, for months on end."

She didn't care if these were the last words she ever spoke. She could say or do anything right now because there did not appear to be consequences in this world. She was filled with murderous thoughts of her own, a burning rage against people she didn't know, the same rage they must have had against her and everyone else in the neighborhood today, and the hot revulsion in her stomach made her feel better than she imagined she'd feel without it.

She gripped the railing for support just as Henry slipped an arm around her waist. She tried to take a step, but then there was no need because he scooped her entire body up into his arms like a goddamn hero, lifting her off her feet with an ease so outlandish that even in her state of questionable consciousness she said, "Are you fucking kidding me?"

He brought her in and sat her on the bed in the corner and the wind shifted, causing another terrible round of coughing. He pulled a pillowcase free, tore it in half, swathed her nose and mouth, and then did the same for himself. He checked her over, palpating her bones from her head to her feet, and then he pulled the duvet around her shoulders, its downy weight like arms, this quilt they had shared, this bed that was hers, did he not understand that? It was hers and hers alone.

TWELVE

IT WASN'T CLEAR HOW MUCH TIME HAD PASSED WHEN she found herself watching the blood from Henry's lip seep into the cotton around his mouth.

"Look what you've done," he said, his voice muffled beneath the fabric. He'd taken hold of her wrist.

It could only have been a minute. They were side by side on the bed. His mouth was still covered in the pillowcase. Hers, too.

The sirens were louder now, a flickering vibrato ricocheting against every surface in the boxy apartment, smacking the high ceilings again and again.

Olivay understood that she had punched Henry, though she couldn't think exactly why, and now as he looked at her hand she realized he'd been referring to the cuts on her palms from crawling across the floor to get away from him, to get the knife.

Shouting rose in the hallway. Her hearing had returned with a high-pitched ringing. She pressed her fingers into her ears.

"Don't move," Henry said, and made a run for the bathroom. She released her fingers, and the crunch beneath the soles of his shoes sounded unusually clear. She was dizzy and shook her head. The room gave a slow spin.

More voices in the hallway.

"Ask them what's happened," she said. "Please."

The room felt chilly. Her teeth chattered, even as she knew how warm it must be with the windows blown out.

"I already did," Henry said.

There he was.

Her thoughts didn't seem to be tracking correctly. Time itself seemed to have collapsed. "Drink this," Henry was saying, the cloth gone from her mouth now, a glass of water at her lips. And then the feel of cold liquid going down, the faint taste of vomit, the gritty film washing into her stomach.

"What did they say?" she asked.

She heard laughter and realized it was her own. Nothing was funny. Except that Henry was wiping her legs with a cold damp washcloth, checking for glass, plucking the slivers from her skin, and she felt so small, like a girl in her mother's care, *Stay still, Olivay.* But she wasn't a girl, wasn't a child at least, still a girl, of course not a *girl*, a woman, she hated being called a girl, but no one had called her that, had they? These thoughts continued to show themselves as laughter.

Henry caressed her open palms with wet cotton balls, so cool and numbing, not quite real.

"Peroxide," he said.

"It doesn't hurt," she said. "Why doesn't it hurt?"

"Shock," he said, and Olivay trembled, recalling the cold, green room, the spinning chairs, the bleached silence in her head. An open skull makes a licking, creaking sound.

"Hey!" someone was saying. "Christ. You're passing out again. Wake *up*."

The encircling sirens and helicopters seemed as loud now as the blasts.

"What?" she demanded to know, reaching for whoever was there.

"Shush, shush, shush," a voice said.

Someone taking care of her.

She was alert, wide-awake, looking herself over. She had not imagined all she'd seen outside. Her palms were red with swelling and heat, even as the rest of her was freezing. She curled her fingers into fists and droplets of blood leaked into her palms.

She remembered Henry kneading his thumb into his wrist at the table in Levine's.

She didn't understand what she had meant to do with that knife.

"You're lucky," Henry was saying. "The cuts in your hands are pretty minor." He glazed the tiny openings with thick clear ointment. "So they won't get infected," he said. "Try not to close your fists like that."

"I can smell fresh blood," Olivay said, unsure if it was hers or if the smell belonged to some greater stench coming in on the wind, or to a memory revived. *Get it while it's fresh*, her neighbor Mrs. Hightower always says of the pies she brings over. Peach had been Will's favorite.

She didn't mean to say that out loud. She wasn't making sense.

Henry was staring at her the way one stares at a drunk, exasperated, half-amused. He reminded her of Will.

"Can you please check on my neighbor? Mrs. Hightower. She's right across the hall."

"You need stitches." Henry had already wrapped her knee tightly in a huge bundle of gauze from the earthquake safety kit in the bathroom, the kit that Will had made fun of her for buying. He claimed that an earthquake big enough to hurt her would probably kill her. "Better to have the Jaws of Life under the sink instead," he'd said.

Henry appeared to be using everything in the box.

Olivay laughed again.

THIRTEEN

"KEEP YOUR LEG AS STRAIGHT AS YOU CAN FOR AS LONG as you can," Henry said. "Let the blood clot. The second you bend it, it's going to open."

"All right," she said, but when she glanced again at the bed the safety kit was gone. Where was Will?

Not Will.

Henry.

She called his name, understanding now that she'd blacked out, maybe more than once. She tried to get up but vertigo whirled her back onto the bed. The air was too thin, and reeked of something awful, and she didn't know if this was why she couldn't quite catch a breath. Could a person stop breathing from shock? She kept thinking of Will, feeling him near, hearing his voice, wanting to understand why this had happened.

People are capable of doing all kinds of things, Olivay. The "why" doesn't even matter.

Helicopters sliced the air so close to the building that Olivay wondered if they had landed on the rooftop garden. She counted three through the windows near the bed alone—vicious looking monsters, the size of which she'd never seen in real life—their huge doors open on both sides where armored men with enormous guns hung halfway out, aiming their weapons toward the ground.

"Are they ours?" she asked.

"Are what ours?" Henry answered.

"The men in the sky. Are they trying to kill us, too?"

"No, Olivay. That's the military. Our military."

"Oh. And the gas lines . . . ?"

"The gas smell is gone," Henry said. "We're all right. You're all right. But the phone lines are blocked. There's no way to find out what's going on." His lip was a little swollen but no longer bleeding. She thought to kiss it—a silly little thought, kissing his wound— but then he'd moved away and she saw bloody fingerprints dotting the front of his T-shirt. When he turned, she saw her palms had left a pair of wings across his back.

She'd liked the smell of his neck.

"Why aren't you hurt?" she asked.

"I hit the floor behind the sofa. I was lucky."

Lucky didn't seem the right word.

"I can't pull up the wireless on my phone," he said. "The neighbors in the hall are saying it was definitely a terrorist attack."

"How do they know?" she asked, hearing her own voice continuing inside her head, all the questions of who and why and how, even as she began numbing herself against the answers.

"The police told someone downstairs. They're telling everyone to stay inside. They think the bomb closest to us exploded in a van near Levine's."

"You were just there."

"Yes. I was."

The nice woman with the myrtle leaf tattoo. The woman with mangled calves, Will on the sidewalk, Olivay in the Egg chair, everyone in the wrong place at the right time, or the right place at the wrong time. Henry in the right place at the right time. It didn't feel like coincidence, everything randomly strewn across the universe. Wasn't coincidence the word we used when we couldn't see the levers and pulleys?

I prefer the beauty of the scattershot, her mother once said. *And you, Olivay, the glory of the blueprint, the calculated master plan.*

Olivay spat a string of charcoal-colored fluid onto the blanket and wiped her mouth with the corner of a pillowcase.

Henry grabbed hold of her leg, and it was only then that she realized she'd been kicking the blanket away. She needed to get out of that apartment. He told her to stay still. Bright red blood seeped into the gauze on her knee.

Other primates have been known to grieve themselves to death.

The next thing she knew, Henry was saying something about a concussion. "Stop falling asleep. Stop laying your head to the side." When she looked across the room, a path to the sink had been carved through the debris. The vomit was gone, and the broken windows above the counter were covered in a patchwork of sheets, sucking in and out with the pull of the wind. Thick lines of duct tape held the edges of the fabric to the wall. Olivay didn't remember having duct tape in the house. Was that part of the earthquake safety kit? Something from Will's toolbox? The fabric reminded her of the taco stand where they'd eaten on their honeymoon in Sayulita, the swaths of cloth bound above them with large sticks to block out the sun, the way a soft breeze ruffled through. *It's like playing fort,* they'd both said at once, and the taste of tequila, the scent of coconut oil transported her back through time, as real as any trip she'd ever taken. "You won't believe what's happened, Will, what's going to happen after you're dead. A stop sign guillotine. Handlebars with antennae in the kitchen. A man who knows what to do with the stuff in that kit. Okay, I'll stop," she said to Henry now. "I promise to stay awake." And then, "A man who knows what to do with me."

FOURTEEN

THE FULL FORCE OF AGONY HIT WITHOUT WARNING, causing a pulsing, nauseating ache behind her eyes. A fire seemed to have caught beneath her kneecap, and Olivay thought she might have fractured the bone when she hit the floor. The stinging in her back and thighs arrived like a thousand little pinpricks.

Henry had told her to take a few deep breaths, drink a lot more water while he found out what he could from the neighbors, and hopefully the police out front. She told him not to leave her, and in telling him, she choked up, not quite crying, not allowing herself to fall all the way apart, and he said he'd be right back, and when she opened her eyes again, he was standing across the room looking out the closed balcony windows through binoculars.

She struggled to sit upright. The achy weight in her head was like the worst hangover of her life. Her words became strangled inside a coughing fit, and every cough crashed like a rock against her skull.

"Easy there," Henry said, sitting next to her on the bed.

She stared with an unexpected spite at the binoculars in his hand. "Whose are those?"

Henry held them up. "Yours, I assume."

"Where did you find them?"

"In the sideboard against the wall."

"What were you doing in there?"

"I'm sorry. I can put them back."

"Why were you in there?"

"I was looking for a phone charger."

"We don't have electricity."

Henry stood as if he were about to put the binoculars back. "I can plug it into my computer."

"Don't put those back," Olivay said. "Leave them here. With me."

Henry tossed them onto the bed near her feet.

Olivay didn't quite understand her own meanness, at least not toward Henry, but that didn't stop her, didn't hold her back from letting loose. She couldn't stand the thought of him touching something so personal to Will. Then she thought of herself, her body, her insides, once upon a time so personal to Will.

She glanced at the windows, unable to erase the footless woman from her eyes. "What a media dream," she blurted. "Think of the news cycle. All the lives 'touched' by what's happened. The Grief Industry is about to explode—*pardon the pun*. But that's a glorious shit-show. A *much* bigger event than the one Will and I put on."

"Listen—"

"Which begs the question, what, exactly, are you doing in *here*? Shouldn't you be out covering all this?"

Henry rubbed the center of his forehead as if he wasn't too pleased with his own thoughts. Wasn't that what her mother would say? Erasing away those opinions, those ideas? And now he was scratching his throat to stifle the words he'd rather not say.

She couldn't remember the last time she'd been in so much pain. If ever. She'd never broken a single bone in her life.

"You've been through more in the last year than most people in a lifetime," Henry said. "But the thing is—just hear me out—I'm sure you have a concussion, and they can make people pretty agitated."

"No seriously. Why aren't you out there getting the scoop? What the hell are you doing in here with me, looking through Will's binoculars like a spectator?"

"I'm sorry for taking the binoculars," he said, his voice suddenly stern, his face no longer showing restraint, and it was as if a set of strong hands had spun her around and sat her down by the shoulders. His words saying one thing, but his tone saying clearly, without question, that she had no right to behave this way. He'd done nothing but make sure she was safe. "I didn't want to leave you up here by yourself," he said. "That's why I'm not out there. You asked me to stay. I told you I would stay."

The words on the edge of her tongue—*People don't always mean what they say*—arrived so abruptly, and with such ridiculously tender anguish, that she dared not say a single one.

She pushed her hair from her face, smearing the ointment through the dirty strands. "I don't know what's wrong with me," she said, like walking through the doors of *Casa del Perdono,* a place she never wanted to eat at again in her life. "Oh, shit," she said, because the last thing she wanted to do was cry, but the tears came anyway, burning tears, polluted tears, as if she'd been hit with pepper spray. "I'm sorry." She shook her head, even as it punished her with pain to do so. She wouldn't look him in the face.

"It doesn't matter," he said, but she could tell by his expression when she finally turned that it did matter, at least a little. He got down beside the bed and held onto her fingertips. "Let's just try to focus on one thing at a time," he said.

Olivay nodded.

"Do you mind if I try your phone for a signal?" he asked.

Where was her phone? She gazed around the ramshackle room, only to see that it was there, all along, in Henry's hand.

"Oh."

"What's your password?" he asked.

Had he gone through the pockets of her shorts?

The throbbing in her head made her nauseous. Henry standing there confused her. She didn't quite understand what he was asking.

"I can do it," she said, finally, reaching for the phone, only to realize her palms were slick with ointment, and pulling back.

She understood how trauma had a way of condensing time, bending and stretching one's sense of it, the rhythms and tempo knocked out of the continuum. She understood how impossible it could be for the traumatized to understand the order of events, the meaning of simple tasks, but she did not understand how she could know these things and remain at the mercy of them.

"Did you forget the password?" Henry asked. "Or maybe you don't want to tell me?"

She stared at the phone, thinking there must be someone she should call. Her mother. Her mother was dead. Will's mother? They hadn't spoken in nearly a year. Another knot formed in her throat.

"Why wouldn't I want to tell you the password?" she said.

She held the top of her head. Small chunks of rubble caked her scalp and she plucked them away. A large bump along her hairline was extremely tender to the touch. Blood had formed a crusted clot at its center. She closed her eyes. "Everything just . . . hurts," she said. "And I think I might throw up again."

"Hold on. Hold on."

She closed her eyes and could hear him moving around the room and then clanging inside the cupboards, and then he placed a large pot next to her. "In case."

"Uh," she said. "Oh."

"Do you want me to get you something for the pain? Do you have something you can take?"

"Don't you think if I take something, it'll come right back up?"

He wiped her cheek with the edge of the quilt. A tear, she guessed. His touch was unusually soft.

"Oh, man," he said. "There it is. You've got an even bigger goose egg right there just above your hairline. No wonder. I didn't see it before you swiped the ointment through there."

"No wonder what?"

He retrieved a soggy ice pack from the freezer and told her to hold it against her head.

She did what he said, and the cold felt good against her skull. It felt good dripping into her hand.

The password was Will's birthday. She spoke the numbers slowly and Henry entered them, and then he held both phones in the air near the windows before checking them again. He shook his head no.

"What does it matter?" she asked.

"What does *what* matter?"

"Who are you trying to call? *Jerry?*"

"My family. I'm sure they've seen it on the news. But yes, Jerry. Of course him, too."

"What family?"

"My parents. My brother. My mother who calls me Henry."

Their time at Levine's seemed like years ago. *I bet your mother calls you Henry.* "What's your brother's name?"

Henry hesitated. "Why?"

"Because."

"George."

Olivay laughed a little to herself, then grabbed her head. "Ow. Of course it is. Henry and George. Sons of the American Revolution. Or Red Coats. Or the Royal Family."

"People will be worried about you, too," he said. "We need to get a phone line."

"Henry and George. A Victorian novel about two gay men." She laughed again, even when it made her sicker to her stomach, even when it pounded her skull. She could hear Henry laughing a little, too. She tilted her head back and drew a deep breath. Her tongue tasted like smoke.

"Olivay?"

"No," she said, slowly lowering her head and meeting his eyes. "No one will be worried."

"How so?"

"That's just the way it is."

"You know a lot of people. A lot of people certainly know you."

"Yeah," she said.

"So—"

"Not the same, Henry." She closed her eyes and clamped her jaw.

"I just meant—"

"Are you going to help me relieve my pain, or are you going to keep trying to relieve someone else's with a phone call?"

FIFTEEN

A MANIC, HOTFOOT ENERGY HAD TAKEN OVER. TOO much adrenaline. Everything speeding up. "Bring me *a lot* of whatever you find," Olivay said. She had fallen too far in one direction, and now she was trying to right herself, ground herself, a corkscrew going round in circles trying to plant herself firmly back into the ground.

Henry had looked twice where she told him to, but the codeine was not where she said it was. The root canal. That was the last time she'd had a lot of pain. But nothing like this. Not even close.

"Try the drawer to the left," she said. "Under the sink. It's there somewhere. I know it is. There are *all kinds of things* in there. You wouldn't believe the variety of prescriptions doctors give people who are grieving. It makes it so easy to kill yourself. Xanax and Ambien and Prozac, which I never took, by the way, in case you're wondering. And son of a *bitch*. Did you find it yet?"

She was shaking, talking more to herself than to him.

"Here." Henry handed her the codeine in a prescription bottle and a small bottled water from the refrigerator. "You've got a concussion. You know that, right? This may not be the best idea. I can go downstairs and try and get you some help."

She gripped his hand and something passed over his face, like some fleeting hope that she'd refuse help from anyone other than him. He didn't want to leave her. She was sure of it. What he wanted was to stay and ride this thing out alone with her, and it was like something was happening to them, something she'd been waiting for day after day after day.

"This will do the trick," she said, releasing his hand. "I'll be fine."

"If it knocks you out, it'll be that much harder for me to wake you every hour."

"Then don't wake me," she said.

"Right," he said. "You're not dying on my watch."

"Who said anything about dying?"

The vibration from the helicopters was enough to hurt her skin.

She tossed a pill onto her tacky tongue and guzzled the water. She stopped to thank him, and he replied with something she couldn't quite hear over swallowing and the noise outside and the sucking of her own breath after downing nearly a full bottle without stopping. She forced a second pill down with what was left.

"No!" Henry said. "What are you doing?"

"I can't stand all of the noise," she said. "How can you stand it? How much longer, do you think?"

"Not long," he said, as if he were fed up with her, and Olivay wasn't sure they were talking about the same thing.

It couldn't have been more than twenty minutes when she felt the world slowing down, when lifting her hand through the air was like moving against the weight of water.

"Yes," she said. "This is . . ."

When she woke later he was saying her name. The clock on the stove blinked 12:00, which wasn't the time, of course. But the electricity was on. The room was cooling down, if only slightly.

Her entire body felt swollen, pumped with water. All she wanted to do was sleep, but a fire truck seemed to have parked directly below the blown-out kitchen windows.

"Hey," Henry said once the siren shut off. He stood at the foot of the bed with his hands on his hips.

"We've got electricity," Olivay said, bristling with a spite that seemed to show every time she came to.

Henry appeared to be searching for something on the floor. "The generator in the basement kicked on," he said. "Who knows how long it will last." He glanced up again.

"How long have I been out?" Olivay asked.

"About an hour and a half."

It felt like most of the afternoon. "You let me sleep for more than an hour."

"Give or take," he said.

"I could have died," she said, a foggy-headed attempt at humor, though he seemed not to notice. "Did anything else happen while I was out?"

"Your neighbors keep gathering in the hallway to check on one another. I don't know their names. I'm sure Mrs. Hightower is one of them. Older woman, long hair? Everyone appears to be fine, at least on this floor. I can't speak for the others."

Olivay liked how everyone seemed to be coming together in the same way people had after 9/11, when a sudden dignity had been arrived at, everyone stepping up and paying attention to all the right things: compassion, mercy, love. A miracle of a moment felt worldwide. Had anything like that ever happened before technology made the world so small? Before we could watch each other suffer with real time intimacy? Was this the upside of media?

"What are they saying?" she asked.

"Some guy on the first floor has a radio. He said the streets have been declared a crime scene." He paused as if to gauge her reaction. "The police keep telling everyone to stay put."

The chorus of sirens had scaled back, long enough for the ringing in Olivay's ears to kick in. Her apartment was ruined. She could see this now, all the furniture she'd been so careful to collect was torn, scraped, embedded with debris and glass. But the bedside table was upright again, its surface full of scrapes. A bloody chunk of glass lay on top.

"What's this?" She picked it up.

"It came out of your knee."

She held it up for inspection, recognizing the width and smooth cut of the edge. It was a slice of the Henning Noorgard table Will had given her for her birthday. She threw it across the room.

Henry watched it whizz past.

It had been several hours since the explosions. They should know something by now.

"Are you hungry?" Henry asked, glancing around the floor again. "Did you have anything to eat this morning?"

Olivay smacked her lips, felt the cottony dry from the pills and smoke, the bitter taste on her tongue. Whatever had been in her stomach was long gone. "No," she said. "I didn't. And the pills aren't sitting so well."

He grabbed a slice of bread for her from the fridge. "There's some pizza left over from last night, for when you think you can handle it."

The mention of last night cleared her mind, revived her like a shot of whiskey. She had to force herself not to tear the bread so quickly between her teeth, to pace her chewing and how fast she let the spongy dough slip down her throat without choking.

Henry had stood the TV upright and was dusting off the screen.

"This must be what it's like to live through a war," Olivay said.

"I suppose," he said.

"I'm sorry for snapping at you earlier," she said. "I think I snapped at you."

"It's fine."

"You're too nice."

Henry laughed. "Not everyone would agree with you."

"Of course not," she said but would have loved for him to name names. "You can't please everyone."

Henry continued to look around for something, picking up junk and tossing it aside.

"Have you ever been in love?" she asked. Why, she didn't know. A stupid question anyway, at their age. If he said no, he was lying. Or a freak.

"Yes," he said.

"How many times?"

"Once."

"What was her name?"

Henry stopped what he was doing. "Genevieve," he said without looking at her.

"Sounds French," Olivay said.

"It was."

"*Was*? What'd you do, kill her?"

Henry went completely still. "That isn't funny," he said, turning his face toward her. "Not even the slightest bit. You shouldn't talk to people like that. You have no idea what they've been through."

Olivay sunk into herself. She could feel the heat in her cheeks. "You're right," she said. "I'm sorry. The medication seems to be making me a little, I don't know. Loose."

"I told you not to take so much."

"That you did." She tried snapping her fingers in the air but they slid past each other with a fumbling thud.

Henry turned back to the TV.

"I'm going to change the subject now," Olivay said.

"Good."

"What exactly did the neighbor hear on the radio?"

"Two bombs, which we already figured, two water mains busted and flooding the streets, which we saw, and a whole bunch of political rhetoric you've heard before."

"Like what?"

"Freedom. America. Destroying our enemies."

"Are they already talking about going to war?"

"Apparently."

"With whom?"

"No idea. Whatever country has been 'harboring these terrorists'."

"But what if it's homegrown?"

"No one's really mentioning that."

Olivay's pain had been replaced with a fleecy kind of warmth, a pharmaceutical tenderness that ebbed throughout her body and brain. *Genevieve.* So touchy.

"Bombs exploding, people dying, on the brink of possibly another war, and yet, here we are," she said. "Like Nero playing the fiddle while Rome burns."

"The cithara," Henry said.

"Except I'm napping, and you're trying to get the TV up and running so we can watch it all unfold—what did you say?"

"It's a myth. If Nero were playing anything it would have been the cithara. The fiddle wasn't invented yet."

"Okay. Well."

"And Nero was a terrible person. I'd rather not be compared to him."

"All right, then. Thanks for the history lesson, Professor Nerd Wilkins."

"You're welcome."

"Was that your major or something? History? Did we talk about this?"

"No," he said, still looking around. "It wasn't."

"Okay," she offered. "Philosophy, then."

Henry stopped and held the top of his head as if she'd plucked the answer straight from inside. "How did you know that?"

"I was kidding," she said, realizing that the more she talked the more stoned she felt, her arms warbling through the air as if her elbows and wrists needed tightening. "No, I wasn't. It's the scruffy hair and shadowy whiskers thing. You kind of look the part."

Henry scratched his cheek.

"I like it, though. This look of yours."

A smirk rose in the corner of his mouth.

A charge shot between them, that spark, like in Levine's, and she thought of the wistful need in his eyes last night, that young-love longing, the way she'd pushed him off and took him in her mouth so she wouldn't have to see it again, wouldn't have to acknowledge any feelings he might have for her, or any she might have had for him.

And now? She didn't look away. For one fractured moment she allowed herself to be seen.

"Then I hope it doesn't come as a disappointment when I tell you that this *look* stems from a kind of thoughtful neglect," Henry said. "I'm well aware of the state I'm in half the time. I just choose to leave it alone."

"See. That right there sounds like a school of thought. *The School of Thoughtful Neglect.*"

Henry stepped to the side of the bed, leaned in, and kissed her so lightly on the cheek, it was as if he'd barely touched her at all. Then he leaned away and held her gaze. It was only then that she realized her hand was hanging midair, grazing nothing at all. She'd wanted to feel him. She wanted him to kiss her on the mouth.

"Thank you," Olivay said, lowering her hand.

"For what?"

"For changing everything."

He immediately looked away and shook his head, as much to himself, it seemed, as to her. "Any idea where the remote might be?" He turned the television toward the bed.

"That's what you're looking for?"

"I can't find the power button on your TV." He slid his fingers along the border of the TV screen the way he'd slid them up her thigh in the night.

"Try over there." Olivay pointed to an overturned basket full of magazines in the corner at the foot of the bed. "Check in that stack shoved against the wall."

She watched the way his body moved through space, her eyes like cameras capturing everything about him. She recalled what her mother once said about the awareness that accompanies tragedies. *The Zen of shock. That strange sense of departure and complete presence all at once.*

When planes hit the Twin Towers, Olivay had been awake only minutes, and yet she would always remember the precise angle of morning light on the wall, the smell and sound of coffee gurgling down the hall, the kitchen radio turned too loud, her mother gasping, cursing, and finally controlling her voice when she entered Olivay's room. Years later when Olivay mentioned this, her mother would tell her how decades after she could still recall with precise detail the wool sofa she'd been sitting on when JFK was shot. *The rough and musty fabric. The taste of lemonade on my lips.*

The magnolia leaves, the smell of warm blood on hot concrete, the licking, creaking sound of an open skull.

"Would you do me a favor?" she asked, an acidic chemical taste rising from her stomach, coating her tongue. "Could you get me my toothbrush, some water, and the toothpaste? I have a terrible taste in my mouth."

When Henry returned, she brushed her teeth over a bowl of water and wondered what details from today would stay with her. Peppermint. The sanitized smell of fresh gauze. The putrid stench and acrid dust of obliterated human beings and asphalt and palm trees and all manner of things that had once existed on her street coming to lay on her floor. The violent noise. The shoestring cutting off the blood in a tattered leg. All of it had already adhered to her senses for the rest of her life, and at the center was Henry, the scruffy-haired charmer forever marked in her memory, the trace of pleasure and pain on her skin, this sensual stranger she'd let go wherever he wanted, do whatever he wanted in her bed.

He lifted the remote from beneath the magazines. "Got it," he said, but Olivay was looking at the cover of one that had fallen out, with a photo of a white ranch house surrounded by a cactus garden, not so different from the one she and Will had almost lived in.

A picture zapped onto the TV screen. A *Breaking News* banner flashed beneath a reporter standing on a corner, squinting against the sun. His tie hung loose around his sweaty neck, the solid flap of hair-sprayed hair going up and down with the wind. Olivay tried to make out where he was. Helicopters filled the sky above him. The smoke had all but cleared, and now the man's mouth was moving without sound. The audio wasn't in sync.

Olivay recognized the gas station over his left shoulder as the man gestured toward drivers in the street who appeared to be abandoning their cars. The traffic was blocked. It was Westwood Boulevard, not too far from the 405, probably half a mile from Olivay's apartment. The reporter fingered his earpiece.

Jets zipped past with a resounding boom, and the reporter covered his ear and looked back to the camera. "Did you see those?" The audio suddenly on. "That's the Air Force. Those are F16s flying over our heads."

The thunderous sound of jets rumbled over the apartment.

"People are leaving their cars in the street," Henry said, and Olivay vaguely recalled a film she'd seen years ago, an apocalypse-themed movie that took place in LA with a famous actor whose name she suddenly couldn't think of, and on some level that was all this felt like, a movie, harmless, made-up entertainment, something to be shut off and put away after everyone had had their fun.

A small dog cowered along the sidewalk, and then set off running between the cars. A cab driver stepped out of his cab and shooed it further away, and a woman appeared from nowhere and held out her arms and the dog ran toward her. She kneeled and scooped it up, and Olivay began to cry.

Crying quickly gave way to laughing, quietly at her own weeping, which she buried in the duvet. Codeine, trauma, concussion, shock. All she needed now was a drink.

Motorcycles zipped past the edges of the paralyzed cars. Henry glanced sideways at Olivay wiping her eyes. She pretended not to notice him looking at her, and she guessed he was pretending not to notice her in tears.

And then, as if out of nowhere, or perhaps because of the motorcycles, something occurred to her about that morning. Henry had left early, telling her he didn't want to go, but he really had to, and for what? Nearly two hours later he was back at her door. And when she'd asked where he got her number, he told her Jerry had given it to him. But that was nearly two hours after he'd left her apartment in a hurry. Two hours to get a bag of sticky buns from Levine's. Where had he gone? If he was late for work, why in the world did he stay gone for two hours (at Levine's?) and then return to her apartment?

And something else, something she was surprised she hadn't asked him before. Where was his car? He had been with her since yesterday afternoon. They had walked to her apartment. He never mentioned having to move it in a neighborhood filled with meters and spaces that required parking passes. Levine's parking lot would have towed him by ten o'clock the night before. Wherever it was, he never mentioned that it could have been destroyed by the explosions.

"As you can see," the reporter said, "motorcyclists are the only ones able to get through. Police are telling us that they are rushing medical supplies to people in need using volunteers on motorcycles. Look at them zipping down sidewalks and alleys. I've never seen anything like this."

No, no, no.

Don't do that.

She wanted Henry to kiss her again.

Needed him to kiss her again.

Needed the thoughts inside her head to go away.

And so she asked him, just like that, if he wouldn't mind another kiss. "On the lips this time," she said. "And harder."

Henry cocked his head back as if trying to gauge if she was serious.

"And then I'll have a slice of pizza, if you don't mind."

"You can be a little hard to read," he said. "Anyone ever told you that?"

"Please," she said, closing her eyes, believing she would somehow know by the way he touched her, by the way he made her feel, that she could trust him, that he was really who he said he was.

Henry was still quick on his feet.

SIXTEEN

GRISLY PHOTOS FADED IN AND OUT ACROSS THE SCREEN
in slow motion, accompanied by a downtempo, crestfallen
soundtrack, and as much as Olivay could not get the images out
from behind her eyes, she could not stop thinking that somewhere,
long before today, some composer had been paid to sit alone in a
recording studio with a terrorist attack as his muse. What was he saying now to those around him? Turn it up, turn it up, that's my song?

Cracked skulls and torn flesh, motionless bodies in the background, faces covered with running jackets in the foreground, others weeping or screaming nearby, all photographs that must have
been taken within minutes, if not seconds of the explosions, and
they were all rolling by now in an attempt to pay homage to the
dead, but the slick production, the soundtrack drained her of empathy, and then filled her back up with disdain.

Olivay closed her eyes as if in prayer when the sound went
out, and when it returned she opened them to video footage from
a helicopter in the upper right corner of the screen. Palm trees
bowed in the wind like skinny showgirls with unwieldy feathered-
heads, a comical contrast set against a street full of charred cars

with blown-out windows, their metal roofs still smoking. The camera cut away to a woman limping through rubble on a sidewalk. A small, bloodied child dangled in her arms.

"Oh, God," she said. "Did you see this?"

The camera continued to follow as the woman turned a corner and waded against the torrent of gushing water, nearly dropping the child as she stumbled. The water reached the woman's knees.

The audio bounced around feedback until the reports overlapped and nothing could be understood fully.

"I think that's here," Olivay said. "Is that right outside? Is this live television?"

"I don't know," Henry said, moving toward the balcony.

"Where is she trying to go?" Olivay asked. There didn't seem to be anyone around her on the sidewalk, and Olivay didn't recognize the blackened storefronts. The water in the street was as high as the wheel wells of cars. The wind was blowing it along, creating small ripples on the surface. The camera zoomed back to the child's sooty leg. The other leg was gone.

"It must be the other main that broke," Henry said. "Not the one down there. It's already slowing down."

She didn't think he'd seen what she just saw. She scooted away from the TV, pushing as far as she could until she was able to lean her temple against the headboard of the bed. "Turn it off," she said. "Please."

She understood as well as anyone that shock didn't wear off all at once. The mind wasn't designed that way, reality needed to unfold slowly, in stages, so as not to shock the system even more, and so it was only now, hours into this nightmare, that she understood the glass from the broken windows and other junk that had blasted into the room were still embedded in her back and thighs. What was in her skin exactly? She began to itch all over. Nausea gained on her again. She searched for the horizon, a focal point to calm the sickness, but the horizon was mucked-up windows coated in who knew what, and she suddenly recalled a term coined after 9/11, *organic shrapnel*, and she felt even sicker at the possibility of being implanted with the bone and tissue of other human beings.

She slipped her trembling hands beneath her to try and gain some control.

"That footage has got to be from earlier," she said, because surely a woman with a child would have already found help. Surely that child had been saved. "Why would anyone do this?" she whispered.

"I don't know," Henry said, and she could hear the crack in his voice. He didn't look at her when he spoke.

She was exhausted, her bones too heavy for her skin. A fine layer of white dusty plaster from the walls coated the headboard and ground against her cheek. She pressed against it, eased up, then pressed harder, and harder until a trace of pain burned past the numbness into her bone. Like sucking on an aching tooth, she couldn't leave it alone, didn't want to leave it alone.

Henry had left the TV running, and Olivay listened against her will as panels of men and women hashed through the crisis, taking turns deflecting the others' outbursts, while at the same time failing to manage their own.

"I do not regard the murder of Americans today as anything less than barbaric, cruel, and abhorrent, and I believe we need to catch those responsible and bring them to justice. But isn't the execution of elementary school students in the same category? Or a massacre at a movie theater? A college campus? A neighborhood Safeway?"

"Cut his mic."

"This is bigotry."

"This is treason."

"You don't have to live in this country. There are plenty of socialist nations that would love to have you. So long as you don't mind paying double the taxes."

"I mean, come on, people! Over 12,000 American gun deaths last year alone, and still not enough to justify any gun reform in the United States, but instead rallying an extremist base to show off open-carries and defend first and second amendment rights."

"Cut his mic!"

"I'm not saying there isn't a threat coming from abroad, if in fact it is from abroad, but there is much work to be done at home before we can police criminals from other parts of the world in the concept of peace."

They cut his mic, and others', though it seemed as if everyone had already had their say.

A woman was reporting on the lack of confirmation about how many people had been injured or killed, but everyone seemed to agree that thousands had been gathered within those blocks—runners and spectators made up of children, parents, spouses, and friends of those in the race.

"My car is in the lot beneath the building," Olivay said. "If we can get it out. If we can get through the streets we can leave. And just keep driving. Head to Mexico or Canada. When was the last time someone attacked Mexico or Canada? *Ever?*"

"We can't go anywhere," Henry said. "We can't just drive through a crime scene."

"What about your car?" she asked. "Where did you park? Maybe it's not on one of the blocked-off streets."

"I don't have a car," he said.

One beat. Two beats. How long should she wait to ask the question? How long before she could ask it without sounding accusatory?

Three beats.

"How do you get around?" she asked, and realized she was bracing for a lie about the bus, or a bicycle, anything other than—

"A motorcycle," he said. "And I'm sure it was blown to smithereens."

It didn't matter that she couldn't quite think of what to say. He was already talking over her.

"I didn't want to tell you." His hands jumped up for emphasis. "I actually thought twice before introducing myself. I didn't want to be a reminder in any way of what had happened to you. It's bad enough that I write for the *Tribune*.

Olivay said nothing.

"But there are a lot of people in this town who ride motorcycles. You realize that. Tens of thousands, in fact—"

"You didn't want to be a reminder in the same way Jerry didn't want you to be a reminder?"

"Yes."

"Did Jerry actually say that, or was it all coming from you?"

"It's exactly what Jerry said to me. But of course I was already thinking the same thing."

Tens of thousands of motorcycles zipping in and out of freeway traffic, riders taking their lives into their own hands in a way that drivers in cars were not. Like a death wish, she'd always thought, watching them weave in and out of traffic on the 10, narrowly missing rearview mirrors, wondering what it must feel like every day, every moment, to be inches from an endless succession of tiny things that could kill you.

SEVENTEEN

MRS. HIGHTOWER'S VOICE ROSE IN THE HALLWAY ABOVE
the others', speaking with the practiced tone of having lived through
a war, even if she'd been a small child when London was bombed by
the Germans. She once told Olivay how it had *formed and informed
her, for better or worse, of the world and mankind at large.* Her English accent was still intact, and this was how she spoke, which was
not so different from the way Olivay's mother often said things,
answering questions with bigger questions, layering innuendos,
meanings always hinted at if not directly pointed out. One of the
few things Olivay had looked forward to this past year was greeting Mrs. Hightower in the hallway, or finding her at her door with
a homemade pie in her hands, and catching up with that pleasant,
jaunty accent.

Now again, here, Olivay smiled at her voice, relieved to hear
her sounding so perfectly well, asking if others had filled their tubs
with water. "So hurry now, then!" she said. "The tanks upstairs may
have already run dry!"

Olivay couldn't believe she hadn't thought of filling pots with
water. No different than an earthquake. It was standard protocol.

Then again, Henry hadn't thought of it either, and he wasn't the one with a concussion.

That kiss earlier. He had done exactly as she'd asked. It felt hard and sure of nothing, but their mouths and tongues moved against one another. Her lips were warm and clumsy from the codeine, a little lost inside Henry's, including the small lump where she'd punched him that morning, and she had wanted him to touch her everywhere just to see if her body felt equally untethered. Instead he held her out from him as if she were a frightened little girl, whispering how everything was going to be all right, that she was going to be fine, and so she'd patted his arm and gently pushed him away, told him of course, and gave a nod.

"Would you mind pulling some pots out of the cupboard and filling them with water?" Olivay asked. "I don't have a bathtub to fill."

Henry no longer seemed quick with an answer, no longer so quick to converse. Maybe he was finally weary from all that was happening, or maybe, as he shoved more trash across the floor with the side of his shoe, he was wondering how he'd made her feel, going on about riding a motorcycle, how he'd been driving one since he was a teenager living in one rural area after another, and was more skilled at riding a motorcycle than he was at driving a car, which she took to mean that he never would have lost control and barreled down a sidewalk into a man. Did he really think she was considering this? Of course it crossed her mind, how could it not? But she never said as much, and what had really interested her was the part about him living in so many rural areas. What was that all about? He'd never mentioned that yesterday. Just the woofing and the crying peacocks. But he'd had an Arcadian air about him from the start. Hadn't he? A dweller from a strange principality that she could not name.

But right now she didn't feel like uttering another word.

"I have to say something," Henry said, standing nearly ten feet away with his hands on his hips.

"Don't feel like you have to," Olivay said.

"I know how selfish it's going to sound . . ." He drifted off a little, holding the top of his head as he glanced toward the windows. He dropped his hand. "I can't stop thinking about what would have happened if you hadn't let me back in."

She sat slightly upright and glanced at her knee, careful not to bend it, and it was only now that she noticed how expertly he'd bandaged it. The right amount of gauze, the careful tuck on the end to hold it in place. If she didn't know better, she'd think Henry was a nurse. A farmhand and a nurse. But of course Henry was neither of those things. Henry was a journalist for the *Tribune*.

"I would have been out there. Right there in the middle of everything. What if you hadn't let me back in?"

Olivay lay on her side and didn't lift her head from the pillow. "Well, Henry. I suppose you'd be dead."

"Exactly."

The old *what if* game. Don't go down that road. *Don't do that.* But old habits were so hard to break, and her own mind was full of heavy tumblers, bowling balls aimed for the gutters.

What if she'd allowed Will to crawl back into bed instead of rushing him out the door? What if she'd gotten up early and they'd gone together, walking side by side when the motorcycle barreled through? What if she'd been hit instead of Will? What if they'd already turned the corner and the motorcycle had gone on to hit someone else? Or never hit anyone at all?

What if she'd never loved him, or loved him even more?

"What if I'd invited myself to breakfast with you at Levine's?" Olivay said flatly. "What if we'd been sitting there with our sticky buns and coffee?"

Henry stared at her.

"It's a riddle never meant to be solved. I don't think it's even meant to be asked in the first place. But trust me, I get the appeal."

Henry appeared to be thinking this through, his eyes darkening into a narrow squint.

"Here's one," she said. "What if Will and I had been arguing just before he left that morning? Do you think it would have been easier to let him go? Or *harder* to let him go? If he'd been killed during one of our darker days instead of in the middle of a more . . . I don't know what to call it . . . a more *stable* kind of love, do you think I would have felt any less devastated?"

"Jesus. Come on. I didn't mean anything like that . . ."

"You know, there were times when I used to wonder, after one of our really ugly fights, what it would be like if he died and left me alone. No, I did, it's true. Just like those awful people on the radio. I don't care what you think, Henry. I don't care that I'm saying this out loud. I don't see what difference it makes. We could be dead an hour from now. A minute from now. Look at Will. Case in point."

"Olivay."

"Camelot. Ha! There was no Camelot. Everyone knows that JFK was a drug addict and a womanizer."

"If I knew I was going to drag to all of this out, I wouldn't have said anything."

"So I ask you, does everyone have those kinds of thoughts about the people they love? Did you ever have those kinds of thoughts about Genevieve?"

"No."

"Well, then, I'm guessing you're special, Henry. Either that or you weren't together long enough. Take it from me, it leaves you feeling pretty awful about yourself. Or it should. Maybe it doesn't at all. You don't strike me as someone who feels too awful about himself."

"We were together plenty," Henry said.

"Plenty."

"Yes."

"Where the hell are you from? Who talks like that?"

Henry didn't even look at her.

"What I'm saying is, all I'm left with is all there is—memories of us telling each other that the love we felt was stronger than the love we'd felt when we first met."

"You really don't need to go on."

"It was electric again, Henry. You know how things are when you're coming out of a dark patch? It's like make-up sex, only it's your *life*. There you are driving in the car all by yourself, or walking down the aisle in the grocery store, and a giddiness pops up in your chest, some revived affection, just like starting over. But are you *really*? The thing is, every time it happens it fools you into believing in a happily-ever-after until you've got two people so committed to each other, so enmeshed in a mutual life, so far *gone*, really, that fighting, when it comes back around, is so fiercely complicated that you're like two scorpions in a bottle."

"Really, Olivay. I've heard enough!"

Oh, she was on fire now, wasn't she? It felt good to get it all out. It felt good to lash at someone this way.

Henry continued to hold his ground, arms crossed as if preparing his own retaliation.

"For what feels like an eternity," she said. "Of course 'eternity' in this case is a relative term."

"Is that it? Is that all you ever did? Fight with each other?"

Look at how skilled he was. How quickly he could send things off in another direction, like a hostage negotiator. How quickly she felt disarmed.

"No," she scoffed. "Of course not."

"Well it sure sounds like it."

"You don't want to know how things were," she said. "Trust me."

He uncrossed his arms. "Actually, I do."

"Forget it," she said.

Henry twisted his mouth to the side.

"Anyway," she said. "I see your point about the thin line between life and death, but you could have just gone to work this morning like you said you were going to. You would have been a mile away from here if you had. Hell, you could have been in San Diego for all the time it took you to return."

Henry's neck and cheeks flushed red. Not like he was embarrassed. Fury appeared to be crawling hot beneath his skin.

"All that talk about wishing you didn't have to go," she said. "What was that all about?"

"I'm working on a story," he said. "I went to Levine's with my computer so I could work."

I would never do anything to hurt you.

Too late for that, Jack Wilkins.

The same need she'd felt that morning returned. To hit him and please him at once. "What if? What if? It's really best not to play the game. That's all I'm saying."

Olivay curled her hands closed. The blood no longer leaked out. "We really ought to fill up some water jugs while we still can," Olivay said.

"You saved us both, you know," Henry said. "First by not inviting yourself along with me to Levine's, then by letting me back in. Some strange luck, don't you think?"

She didn't like the way he said that. As if she'd had something up her sleeve, as if she knew more than he did about something she wasn't saying. Could he see what she was thinking now, see all the way into the back of her mind where her thoughts no longer struggled, no longer were afraid to let loose? If so, she didn't care. There was plenty more to this guy than met the eye. Let him see what he wanted to see. *I believe you're the one with the strange luck, Henry. You're the one with a thing or two up his sleeve.*

EIGHTEEN

HENRY STOOD AT THE SOUND OF KNOCKING ON HER door, looking down at Olivay with a stranger's stare she did not know how to read.

"Do you want me to get that?" he asked.

"Olivay, dear?" Mrs. Hightower called out. She banged with what Olivay knew was a brittle fist. "Are you home?"

Olivay pulled herself up and nodded.

When Henry opened the door, Mrs. Hightower stepped back.

"Sorry," he said. "I didn't mean to startle you."

She charged past him and straight toward Olivay. She hadn't brushed her long gray hair, which, until this moment, Olivay had never seen down. It wisped around her shoulders as she trudged across the room.

The sight of Olivay must have frightened her. "What on earth?" She looked around the floor and broken windows covered in sheets, and then at Olivay.

"I'm *fine*," Olivay said, almost cheerily. It was part codeine, part wanting to spare her any worry, recalling how upset she'd been when she drove Olivay to the hospital behind the ambulance, holding her hand as Will's blood dried like glue between them. She'd wept easily and openly while Olivay stared straight ahead into the red lights of the ambulance, and then down at the way they lit up her skin.

Now she brushed Olivay's hair to the side and checked her forehead. "Nasty great lump," she said, and lightly touched the bandage on her knee.

"I fell on the floor," Olivay said. "It's nothing. Henry . . . this is Henry . . . bandaged me up."

Her small, spotted hand patted the side of Olivay's hip, and the motherly gesture caught Olivay unaware and a sting of tears rushed along her lids. "Oh darling," Mrs. Hightower said. "You poor thing."

Olivay didn't mention she was feeling a little high, and that the pills might be making her weepier than she would have been without, and anyway she didn't want the attention from Mrs. Hightower to stop. She made Olivay feel as if she were being absolved of some terrible thing.

Mrs. Hightower glanced between Olivay and Henry, and then toward the Egg Chair with the stop sign jammed through the back. "Mother of God," she said.

Olivay didn't tell her she'd been sitting there a fraction of a second before it flew through the window.

"You've no tub," Mrs. Hightower said, and turned to Henry. "Can you fill some pots with water while there's still some left in the tanks?"

"I already asked him," Olivay said, as if to keep herself from looking stupid. Making herself feel better by making him feel worse.

"I was just about to," Henry said.

Mrs. Hightower stood. "I wanted to make sure you'd heard. The police are asking everyone to remain indoors. There could be other things to come."

Olivay nodded.

"What else did they say?" Henry asked.

"They're going door to door. Asking questions. They're headed up here, no doubt. Making sure the suspect or suspects aren't hiding in plain sight."

Olivay glanced at Henry.

"Is that it?" he asked. "Did they say how long they wanted us to stay here and wait?"

"People have been electrocuted in the water."

Olivay closed her eyes, but behind her lids sparks from the dry cleaner's appeared as real as if she were seeing it happen again, and she sprang them open.

"It's beyond dreadful. They're working to get the lines out of the street. But there's no way to shut the water main off quickly. Apparently a sudden shutoff would just cause others to break."

"This is unbelievable," Olivay said.

"Everyone is to remain indoors unless they're in need of medical attention. But even then, what's one to do? You can't run out into the street."

Henry covered his eyes and shook his head at the floor.

"I don't know any more than that. But you. Are you sure you aren't in need of medical attention, love? I suppose we could try for an ambulance, or carry you out the back through the alleyway. Oh, but I believe there's water there, too."

Olivay shook her head. "I don't need anything. Really. I've got Henry here." She tossed him a smile, but the string of tension between them had not yet been cut. He nodded politely toward Mrs. Hightower in return.

Mrs. Hightower whispered next to Olivay's ear. "He's your boyfriend, then?" She leaned back.

"Yes," Olivay said. "Yes, he is."

Olivay glanced at Henry with a grin.

Mrs. Hightower winked at Olivay.

"Did they say anything about the building?" Henry asked.

"The building?" Mrs. Hightower asked. "What do you mean?"

"The cracks in the walls," Henry said.

Olivay studied them closely. They were larger than she'd first thought.

Henry was looking directly at her now and it took a second to realize he was really posing a question to her because she was an architect, as if that were the same as being an engineer. She had, in fact, seen the design plans when she bought the place while she and Will were still dating, and the thought had already crossed her mind that a lateral shift from an explosion might be similar to an earthquake. But the truth was, she'd felt the walls slide sideways just like everyone else, and had no idea what the consequence would be. It was a new building. Earthquake safety and all that—

"Fuck if I know," she said, and Mrs. Hightower swung her head around. "Sorry. No. That's not what I meant. I'm sure the cracks are just superficial." The image of the Twin Towers flashed before her, their haunting, inconceivable collapse. The skin on her back had really begun to ache.

"How about you sit here with her," Mrs. Hightower said to Henry as she stepped lightly across the messy floor wearing high-waisted jeans and a deep blue cardigan that appeared as clean as if it had just been laundered. She didn't seem to have a scratch on her, but of course her apartment faced the courtyard, away from the street. She shoved pots from the lower cupboard beneath the running faucet, which sputtered in loud, pressurized fits.

"Don't forget this one," Olivay said of the metal pot near the bed from earlier when she thought she might be sick. Henry reached for it, but Olivay held tight to the rim a second too long before letting go. He looked at her as if she'd come a little unhinged. But she was just being immature, wasn't she? "Just like your days in the pink Safari Park," she said. "No running water."

Henry jerked the pot from her grip and held it to his chest as if protecting it from some other plan she might have had until he walked over to Mrs. Hightower and let it go.

The TV popped back on, and Henry sat on the end of the bed and strained forward to listen. The news now came from reporters in a studio. Ricardo and Miranda, the team who had spent weeks "updating viewers" on Will's story.

"Oh, kiss my ass," Olivay said, and all eyes in the room turned to her. She had been wrong about the revolver. If she had one now, she would lift it from its cedar box and empty the chamber into the TV screen.

"We now confirm that all flights coming in and out of LAX have been suspended until further notice," Miranda said. She went on to explain how everyone in the area of the bombings and water main breaks was to remain indoors.

"As I said!" Mrs. Hightower called out over the sputtering tap and TV.

"But it's not an *order*?" Olivay said. "Not an actual lockdown."

"She's not calling it that, in any case," Henry said.

"So, you could leave if you wanted to?"

Henry stared.

"I'm not suggesting you go," Olivay said. "I could leave. We could leave."

"Oh dear," Mrs. Hightower said. "You're in no shape to go anywhere even if you could get out of here safely. You're better off in your own home. Even in the state it's in."

Miranda's voice suddenly took on a frenetic tone, and Mrs. Hightower turned down the faucet to hear. "Can you make it louder, please?" She switched the water back to full force, but it seemed to have already lost pressure.

A look of fresh panic had filled Miranda's eyes. She held up a finger to the cameras and began nodding, apparently to the person in her ear. Her mouth hung slightly open.

Wind whipped the windows above the bed and Olivay gripped the duvet. Something else was coming. The cruelty of the day wasn't finished with them yet.

"Okay. This is breaking news, just now coming into us here at News 7. There have been reports of fires. Several, in fact. Fires spotted in the Santa Monica mountains near Topanga, and . . . and also this as well—this as well." She paused and repeated *this as well* several more times as if trying to speak over the person in her ear. "Coldwater Canyon. We now confirm that more than one large fire has been spotted in Coldwater Canyon."

"Mother of God," Mrs. Hightower said, and banged a pot of water down onto the stove.

The Santa Ana winds. It couldn't be a coincidence. "Did someone set them on purpose?" Olivay said, thinking of the way they whipped east to west, picturing the fires meeting up with the disaster already in progress and fueling it anew. When she looked over at Henry, she saw for the first time since the bombs had gone off that his hands were shaking. He curled them into fists, ran them up and down his thighs. Then he drummed his knees nervously, while his breathing beneath the bloody wings on his back rose and fell a little heavier.

He seemed not to hear her question.

"The president has addressed the attacks," Miranda said, and it was clear that she was shaken in a way she hadn't been before, her voice breaking in her throat, unable to coat her fear, and Olivay realized that the Studio City newsroom she was sitting in was located in the center of the encroaching fires she'd just been forced to report. Olivay no longer wanted to shoot the TV screen, no longer hated Miranda in the same way.

"The president has said, and I quote: 'We still do not know who did this or why. But make no mistake—we will get to the bottom of this. Anyone responsible will feel the full weight of justice.'"

"I can't sit here anymore," Henry said, jumping up and shutting off the TV. "Do you have a broom?"

"What?"

"A broom," he said.

"Of course I have a broom." Olivay slowly pointed to the closet near the bathroom.

Mrs. Hightower cocked her head, her expression a fleeting mix of distaste and bewilderment, and then she saw Olivay looking and turned to peek inside the four pots she'd filled, two of which were smaller sauce pans. "Not much here, but it's certainly better than nothing," she said.

Olivay didn't understand. With all that had happened in the last twenty-four hours, Henry might have shown a range of emotions, but instead he'd remained a fairly good study in calm. A soldier trained for a crisis. A journalist, a man who could take whatever was thrown at him. But now, with the fires, he was quickly veering off from the script, from the person he had seemed to her to be. Why would *this* be the thing that seemed to be pushing him over the edge?

He snatched up the broom as if it were a rake, shoving the entire mess sideways across the floor, dragging it into a large jumble in the corner.

Mrs. Hightower exchanged a look with Olivay. "The pots are as full as they're going to get," she said. "I think you may have gotten the last drops."

"Thank you," Olivay said.

"Right, then." She crossed the room and kissed Olivay good-bye on the temple, and Olivay asked her to please hand her the remote, which she immediately gave her, and Olivay turned the news back on because somehow Miranda's voice in the room had turned into a comfort.

Henry never looked up from his sweeping.

"Everything is going to be fine," Mrs. Hightower said. "That's the National Guard floating around above our heads. This country is full of might. Don't you worry yourself over a few bad men."

But Olivay couldn't help thinking about Hurricane Katrina. The thousands of people abandoned to that disaster. They had known the might of the country, too. Watched it fly right over their heads for days, everyone waving at it, everyone waiting for a rescue that never came.

NINETEEN

THE SANTA ANAS WERE LIKE HURRICANES, MIGHTY
pressures churning away from civilization, spinning first in the
desert in the same way hurricanes formed in distant oceans until
their full force was unleashed on cities and towns and islands where
people made their lives. It was only there, among the living, that
their strength would finally be extinguished.

The winds sped east to west—everyone knew this was how they
traveled—everyone knew they whipped viciously and without warning to the north and south, too, in swift, unpredictable gusts, turning fires into erratic, mercurial beasts nearly impossible to contain.

Whoever had attacked them knew this, and it was hard not
to admit, no matter how evil the intent, that it was also a brilliant
plan. The real surprise was that no one had tried it before.

Henry had changed his mind about the TV. He would not stop
watching now, even as he shoved the broom around harder than
before. He continued to glance up and pause at it with a peculiar
expression. Anticipation? Expectation? It was as if a specific question had come to mind and he kept waiting for the TV to answer.

"Now you've got religious leaders in this country going on television claiming that God has taken revenge on the gays in Hollywood," the TV blared. "That God himself started those fires."

Olivay picked up the remote and lowered the volume. "You seem pretty upset. Is there someone on the Eastside that you're worried about? Does Genevieve live near there?"

He spun on her, gripping the broom so hard she could see his knuckles had gone white. "Why *wouldn't* I be upset? It's like some kind of fucking Armageddon out there. Why aren't you *more* upset?"

"*Me?*" What on earth could he mean? "Me? Are you joking?" What did he see when he looked at her?

"And, *no.* Genevieve *does not* live over there. Not that it's any of your damn business."

"Jesus Christ, Henry! What has happened to you? I mean, you've acted like Mr. Calm and Collected throughout this whole bizarre thing, and now suddenly your hands are shaking and you're *sweeping!* You're like, I don't know, attached to a *broom*, and yelling at me." The broom made a loud crack when he shoved it to the concrete floor. "Maybe it's because I've lived through worse!" he said.

Olivay squinted, realizing only then that her eyes had continued to sting from the smoke. "Really? Worse than what? The apocalypse outside our door?"

Henry grabbed the broom back up off the floor. He didn't look at her. Didn't speak.

"What are you talking about?" Olivay asked.

"Nothing," Henry said. "Never mind."

"Oh, come on!" she shouted.

But Henry didn't say a word, and for a moment Olivay felt a familiar isolation, once again a castaway shipwrecked on the same bed she'd been lost to for nearly a year.

"And anyway," she said, "how would you know if you've lived

through worse when we don't even know what's happened? Or what might be happening still?"

"Never mind," he said, sweeping again. "I didn't mean it like that."

"How did you mean it?"

"Can we just drop it?"

Olivay couldn't. "I know I asked you to stay with me. But why didn't you go out there when it first happened and take pictures? Or maybe after I'd drifted off or something? Don't you think Jerry is going to be pissed?"

"I hope his main concern is that I'm alive. That *we're* alive."

"Well, sure but—"

"Besides, I *did* go."

"What do you mean?"

"I slipped out a little while ago when you were asleep."

"What?"

"I wasn't gone longer than ten minutes."

"Why didn't you tell me?"

"What does it matter?"

God, how she hated that phrase. *What does it matter, Olivay? I love you, Olivay.*

"Well, I don't know, Henry, it just *does*. Like the kind of information anyone else might have let me in on. It seems a bit pertinent, wouldn't you say?"

He didn't answer.

"I mean, what did you see?" she asked.

"The same stuff you saw from the balcony."

"Did you take photographs?"

"Every bit of debris is considered evidence. I couldn't get close to where the second bomb went off."

"But did you take pictures?"

"Of course I did."

"Did you see anyone who needed help?"

"I would have just been in the way of professionals trying to help."

"But did you see anyone?"

"Yes! Okay? I saw a little kid get pulled out from under a car. And if you want to know, he was dead. All right? And an old man, too, a runner with half his face missing, but he was very much alive, very much aware of what was going on when they found him beneath a concrete slab."

"My God, Henry."

"I didn't want to upset you."

"*Me*? What about you? How in the world could you come back in here and behave so normally? What about having some kind of *human reaction*? What is wrong with you?"

At this, Henry tightened his lips against his teeth. He was mad now. Boy, was he ever. "I'm going to pretend you never said that."

"Yeah, well, do whatever you like, Henry."

"Damn it, Olivay. Your meanness really doesn't know when to quit. It just keeps climbing and climbing until you've got your opponent by the throat."

She stopped. Was this really how he saw her? Was this really how she was? She didn't think she would sit for that from Will. But for whatever reason, she was taking it on the chin from Henry.

"What did you do with the photos?" she asked.

"Nothing. I'll send them to Jerry as soon as I get a signal."

"Shouldn't you be sending them to the police?"

"Look, I'm a journalist, for god's sake. I can see what you're thinking."

"I'm not thinking *anything*," Olivay said. "But I'm *guessing* that Homeland Security might really like to see whatever you have. There could be something on there that you aren't even aware of."

"I realize that. But I can't send them to *anyone* until I get a signal. This is part of the reason I keep trying."

"Well. You didn't even mention sending them to the police."

"I'm a *journalist*! It's my role to document, just like it's the role of the police and firemen and doctors to do what they do when a crisis hits. And there were plenty of them down there, I assure you."

"*All right!*"

Henry shoved the broom into the mess even harder.

She shoved the duvet from her legs. The codeine was starting to wear off.

God, how she hated that unsteady feeling after a fight, that need for solid ground while being driven by pride and hurt feelings, the impossibility of avoiding being trampled while trying to find a way back.

His phone was on the nightstand next to hers. His backpack slumped on the kitchen counter, and she recalled how, right after the first bomb had gone off, Henry had snatched it up and attached it to his back as if he were leaving, or trying to protect what was inside. But from what? How did he know it might get damaged? How did he know to duck behind the end of the sofa? Olivay hadn't thought to protect anything other than herself; in fact there had been no time to think. In an instant, she had become a body scrabbling blindly for cover, taken over by a reptilian brain whose sole purpose was to keep her alive.

TWENTY

"FUCKING TOWELHEADS!"

The screams were so loud that the strain and crack in the man's vocal chords reached all the way from the street into the apartment.

"What the hell is going on?" Olivay said.

Henry opened the balcony door.

"Go back to the desert, you rotten pieces of shit!" the man screamed.

"Oh, my God," Olivay said.

Henry ducked his head back inside. "It's a guy with no shirt or shoes out on his balcony. About a half block down. He's throwing something at Hassan's Deli across the street."

"You think you can come over here and do this shit to us?" the man yelled. "We're going to destroy *your* families. We're going to burn your babies on sticks."

"Holy shit," Olivay said. "Is someone trying to get him under control?"

"Some cops are coming out on another balcony below him, a couple of apartments down. Oh—"

"He's insane," Olivay said. "What? What's going on?"

Voices were rising at once, men and women yelling for the man to raise his hands and drop to his knees.

"The guy just ran inside his apartment."

"Good."

"But now someone else is yelling at the cops. There are five cops now. Two on one balcony, and three on another. And they all just drew their guns."

"Tehrangeles, my ass!" the man yelled.

"He's back," Henry said.

"Little Persia, my ass!"

"As you can hear," Henry said.

"Your hands up and your knees on the ground!" a man yelled. "*Down!*"

"Now!" a woman yelled.

"Does he have some kind of weapon?" Olivay asked. "What does he have?"

"I don't know."

"They *aren't* going to shoot him," Olivay said.

"The way their guns are pointed . . ."

A crowd of voices exploded until it was impossible to understand who was saying what, and now a wailing siren approached, drowning everything out, including Henry.

"Shit," Henry said.

"What?"

"It looks like a gun in his hands."

"Down, down, down!" they all yelled, and Henry winced and grabbed his head, and the crackling sound of fireworks was surely the spray of bullets.

Olivay cupped her ears and closed her eyes as Henry rushed in and slammed the door behind him.

When she looked up, he was staring across the room at nothing she could see, like a man gazing into the future or the past—either way, what he saw clearly appeared real to him, his mouth gaping like a bird's, and then, only twice, his bottom lip quivered. If Olivay hadn't been looking, she would have missed it.

"Henry," she said.

He leaned his back into the glass door and closed his eyes and mouth.

Another siren. An ambulance, she guessed.

"Henry, come here."

He didn't move.

The sound of bullets rattled her brain, and she tried to picture who the man might have been, this neighbor so close, someone she had surely passed on the street. Maybe he was scum every day of his life, but he could have been generally kind, too. She recalled the horrible things she'd said to the social worker in the hospital the day Will had died, and to the doctors, too, who'd tried so hard to revive him, but her mind had clouded over, slipped away entirely, really, and in its place something dark and vile had taken hold.

She never should have said what she did to Henry about "being *human*," never should have accused him of being insensitive to what he had seen. That quiver in his mouth, she could barely think of it seconds later without verging on tears. She couldn't say his name without loathing herself so completely that she wondered why he hadn't walked out. He should have walked out and left her there.

"Please," she said. "It's not easy for me to get up from here."

He shook his head, pushed himself away from the door, and began rolling up the rugs.

"What are you doing?"

"I'm going to mop."

He squirted cleaner from beneath the sink into the smallest pot Mrs. Hightower had filled, plunged the mop in, and she said nothing about that water being meant for them to live off of for who knew how long. She said nothing as he swiped the mop across the concrete floor until the room smelled more lemon and pine than smoke and destruction.

He used a hand towel to protect his palms while trying to wedge the stop sign out of the chair. Olivay didn't understand why he bothered. It wasn't as if the chair could be used again, but she still said nothing, just watched him struggle, understanding that he needed to do something physical, to push his body until whatever was resisting him gave in. As for the chair, he finally shoved it into the corner pile with everything else. He dampened a white sheet in the mop water and threw it over the mound to keep the dust from lifting off into the room, then looked around as if for another task.

The sirens were fading now for longer stretches of time.

By four p.m., they had eaten the remainder of the bread, two apples from the crisper, yogurt, and half of a dark chocolate bar. Several slices of pizza remained for later. Olivay tried to read her novel again but couldn't find the thread, couldn't makes sense of the jumps in time and place, and gave up after reading the same bar scene five times in a row without knowing what she'd read. It seemed the only proper thing left to do was worry and wait.

Henry wrote in a notebook at the table, the same thin notebook style Will had used, the kind he'd had in his messenger bag when he died.

Rumors had started to swirl in the news about a man with Middle Eastern features being picked up for questioning. But less than an hour later, the story was that no man with Middle Eastern features had ever been picked up—in fact, there was no suspect, much less a man with Middle Eastern features, and apologies were doled out across every station. After that, attention was diverted to a van parked near the first bombing. It had been rented through U-Haul.

"In whose name?" the contributors on TV asked.

People calling in wanted to know.

"Was he a *Joe* or a *Mohammed*? What? There's nothing wrong with asking that question. If we'd been asking these kinds of questions years ago, we would have never had 9/11."

"Oh, for crying out loud! Somebody take his mic."

"The van near the first bombing actually belonged to the Cup Cake Shoppe on the corner. We apologize for the misinformation."

Al Qaeda, Jihadists, Domestic Terrorists, Revelations, Armies of God. Everyone had a candidate. No one had an answer.

Why hadn't anyone come forward yet to take responsibility?

Leaders from around the world condemned the acts, spoke in support of their friend, the United States. Saudi Arabia was quick about it. Great Britain, too, though they included a loose reference to the IRA, which drew a nasty rebuke from Ireland about how *now was not the time*.

"Do you think you could get up for a minute?" Henry asked out of the blue. "I can help you sit at the table. I want to change the bedding, if that's all right."

He had shaken the dust and debris off earlier, but the blood stains and dirt remained.

She could see him making an effort to bridge the gap that had opened up between them, and she nodded and stood and placed her arm around his shoulders while he held her at the waist, and now he smiled at her when his mouth was only inches from her own, and God help her having him so close, and then she hopped down with her good leg and gravity took over, yanking at her bad knee like a set of strong fingers. How bad might it hurt without the codeine? She couldn't imagine. Henry told her he was sorry in that voice of his, everything about the way he took care of her seemed sincere. He picked her up once again and sat her on the kitchen chair. He grabbed the second chair and propped her leg across it.

Sweat prickled her hairline. He handed her a bottle of water.

He set the binoculars back on the sideboard and she pretended not to notice. She watched him change the sheets like a soldier, snapping and straightening with a quickness that wore her out. He'd chosen the white and orange set from the closet that Olivay had bought with Will in mind. It had given the room a more masculine feel, and here again with Henry standing over it.

"That's better," he announced.

When Olivay didn't say anything, he asked her if she was all right.

"I'd say it's all relative," she said.

"Sure it is," he agreed.

"How about you?"

"I think you're watching me." He stuffed his fists deep into the pockets of his dirty jeans, but didn't turn away from her eyes. "I don't think you trust me."

"Well," she said.

It was only partially true.

"Well," she repeated like an idiot because she just didn't know what else to say, and anyway, saying "well" twice had the feel of two strong columns holding up her lie. "That's just not true."

TWENTY-ONE

"WHO ARE YOU, HENRY?" OLIVAY ASKED. "I MEAN, where'd you come from, what's your family like? In all of our chit-chat yesterday, you never really told me."

He sunk his hands into his pockets. "Why do you want to know?"

Olivay laughed. "It's an innocent enough question, don't you think? Considering all we've shared to this point?"

Henry leaned his hip against the sink. Then he switched and leaned into the other. He hadn't been able to sit still for more than ten minutes at a time without getting up to do something.

"The answers will just bore you. Or worse."

"Worse?"

"You'll find out how boring I am."

"I'll be the judge of what's boring and what's not."

He pulled his hands from his pockets.

"Come on," she said. "We appear to have nothing but time."

"You really want to know?"

"I do."

He sat across from her at the table and flashed his eyes to the right where memory is stored, according to her mother, which meant he was about to tell her the truth.

"Where do you want me to start?"

"Anywhere. But cut to the chase. The real stuff. We may not have as much time as we think."

The small wince in the corner of his mouth surprised her.

"Tell me a story, Henry. The one about you."

"All right. Okay. The story of Henry. The *real* stuff."

"Exactly."

"Let's see . . ."

"Don't think too hard. What's the first thing that comes to your mind about growing up?"

"When I was a kid my parents' optimism about my future used to fill me with dread," he said.

Olivay laughed. "Sorry. That's. *What?* No. Go ahead. Please. I've got to hear this."

Henry tilted his head.

"I'm serious," she said. "That's one hell of a topic sentence."

"Actually, it was really more like a *low-grade* kind of dread."

"Now you're just showing off."

"I'm not making this up. I was convinced that my life was going to be a huge disappointment, and there was nothing I could do to stop their constant good cheer."

"Wow."

"What?"

"I thought *I* was a sourpuss of a kid."

"I can see how that might be."

"Takes one to know one."

Henry shook his head.

"Anyway," she said. "You were saying?"

"I don't know. I think I just wanted something dangerous to happen to me," he said.

"When you were *a kid*? You thought that, when you were a *kid*?"

Henry shrugged.

"So, did something dangerous happen?"

He laughed.

"I mean, besides all of this."

"Yes," he said, no longer smiling.

"Are you going to tell me about it?"

"I don't know."

"Fair enough," she said. But why not say it? They could be dead an hour from now. A minute from now. If she had not understood before just how short life was, she certainly understood it now. Why hold the truth of who he was from her? What if he never got the chance to say?

If this were your last day on earth, would you be satisfied with how you were living it? her mother used to say. Olivay always joked that she wanted to go out with guns blazing.

"I can only imagine what your family must be thinking right now," Olivay said. "Watching the news. I keep wondering about that woman on the street with the child in her arms. People who know her would have seen that. If my mother were alive, I'd be desperate to tell her I was all right."

"I'm sure they're worried. But they've more than likely already studied a map of Los Angeles, located my address, checked to see how close it is to the bombings and fires, figured out that I live and work approximately fifteen miles from it all, and devised an equation that soothes them with its very slim odds."

"Jesus, Henry. What are they, mathematicians or something?"

"Cartographers. And life has always been mapped out for them. No pun intended."

"A wise guy. All right." She was smiling at him when something occurred to her. "But, hold on. The *Tribune* is on this side of town."

"They don't know that I work there."

Olivay's eyebrows shot up.

"They think I'm teaching high school French near my house."

"Whoa, whoa, whoa."

"Listen. It's a long story." He put his hand out, clearly not wanting to get into it.

"So is life when it's made up of little white lies," she said.

Henry stood.

"I'm kidding," she said. "Half-kidding. Okay, *not kidding at all.* Why are you standing? Please sit back down."

Henry sat. "I have a very good reason for not telling them the truth."

"I'm sure you do."

I have a very good reason for not calling, Will had said. *A very good reason for not answering my phone. A very good reason for being late.*

Late.

Late.

Late.

"Come on," Olivay said. "What would make you lie to your parents about working for one of the biggest papers in the country?"

"I know. You would think . . . Okay. All right. I'll tell you. Remember how I mentioned the Peace Corps?"

"Yes. In the Central African Republic."

"It has to do with that."

"What does?"

"The lie to my parents."

"You realize this isn't making any sense? We've known each other twenty-four hours, and in that short time there have been three instances where you've lied or withheld the truth from me—which is arguably the same thing—and so forgive me if I'm thinking you're stalling here out of a need for deception."

"I'm well aware," he said, his annoyance clearly rising. "I've explained myself the best way I could about the other stuff. But this. My time in Africa. It's not the same. I'm not used to . . . I've never talked about that, other than what my parents already know. And they don't know the whole story."

Olivay could tell by the look in his eyes that he was moving away from the conversation. She shouldn't push too hard or he was going to steer it somewhere else within seconds, and she didn't want that to happen. Things were just getting interesting.

"How long were you in the Peace Corps?" she asked.

"Almost two years."

"Almost?"

"Yes."

"I don't know much about it, but I've heard you have to sign up *for* two years."

"Right," he said.

"You didn't make it 'til the end?"

"No."

"I see."

"The reason I went in the first place was because it seemed like the most logical fit for me after college. A degree in philosophy. I mean, what else is someone supposed to do with that?"

"Become a journalist?" Olivay said.

"Well. Yeah. Eventually. But I had to find my way to it first."

"Whatever that means."

"I'll tell you what it means."

He went on to explain how his family had traveled constantly when he was growing up, his most faithful companions had been his dogs, used as trackers and protectors by his parents, and of course his brother, George, whom he'd been so close to then, though he'd been lost to him now for years. They'd lived all over the world in places like rural Mongolia and Australia and several other African nations whose names had since changed. The Peace Corps seemed an extension of a life he already knew. In a strange way, it was the safest and easiest option for him, familiar and not difficult to navigate, whereas for most everyone else he met in the corps, it was the complete opposite. For them, it was the unknown and the struggle they were after—that, and an overwhelming willingness to help.

"I'd always lived in the safety of a bubble, no matter where we went. Locals cooked for us and looked after me and George. We were educated alone in the same way. Tutored in a house kept orderly by a hired staff. Our existence was more or less walled off from the real world outside."

Olivay shook her head in disbelief. Boring? There was nothing boring about him.

"Don't get me wrong," Henry said. "Everything was bare bones. When I say *staff*, I mean people who were paid a dollar per week. I understand why we were often separated in this way from others. It wasn't always safe or sanitary in some of the more remote areas. But I couldn't help thinking that life was always taking place *out there*. Somewhere else. It wasn't until I was grown that I understood what a great paradox it was. Growing up a citizen of the world while completely missing out on what was really happening in the world, being forced every single day into a life that wasn't quite real."

"Your childhood makes you sound a little like Siddhartha. Buddha, the young prince walled off from the sick and suffering."

"You're not the first person to say that."

"Genevieve?" Olivay asked.

"Anyway, even as I was trying to break out of the familiar, I didn't quite understand until I got there that it was the same kind of life I'd always known."

"Sounds disappointing," she said.

Henry gave a small nod, and then switched back to his parents, how they'd thought philosophy in college made perfect sense. They said his inability to take a stance made him more compassionate.

Olivay laughed. "That sounds a bit passive-aggressive, if you don't mind me saying."

"No. I don't. But it's not that. They're just pretty complicated people."

"Okay. But for what it's worth, you don't strike me as wishy-washy, like someone who lacks the ability to take a stance. In fact, you strike me as the complete opposite of that."

"Maybe I've changed. Of course I have. That was a long time ago."

It was quieter now, the quietest it had been all day, as if all the rescuers and everyone left in the neighborhood had calmed at once. The ringing in her ears was louder now, and she wondered if it was there to stay.

"But who can say why we end up where we do?" Henry seemed to be thinking a whole lot of other things attached to that one sentence that he hadn't bothered to mention. He had a faraway look now, and his speaking voice slowed. "My mother likes to tell people that I was born with extra empathy, which is, I don't know, just a mother talking, I assume, but it got me thinking that help-ing people out in a place like the CAR might be something I was suited for. I already knew how to speak French from all the colo-nized countries we'd lived in. So I minored in it in college, along with creative writing, and decided to teach English to the French-speaking students."

"And what about your dad?" she asked, but it was Genevieve she was thinking of, Genevieve she really wanted to know about. "You haven't said much about him."

"He's a little odd. Extremely intelligent like my brother, in a drier, scientific, absorbing-numbers kind of way. He once told me that he'd thought the two sides of my brain were like the scales of justice themselves."

"Jesus, Henry."

"I don't think it was a compliment."

"And you thought I would find you boring, because?"

Henry shrugged. "I feel boring? Or maybe I just feel *dulled*."

"Ah," she said. "Not the same thing."

"No."

"And so you lied to them about where you work because—?"

"Because after I left Africa, I started writing about my experiences there. Some of them, anyway." His hands started shaking again, and when he saw her looking, he held one in the air to show her he knew well enough what was happening to him. "There I go again. Nervous, as you can see."

"It's not a judgment, Henry."

But of course, it was.

"Anyway." He lowered his hand. "I had some difficulties." He paused as if waiting for her reaction.

"Difficulties," she said.

"Yes."

"Well."

"It's that my parents thought the writing, some of the things I had written, were making matters worse for me. Emotionally. You know, stirring things up. So to keep them from worrying about me, I told them I had gone back to teaching."

Olivay studied his eyes and hands for traces of a lie, for some assurance of the truth. She couldn't quite tell either way.

"What about your name in the paper?" she finally asked. "It's not like it's some local newsletter in Idaho."

He looked away.

"Oh, no. *No.* You are *kidding* me! You're not using your real name, are you? It isn't Jack? *Or* Henry? *Or* Wilkins?"

Henry squeezed his eyes shut and patted the air for her stop. "Just listen to me. It's Henry. It really *is* Henry. My family sometimes called me Jack. My brother likes to call me Jack. But no one else. But Wilkins is the name of a street in my neighborhood."

"Terrific. And at what point in the future will you tell me that what you *just told me* isn't true?"

"I won't, Olivay. My real name is Henry Bearden. I grew up all over the world, and everything else that I have told you is the truth. What I haven't told you, about my time in the Peace Corps, I was honest about saying that I didn't want to."

Olivay crossed her arms and glared. "Does Jerry know?"

"He knows my real name."

"Does he know why you use a fake name?"

"No. He never asked. Lots of writers don't use their real names."

Olivay was willing to let that one go. It was true. It could be true for him, too.

"So tell me, *Henry*," she said, trying not to press her lips too tightly, trying hard not to push him away. "What was it about your future that filled you with dread?"

"I don't know." He held up both hands at his sides like surrender. "That's the truth. It was just something I knew about myself, the way people know things about themselves, even from a young age. From the time I was a kid, my parents tried to convince me that I could be anything I wanted to be when I grew up, as if it were as simple as making a choice. And the whole concept of that really bothered me."

"What are you talking about?" She was still a little angry, her voice a little too harsh, and she made every attempt to calm down. "It's *not* a choice?"

"No. Not really. Not the way I see it, which isn't for everyone. If it were true, I'd have to believe that people around the world had chosen lives of suffering. Then again, I get it. My brother had a clear talent for science by the time he was ten. He always knew what he wanted, and he came from a family who supported him. All he had to do was play by the rules, which, for whatever reason, never came easy to him."

"Well. I'm afraid I fall in the same category as your brother, *and* your parents. I knew what I wanted from around that same age. Filling notebooks with houses and landscapes. Fascinated by color palettes. My mother encouraged me. Pushed me in the right direction even as I rebelled—skipping school, getting high."

"And your father?" he asked.

"I never had one. Never even knew who he was. He was a one-night stand, according to my mother."

Henry raised an eyebrow.

"What?"

"Nothing. I'm just listening."

"Are you sure you aren't thinking, *like mother, like daughter*? Because you can relax there. It's a little late to say now, but I *am* on the pill."

"No. I wasn't even thinking that."

"Why not?"

"I don't know. You're right. I guess I should have been. But like you said, it's too late, anyway, for that discussion now. We are really going off the rails, here."

"All right. Back to you. To the story of Henry."

But of course the mention of the night before hung in the air, the pleasures tracing them again.

Olivay closed her mouth and touched her lips.

"No, I was just . . ." Henry stumbled on his own words, glancing around, kneading his wrist. "I was saying that I never had much of anything going on for myself. No clear ideas about what I wanted to do. No obvious talents, or direction."

"Come on. I don't believe you."

"It's true. Unless you count all my hazy, lazy hours of day-dreaming."

"Well. *I* would count those, but I've clocked a lot of hours in that bed doing exactly that, so maybe I'm not the best judge."

His mournful smile had returned, and Olivay wondered what her own face was doing. She touched her cheeks and slowly let her hands fall.

"I was always a little obsessed with planets and stars," Henry said, "but had no interest in astronomy, at least not in the traditional sense. I felt like I was somehow learning more about a sense of time—in the infinite sense—by tracking their arcs than about the planets and stars themselves."

"I think you were an original nerd, Henry."

"Indeed. I imagine I'm even nerdier now."

Her attraction for him billowed up, and when he reached his hand across the table and took hers, she felt the blood race from her chest to her head.

"Thank you," he said.

"For what?"

"For asking me about myself. I never talk about this stuff. Well, that's not true. I tried once, and when I saw the look on—" He stopped and for a second Olivay didn't think he was going to continue. "When I saw the look on her face, I changed the subject."

The sting in Olivay's chest surprised her. "Her, being Genevieve?"

Henry nodded.

"Well. You'll get nothing from me but a poker face," she said. "Say what you will. Out with your dark secrets, Henry Bearden—if that's really your name."

"Sure. That's what you say now."

"Try me." She waved her free hand across her face and played it straight.

"Nice poker face," he said. "You already cracked."

"No, no. I'm good." She dulled her thoughts, her expression. "Keep going."

Henry eyed her with a smirk. He pulled his hand away.

"That 'gloom and doom' you mentioned this morning about my face when I saw something good in yours?" he said.

"Yeah?"

"I think it goes back to when I was a kid. I used to have these moods or whatever you want to call them, bouts of melancholy, that left weird, prickly sensations across my skin."

"Uh huh," Olivay said.

"I know you want to laugh."

"Not true," she said, but she did, a little. When she tried to picture him as a moody child, the image that came to her was that of a miniaturized, brooding little man.

"It was pretty impossible for a kid to voice such things. I know how odd it sounds, I can hardly explain it, even now. It was kind of like that feeling in the fall when things cool down and the leaves turn red and yellow—all of that used to affect me in this strange, moody way. It was the same sort of thing when I was looking out the window into the yard from one of the houses we lived in, and I could hear my mother singing in the kitchen. I remember that so clearly. I was aware of the feeling while I was feeling it, and ended up deciding it was a kind of nostalgia—a word I looked up in the dictionary after hearing my parents throw it around, but I understood even then that it also applied to things that weren't yet lost."

Olivay lowered her hands into her lap, one holding the other, and tried not to think about the mixed feelings worming inside her, that Henry could have been describing her own childhood, the loneliness of it, the unaccounted for annoyances with her mother, who now seemed to be a saint. They didn't move around at all, it wasn't that, but there was no one else in their house besides them, no siblings, no father, no cousins, only Oskar to create a little contrast to what often felt like a walled off existence, a suffocation Olivay could never quite breathe through.

The pain was returning to her leg. She didn't know how much longer she could sit there, but she didn't want him to stop. She didn't want it to end.

"We had a plum tree behind one of our houses," he said. "I don't even remember which house it was anymore. But I remember looking right at it and missing it at the same time."

Now Olivay was the one who raised an eyebrow.

"I was forced to come to terms with the idea of impermanence at an early age," he said.

Olivay nodded, slowly, in agreement. "I think I know what you mean. My mother used to drive me crazy at times, but she was all I had in the world, and there were days in kindergarten when I cried myself to sleep at night, missing her before she was gone."

"And yet, there was some weird pleasure in that, too, right?" he said.

"I don't know. I suppose."

"I remember feeling that way at random moments, like holding a book in my hands, imagining it already read and gone, left behind in another move. Or staring at my juice at breakfast, switched from orange to apple, noticing the way the kitchen smelled like cinnamon most everywhere we lived, but that was never enough to make it feel like home. It all filled me with something I couldn't name until I grew up and understood I kept getting caught in a perpetual state of melancholy. A pleasurable kind of ache."

"Jesus, Henry."

"You told me to go straight for the real stuff."

"I did."

"So what I'm saying is maybe that's what you saw on my face this morning when I came back, that sorry look in my smile when you lit up. I'm guessing it's a kind of melancholy I've carried around since before I could articulate it. I don't mean to lay it on thick, but

I've always felt that deep inside that strange kind of sadness is a different kind of beauty, and *that* was exactly what I was thinking. That was what I saw in you."

Olivay felt a tightening in her throat and chest. She reached across the table and took his hand back.

"What happened to you?" she asked. "Over there. In Africa."

The blood appeared to drain from his face. He shook his head. "I'd really rather not say."

"What if this were your last day on earth? And let's face it: it could be. Would it really matter, you keeping it all to yourself?

"I'd just rather not," he said.

"Our last day, Henry. Last rites."

"If it comes to that. If I see it come to that, then maybe. But right now, I'll take my chances. I'll keep hoping that we're both going on to live long lives."

"I wish you wouldn't," she said.

"Hope for long lives?" He squeezed her hand.

"Very funny."

"Bear with me. I've only known you for twenty-eight hours."

"But who's counting?"

He brought her hand to his face and pressed his cheek into her palm. He brought it to his lips and kissed it, then laid it back onto the table and covered it with his own. "But there is something else. That I'd like to tell you. That I feel you deserve to know, and not telling you seems too much like lying."

Olivay slipped her hand away. "You're kidding, right?"

"No. But it's not about me. It's about you."

"Me?"

"Yes. You. And Will."

TWENTY-TWO

BEFORE HENRY EVEN OPENED HIS MOUTH, OLIVAY FELT herself split in two. Half of her eager to hear what he had to say, even as she bristled at the sound of Will's name on Henry's lips, even then she understood he was about to offer up some kind of answer, a confirmation she had been needing for such a long time, while the other half of her had already checked out, run for cover, was devising ways to get another pain pill, which she needed desperately now, but first—

"Yesterday," Henry said. "When I finally talked to you at Levine's."

Olivay braced herself.

"I was glad to see you there. Finally getting out."

"So you've been paying close attention."

"Of course I knew, Olivay. I mean, the staff at the *Tribune*. They talk. The whole thing affected everyone."

"What are you getting at, Henry?"

"I was so glad to see you there."

"It wasn't a coincidence, was it? You being there at the same time?"

"Yes, it was, actually."

Olivay narrowed her eyes at him.

"And no, not completely."

"Henry."

"The first time, yes. I was writing in one of the booths, and I saw you walk in. I couldn't believe it was you."

"Meaning what?"

"Meaning, that I had wanted to talk to you for some time."

"About *what*?" she asked, afraid she already knew, afraid this was all about investigating Will's death.

"Let's just say I've liked you from afar. And no, not in the creepy starfucker sense. It goes back to before all of this mess. And it doesn't really lend itself to an easy explanation. So I kept coming back to Levine's hoping you would turn up."

She wasn't quite expecting this.

"What do you mean from *before*?"

"It's going to sound lame."

"Try me."

He took his time, as if every word were under careful consideration. "All right. You know when you see someone and instantly feel this—hell, I don't know. You're just, it's simple, really, you're just drawn in, and who can say exactly why—?"

"Lame."

"Come on."

"I'm kidding. Keep going."

"That *thing* between people. I don't necessarily mean romantically, I mean anyone, really, just people. You don't even have to speak the same language." His foot began bobbing beneath the table.

Genevieve. Sounds French.

"Did you see me before that day in Levine's? In person?"

"Yes."

"Where?"

"At the *Tribune*."

"What do you mean? I thought you said you started working there *after* Will died. That's what you said. I know that that is what you told me."

"I did. It's true. I was telling you the truth. They didn't hire me until after he was gone."

"Then what are you saying?"

"It was in the lobby. I was there for an interview a month or so before the accident, and you were waiting for Will to come down and meet you. I didn't know who you were. I saw you standing by the window. I'm going to sound like an idiot now, or a stalker." He ran his fingers through his hair. "But I was so attracted to you. Not just the way you looked but . . . I don't know what to call it. Your *presence*? The way you were standing . . . I just felt like I knew you before I knew you. There. I said it."

Olivay recalled looking up from her book in Levine's, and seeing him, and then the rush of feelings that overtook her. Afterward in her apartment—she had never experienced anything like it in her life.

"I walked over and asked if you were reading some magazine on the table nearby," Henry said. "I really just wanted to hear your voice. You said *no* and you barely looked at me. But up close I could tell you were upset. As if you'd been crying."

"Oh, Jesus." Olivay remembered now. This was why she'd asked if they'd met before in Levine's. She hadn't seen him in Levine's. She had seen him in the lobby of the *Tribune* the day she went to confront Will about the affair she suspected he was having.

"And then what happened?" Olivay asked.

"Then Will came out of the elevator and crossed the lobby and led you out the front doors like a man who didn't want to make a scene."

TWENTY-THREE

GET TO THE POINT, IS WHAT SHE WANTED TO SAY, BUT SHE knew where he was headed. That look in his face, apprehension, pity, if she wasn't mistaken. *Just say it and get it over with.*

It wasn't until Will was already dead that Olivay began to understand how he'd possessed the same kind of forced optimism her mother had had, and how he, too, had tried to push it like the law of the land on Olivay. He had a way of making her feel badly about herself, as if the sober feelings she so often carried around were somehow flawed. As if living a life where questions never quite came with satisfying answers—where she was often left feeling more alone and distressed in the company of other people than she felt being by herself—was a kind of defect, someone who was missing the point of life, which was a kind of happiness that never seemed quite real to her in the first place.

What she was thinking she couldn't bring herself to say. It occurred to her that somehow, in the last hour, she'd grown more concerned about what was happening inside her own apartment with Henry, inside her own life, her history with Will, than with trying to figure out what was happening outside where people were *actually dying*. This was all so pathetic. "Fuck," she murmured. She had waited too long to take another pain pill.

Henry gulped down a bottle of water. "So," he continued.

"I need to wash my face," she said, aware of him staring at her, realizing how truly awful she must appear. She stood, and quickly fumbled against her own weakness.

"Let me help you," he said, but she said no, no, she was fine, she didn't need his help, the bathroom was only a few hops away.

He covered his eyes as she winced and hopped and tried not to cry at the pain.

In the bathroom mirror she barely recognized herself, gritting her teeth, shivering with adrenaline. Her eyes had the puffiness of early morning. A bruise was spreading down her forehead from the blow to her head. She parted her hair to see black clots of blood. She was filthy. And Henry had kissed her anyway. Kissed her more than once.

She washed her face with the bowl he had left on the sink. She patted herself dry and spread moisturizer from her blue bottles across her skin. *The human head is nothing more than a tiny walnut under the right circumstances.* She found a hair tie in the drawer and fastened her hair into a ponytail at the base of her neck. She brushed her teeth in the same water and then swiped her lips with clear gloss. She felt a little better already.

She sat on the toilet, though not without trouble. She gave out a yelp trying to keep her leg straight.

The toilet wouldn't flush without running water, so she closed the lid when she finished, poured the bowl of water over her hands in the sink, and dried them. After that, she hopped back out to Henry at the table.

He looked a little lost. He looked exhausted.

"So tell me," she said, trying not to show how fiercely the pain was traveling up her leg. She only had a couple of pills left. She could take it a little while longer. She believed she could. "Did the people Will worked with miss him?" she asked. "I mean, what was the mood like when you started working there?"

Something crossed his face.

"What is it?" she asked.

"Of course, they missed him."

"Not that. I mean the thing you didn't say just now."

Henry nodded once.

"You think it's going to matter now, after all this time?" she said. "I want to know."

"That day I saw you in the lobby . . . I was still up in the newsroom talking to Jerry when Will came back from lunch with you. I saw him go over to the desk of a female reporter whose name I didn't know at the time. They were whispering. Then she drew back, and . . . she kind of covered her mouth, like he had just told her something that shocked her."

"I see."

"I didn't want to say anything. I mean, what's the point now? But I didn't want to lie to you, either."

"It's all right," she said, feeling a little too far outside of herself. "What else? That can't be everything."

"What I saw, well, what everyone saw, in that first month after I was hired, after Will had died, this woman—"

"What was her name?" Olivay asked, even when she didn't need to.

"Daphne."

Olivay laughed, though she could not stop her eyes from watering.

"If you don't want me to—"

"No, no. I certainly do. Tell me the rest. I want to know."

"Well. I kept seeing her, she would just sort of break into tears in the middle of the day at her desk. She'd put her head in her hands, but no one would go over to her. They just left her alone. She . . ."

Are you crazy? Will had asked her. *I mean, seriously. You actually think I'd be interested in someone else?*

They weren't even married then.

Ask me that again and you'll find out, Olivay had said, and Will had apologized. He was good at apologies. So good that after he died, Olivay believed it was only a matter of time before she came upon a note explaining how sorry he was for dying.

"Thank you, Henry," she said politely, even managing a small smile before she began to feel sick.

TWENTY-FOUR

"IT'S LIKE SOMEONE DROPPED ME IN ICE," OLIVAY SAID, or thought she said, thinking at first that Mrs. Hightower was still there, realizing she had already gone, that she had kissed Olivay's temple on the way out the door.

She wanted to lie down and so she sat on the bed, telling Henry not to speak to her, that it was a kindness she'd appreciate for just a minute or two, and he said that was fine, that he wouldn't make a sound.

Thirty minutes later she was still sitting on the edge of the bed, her leg stretched before her, as she stared across the room at the cracked and bare Snow White wall.

And then, "Lean back," Henry was saying. "Against the pillows."

"I can't," she said, shivering, realizing that every time she'd fallen asleep she'd been on her side. "I've got some stuff in my back and behind my thighs. The sheets are clean. My clothes . . ."

Henry folded her shoulder toward him and looked behind her. "Oh, man. You've got specks of stuff all over the place."

Olivay shivered. "I'm freezing."

"It's hot in here, Olivay."

"I need a shower."

"There's no water."

"I know that."

"You've got pieces sticking out of your shirt." He sighed. "Hold on. Sit right here for just one second."

Olivay closed her eyes, but the shivering continued. It didn't seem as if more than three hours had passed since she'd taken those first pills but they had, and the pain had returned like a hammered claw. She was feverish.

"What's happening?" she asked, opening her eyes to another pill from Henry.

"Take this. I need to clean your back. It might be making you feel worse. You could already have infection setting in."

"No," she said, but she didn't even understand what she was saying no to.

The TV was blaring again.

"It's too hard to believe," Henry said, and now his voice was overlapping with other voices.

Terrorism, terrorist, terror.

"Trauma," Henry said.

Something else had happened. Had something else happened?

"The mayor of Los Angeles has declared a lockdown on the Westside," a reporter was saying. "No one is permitted in the streets within the twelve-block radius of the explosion site. They are telling us that the suspect or suspects responsible for this attack are most likely still in the area."

"Fuck," Henry said from somewhere across the room.

"He has declared mandatory evacuations on the Eastside from Griffith Park all the way over to Coldwater Canyon Park, including Runyon Canyon, and all traffic on the 101 has been blocked and rerouted south to the 10 and then east up toward Pasadena for those trying to go north. The section of the 101 between Central

LA and North Hollywood is completely closed. For those of you unfamiliar with Los Angeles, the 101 is a major freeway through the center of town and the section closed off is approximately fifteen miles long. Thousands of homes—as well as these landmarks: the Griffith Observatory, the Greek Theatre, and the Hollywood Bowl—are all in grave danger of being destroyed, as is the iconic Hollywood sign. We are watching the winds closely and will keep you updated on any and all news on this terrible, terrible day in the great state of California."

How small Olivay felt in the face of this. How insignificant she was against it.

"How long can this possibly go on?" she said, but of course it was rhetorical, she wasn't expecting an answer, and Henry didn't try to offer one.

There wasn't much food in her apartment. She too often ate like a college student, cereal for dinner, boxed mac-n-cheese, crackers and a coke.

Henry was saying something. Was he talking to her? Talking on the phone?

Shock was having its way with her. *Was that what this was, this feeling of being swallowed whole?* She'd thought she was tough. Now all she wanted to do was curl up on the bed like a child desperately in need of her mother, and the need only served to remind her that her mother's death was the first time Olivay's heart had cracked in ways that would never quite seal. *What a time we had*, her mother used to say about everything—lunch on a patio, a day at the beach, shopping for shoes. *What-a-time*, pointing out how extraordinary life was, even during her bouts of quiet depression, the ache right there beneath the surface, and still, what a time.

Olivay made a mental note to tell Henry about her mother. Maybe he'd want to write down her story. Will had said it was out of his league. Fuck him. *She* was out of his league.

"Henry?" He wasn't there when she called his name. She wanted to tell him about her own life, too, the way her mother had played piano all those years ago when Olivay was still a restless, antsy child with no interest in Brahms, Schubert, or Bach; she didn't hold back from making faces when she heard it, or from telling her mother how much she hated to hear her play, that she was ugly with her face scrunched up, her back hunched over the keys like a witch, and yes, just as Henry had said, her meanness climbing and climbing. Once her mother stopped abruptly, and said she should listen, try really hard to listen how the whole of life was contained in a song—the rise and fall, the violence and forgiveness, the suspense, the tension, the not knowing how it might end until you felt that very last note. Olivay wanted to tell Henry how she was already in her early twenties when it finally dawned on her how cruel she'd been to her mother, and her latent understanding was made doubly cruel because, by then, her mother had developed arthritis in her fingers and never touched the keys again.

This essence of Woman, the beginning of us all, what it was to be human and love in the face of death.

What might her mother have said about today?

No, no. Look at me, Olivay. There is no sense to be made.

Her mother, laughing at nearly everything—the *Sunday Times*, the children messily planting marigolds next door, joking with Olivay after her first big fight with Will, pointing out the nonsense of it, the petty ways people stood their ground against petty things. *It's ridiculous and funny when you compare it to the world at large and its capacity for evil.* A trace of her Polish accent snuck into her California vernacular every now and then when a word contained a *W* and an *R*. *World* sometimes made her sound a little like a vampire.

Her mother could dismiss every injustice that crossed her path as worthy of ignoring because it didn't measure up to the Holocaust, but what her mother had never understood was that the worst thing that ever happened to a person was still the worst thing that ever happened to that person.

Look, Mother. Look at this. Look at my dead husband on the sidewalk. Look at what he was doing to me before he died. Look at the death and destruction in the streets, our city of angels being destroyed. How can you go on laughing? What exactly do you find so *funny?*

What was funny was that the two people in her life, who too often struck Olivay as having a kind of false optimism, who chided her for her darker, moodier ways, were both dead.

And at least one died a liar.

Even so, she wasn't finished arguing this point, what point was it? What was the point of that bloody child with the missing leg? What should Olivay take away from that? And how was it that Olivay had a *strange luck* for saving herself without even trying? Why did she get to be an unlikely survivor of an unlikely survivor, living to see another day? Maybe the truth was more slippery than that. Maybe death had actually been coming for her all along and somehow she continued to outsmart it. Strangers filling spaces in the street where Olivay should have stood. How was it that her life was any more important than theirs? Those sitting in Levine's, where Olivay should have sat with Henry—*Yes I'd love to come with you, Henry. Thanks for asking.* As if her death were a special case, a karmic retribution from long ago set in motion like a tortuous plodding, a giant black beak meant to peck her bit by bit by bit.

She wished there were someone to say this to, someone who understood her without her having to say it.

"Henry?"

"I'm right here."

"What if my mother *hadn't* been dazed by homemade vodka at six months old and scuttled out of the Warsaw Ghetto inside a man's toolbox? What if it had been another baby instead?"

"I'm not sure what you're saying," Henry said.

"What if she'd cried when they slipped past the line of guards and into the carpenter's truck? What if someone had found her real name, and all the others', buried for years in a jar beneath an apple tree before the war was over?"

"Olivay? I think you're running a temperature."

"Existence is a finer line than anyone cares to consider."

"I can't argue with that."

"You would have liked my mother," she said.

"I'm sure that's true."

"She used to say, *Your existence, and mine, are a bit of a miracle, Olivay.* And from that the rest of her thoughts seemed to take shape."

Henry was laughing. What on earth could be so funny?

"She was forty-five years old when I was born, Henry. I was premature, arriving with the early morning sunrise—that's how she liked to tell it—ten thousand miles from her 'scorched beginnings.' My mother was so sure of life in the face of death. She waved off warnings from the doctors that I was arriving too soon, too small, a five percent chance of survival. *You see, you see!* my mother told them. How I clung to life with viscous red fists, small as cherry suckers, my tiny fish mouth gasping to fill a ribcage too big for the body it housed, which, uncannily, or rather *cruelly*, my mother said, resembled the hungry neighbors of her youth."

"Your fever is really spiking, Olivay," Henry said. He'd taken her warm face in his cool hands. She closed her eyes.

"If I knew better, I'd stop myself from saying I think I love you," Henry said. "But I don't know any better." His lips were cold on her forehead and cheeks, on her hand held up to his mouth.

"Don't make me laugh," Olivay said, but Henry was the one who started laughing.

Viscous red fists. They ached only slightly now, but her lids were so heavy, and this hand, so good at caressing her side, her hair, like smoothing feathers, like saying the world had not ended, not here, not yet. "It's over now," he whispered just inches from her back, his warm breath touching her ear as if proof that it wasn't a dream.

"Stay," she said, and he said he would. He said there was no place else he'd rather be. He lifted her shirt from her back, undid her bra, and gently peeled each from her battered skin. He did the same with her shorts and underwear, sliding the fabric carefully down her legs and around her hurt knee, until she lay completely naked on the bed, her right leg splayed sideways on a pillow to take the pressure off her knee.

She closed her eyes. Henry was staring at her from behind, she was sure of this, taking in every last inch of her. She could hear him sighing, moving around, and now climbing along the bed, making small noises with his breath and lips as he extracted shards from her skin. She drifted in and out, awareness coming quickly when it stung, more slowly when he was quiet, and more than once when he hummed a song to himself—too softly for her to recognize the tune, but the refrain he repeated again and again, and she tried to unravel what it was as she dozed and came back. He had mentioned the word love.

The last thing Henry did before she drifted too far away was plunge a washcloth into a bowl of cold water, and the rippling sound made her feel as if she'd fallen to rest on the bank of a creek, the heat of the sun was the warmth she felt against her skin, like maybe she was laid out across the huge expanse of shadeless lawn next to Will, and then the cloth cooling her like rain, like a ritual, a baptism freeing her up from her past. Olivay felt absolved from all she'd done wrong in her life, from all she was about to do, as he wiped her body clean.

PART TWO

TWENTY-FIVE

ACCORDING TO WITNESSES THAT MORNING, GENEVIEVE was spotted shortly after seven a.m. on her way to teach at the Perouix School of Music on the edge of the village. She was dressed in a lapis blue blouse and matching pagne, delicately tucked around her thin frame. She wore double-strapped leather sandals she'd bought in the village six months before, and on her head she'd wrapped a black head-dress to protect her white, pixie-cropped hair from the blowing sands.

She was stopped at the dusty trail by a young CAR soldier who engaged her in what appeared to be friendly conversation. Genevieve pointed toward the thicket of brush, a footpath which led directly to the school, the same direction she headed five days a week, the direction she was headed now. Many of the soldiers in the villages were no longer locals, and this man, known to no one, seemed to be asking for directions. Perhaps he'd been sent to guard the girls and their teachers at the school. "Yes," a pair of young adolescent boys said. "He was pointing. She was pointing." A country on the brink of civil war put women in particular at risk, and the thought of a soldier protecting a school of teenage choirgirls, if anyone had thought about it, would have come as a comfort.

Genevieve talked to him, why shouldn't she? Even if she didn't know him, even as his assault rifle hung over his shoulder, such sights on the brink of war were common. If not for Genevieve's white skin and hair, like flour and sugar against the black and woody camouflage of the young man, those who had walked past that morning might have noticed nothing at all.

"He seemed to be asking for directions," the witnesses said. "Genevieve was friendly. She was always friendly." No one mentioned that she would have been singing to herself as loudly as if she were alone just before he approached, her hands swinging at her sides like a conductor in a trance, but Henry knew exactly how she moved through the world, exactly how happy she would have appeared before she died.

TWENTY-SIX

WHEN OLIVAY WOKE IT WAS DARK, AND HENRY WAS ASK-
ing her what clean clothes she would like to wear. The only light
in the room came from the glow of a tall "Mary" candle on the
bedside table.

"What the hell?" she said.

"The generator ran out of fuel. Your super kept them in a stor-
age unit downstairs. He's Catholic. Said he couldn't bear to throw
them away."

Olivay realized she was naked. She raised her head and it began
to throb but without the pain, just the drumming pressure of blood
pulsing through her veins.

"What do you want me to grab for you? To put on, I mean?"

She sat up all the way up on the bed and faced him. "The nightgown in the drawer."

He pulled it out and held it up. "Are you sure?" he asked. Maybe
he was thinking it was too similar to the one she'd been wearing in
the video with Will—her breasts visible through the fabric.

"Yes," she said, "I'm sure."

Henry gazed at her body with the look of a forlorn lover, a man in need of something Olivay wasn't sure she had to offer. Maybe it was just the contrast of what was happening outside, the apocalyptic backdrop for which her body was no match, her sex unimportant in the scheme of things. No, not exactly that, but she guessed it was along those lines. Maybe she'd only imagined him saying something about love.

"What is it?" she asked. "What are you thinking that you're not saying?"

His eyes trailed down the front of her, stopping along her right side, where earlier she'd felt a deepening ache. She glanced down. A large purple bruise spread at the base of her ribs.

"Ouch," Henry said.

"Whoa," Olivay said. "You must have done that with those cage-fighting moves you used to get me on the bed."

"Are you referring to this morning or last night?" The humor in his voice surprised her.

She rolled her eyes up from the bruise. "Either way, I'm sure your intentions were true."

She was back in the graces of codeine.

He sat very close, brushed her hair from her shoulder, and met her eyes. He parted his lips several times as if readying to tell her the thing he hadn't said before, and it must have been difficult, she could see that it was, so difficult it appeared to have finally won out and fastened his jaw.

He leaned slightly away. "Arms up," he said.

If anyone had ever dressed her besides her mother, she had no memory of it, and no idea before now that the quiet, careful act of tucking her arms into the fabric, of guiding her head through the opening and the slow drop of the pale thin cotton down her chest and torso could contain such intimacy, such a gauzy, dreamy warmth.

Her skin continued to resonate from his touch, from his eyes lingering on her body, from the sore burn of disinfected skin.

The apartment was warm, which she took as a good sign. Her temperature must have dropped.

"When I was a kid I could cry hard enough to give myself a fever," she said.

"I didn't know that was a thing."

"I was an especially awkward, fragile child, which I'm sure was part of it. But it actually started when I was a little bit older. Twelve, in fact. Late bloomer. When most other kids were growing out of their crying phase, I just started entering mine."

"Did something happen to you?"

Olivay laughed. "Yeah. I read these two books, back-to-back, from my mother's shelf."

"Must have been some pretty crazy books."

"They were full of all kinds of things that terrified me."

"Terrified you?"

"You're going to laugh."

"Am I not supposed to?"

"No, I suppose you should and will."

"Let's have it."

"*Carrie* by Stephen King, and *Everything You Always Wanted To Know About Sex*, by whoever wrote that."

Henry swiped his hand down his mouth as if erasing his grin. "That's one rude awakening for a twelve-year-old."

"I'll say. And what was just as upsetting as the books was the feeling I suppressed for weeks afterward, the way it built inside of me, like layers of disease, until, well, the fever."

"What do you mean?"

"I felt like an imposter, walking around in a body stuffed with secrets. It was physically heavy. I remember thinking that secrets had weight."

Henry said nothing, but she could see him thinking.

"And no, I'm not playing some kind of mind game with you so that you'll tell me your secrets now."

"I didn't say a word."

"You didn't have to."

"If you're such a mind reader," he said, "then I don't have to tell you anything anyway."

"Wise guy."

"Tell me the rest."

"Well. I was sure that no one else had understood what was in those books, including my own mother, because I couldn't imagine how anyone would know such things and go on behaving as if they didn't. I mean, I couldn't even sleep. I couldn't eat. And within a couple of days the fever showed up. There was no other way to explain it."

"That's a pretty heartbreaking story."

"Is it?"

"You don't think so? A young girl suffering like that in silence."

"I don't know. I never told anyone before. I didn't know how it sounded."

"Not even Will?"

Olivay shook her head. "I never told my mother, either, because I couldn't bear to hear what she would think of me knowing such things, and I couldn't bear to hear what she thought of them herself. But it was impossible for me to look another person in the eyes after all those images of sex combined with supernatural violence. Just the thought of all those *things* people did to one another, or could do if they had the right kind of powers, and the thing that struck me as much as anything was how each book considered everything that was happening in them *normal*. I just couldn't wrap my mind around it." She remembered how the blood in her head seemed to have dropped, and then filled back up too quickly, making her feel a lot like she did now. "I couldn't get out of bed for days."

The sirens had all but stopped, the helicopters, too, but the winds were growing stronger, beating against the sheets, yanking them with a snapping thump. And then they hit with such force that Olivay braced for the fabric to tear loose from the duct tape and disappear into the street.

Henry grabbed his backpack, rifled around inside, and then held up what looked like an old Swiss Army knife, except it was nearly twice the size of the ones she was used to seeing, this one was more of a hunting and fishing knife, with rubber grips on the handle. He opened the blade and it stretched at least five inches, with a jagged edge cut out on one side.

"What are you doing with that?" Olivay asked, and it wasn't until she said it that she realized she'd meant it both ways—now and in general, *what was he doing with that knife?*

Henry said he'd show her and climbed onto the counter, checked his balance, and began slitting holes in the fabric, swiftly, as if puncturing the membrane of a soft balloon. She studied the silhouette of his body, legs spread, his bare feet gripping either side of her sink. His long arm stretched out as he pressed his hand onto the wall to steady himself, and she was instantly aroused. She wished he would stay there and allow her just to look.

The blade of his knife sliced again and again through the sheet, and now the strength of the wind weakened as air seeped through the openings, bringing with it the smell of tar and burning wire.

What had stirred inside her a second ago quickly extinguished. She had always thought of the inner workings of construction like bones and veins and muscle, functioning only when sealed safely inside, and the smell, the vision she had of cables, plumbing, plywood, and metal all spilling into the open, made her bones ache.

Henry hopped down and snapped the blade closed, dropping it into his backpack. He wiped his hands on the hips of his jeans. He was badly in need of clean clothes.

"Why do you carry that knife with you?"

"In case I get in an accident on my bike. It'll cut away my clothes, if need be."

"That's a weird way to live," she said.

"I like being prepared."

Olivay let that one sink in. He'd never mentioned having condoms before they had sex. He'd never asked if she was on the pill.

Henry shrugged. "It is what it is."

"Listen. Check the two bottom drawers of the bureau in the walk-in closet."

At first Henry seemed not to understand.

"The T-shirts should fit. I don't know about the pants. Feel free to try whatever you find."

His eyes narrowed with a pained expression of understanding, and then a questioning look as if asking if she was sure.

"It's all right," she said. "I don't mind if you don't mind." She wasn't sure if that was true. She was embarrassed for him to know she'd saved Will's clothes. Embarrassed that he was sure to imagine her holding one of Will's T-shirts to her face, breathing him in, crying back out. And it was true. She had done exactly that. She was embarrassed that no one had offered to come take Will's things away. Not his sister or father. Not even his mother. Perhaps least of all her. But Olivay had shut them out completely. It was an impossible situation. She had given them little choice, and she understood this now, everything coming to her in a flash. Without Will they were nothing to one another but reminders of his absence. There was no escaping this. No way to pretend it could ever be anything other than that. She might have gotten rid of Will's belongings herself if she could have been certain that no one would snap photographs of her dropping his clothes off at the Salvation Army. So she'd kept everything, even the bloodied backpack from when the motorcycle hit. And all the items stuffed inside. It lay in the back of a small closet she never used.

Henry came out of the bathroom wearing Will's vintage Peter Frampton T-shirt and blue and white striped pajama bottoms. She curled her fists around the duvet. It wasn't just seeing him in Will's clothes that struck her so profoundly; it was absorbing the realization that Daphne had been here, after all, right here where Olivay lay on the bed. She had seen Will step out of the bathroom in his pajama bottoms, or some version of this, just as Olivay had done so many times over the years. Two cups, two spoons, two bowls in an otherwise empty dishwasher when Olivay returned from one night out of town. It was the start of another argument. "I had the same thing for breakfast that I had for dinner," Will told her. "You're paranoid, Olivay. Come on."

She had held both cups to her nose when he went into the bathroom. She examined them for a trace of someone else's lips, and found nothing.

"You look comfortable," she said to Henry, but didn't meet his eyes when she said it.

"You were right," he said. "The pants were a little too short."

Olivay guessed they were a little loose around the waist as well.

He retrieved his notebook and began writing at the table, using one of the Jesus candles for light, and again Olivay's heart kicked around her bony chest at the sight of another man in her dead husband's clothes, writing in the same kind of notebook, sitting in the chair where he'd so often sat. It prickled her skin with goose bumps, and she flattened the tiny white hairs on her arm. *Horripilation is the technical term for goose bumps*, Will had once told her. *Comes from the Latin for hair standing on end. Sounds hor-rible*, Olivay had said, and Will had said, *The funniest woman alive.*

Like polishing a mask every morning before fastening it on.

Henry continued to check his phone for Wi-Fi, and then his laptop, which he'd taken from his backpack, and several times he went out of the apartment, taking his backpack with him to check for Wi-Fi downstairs, leaving her alone in the dark with nothing but the flickering glow of sacred candles. And each time she could hear him talking to neighbors whose voices she didn't fully recognize, their conversations never quite clear before the large metal door slammed closed on the stairwell, and then slammed again minutes later just before he walked back in and shook his head. Olivay hadn't even tried her laptop. She was tired of the news, tired of the outside world at large. She was tired, too, for far too long, of not being able to live inside her own skin, and so she lay without speaking in the candlelit room, resigning herself to plan for a different life. And to something else she couldn't yet name, that had to do with the fevers of her childhood.

"The lump on your head is going down," Henry said, crawling in next to her, and blowing out the flame. "We should try and get some sleep."

Olivay lay against his shoulder, and his long fingers wrapped inside her hair, and there was something she wanted to tell him about what being with him was doing to her, but within seconds she was gone.

TWENTY-SEVEN

THERE WAS A TIME, MONTHS BEFORE, WHEN GENEVIEVE came close to dying. During their nearly two years together, she and Henry had been ill so often that it was considered part of their daily life. To be sick was, strangely and simply, to be alive. Parasites found a way inside their bodies no matter the precautions Henry and Genevieve took. The water they drank was purified, but the food the locals served them was not, and to turn away a meal in a place where poverty and, paradoxically, generosity was seen at every turn, would have been its own kind of death sentence by breaking the trust, and defeating the purpose for being there.

They had come, just as JFK had intended, to promote world peace and friendship. They had come to help.

After a night of chills, Genevieve's fever had spiked to 104 degrees. Neither of them had ever had a fever so high. By sunrise, Genevieve was too unstable for Henry to put her on the back of his motorcycle and ride two hours to the mission where they could give her an IV of antibiotics and the cocktail of medications she needed to clear the parasites from her system.

She was partially delirious, unable to understand half of what Henry was saying. "You have to get on the mat," he demanded. "On the floor. I need to take off your clothes, Genevieve. You need to let me help you."

She thrashed and clawed to get away from him, and they wrestled across the dirt until her damp white arms and face were caked with brown soil. She called him names in French that he did not understand, a slang he had never fully learned.

"You have to listen to me!" he shouted, but she would not, and Henry found that he had no choice but to overtake her small body, to rip the pagne from around her while she screamed for him to let her go, screamed that her skin was hurting, but he refused to lessen his grip. He pressed her down onto the mat, and her scream was a sound he would never forget. A vocalist with a large capacity for air and for holding a note, and even now as she cried, her voice was horrifically glorious. There was no other way to describe it.

Her neighbor Vera had come running, and she gasped at the heat from Genevieve's forehead beneath her hand. She pinned Genevieve's arms above her head against the dirt floor while Henry straddled her naked body and poured cold water down her face and chest, and she screamed and screamed in the same way she surely would have if they'd been killing her.

When the first bucket was empty Henry fanned her wet body with a towel, and God how she shivered and cried and begged for him to stop.

TWENTY-EIGHT

THEY WOKE IN THE NIGHT TO NOISES OLIVAY COULDN'T quite place.

"Can you hear her?" Henry said.

"Who?" Olivay asked.

"The woman crying out her window. People are saying it was her husband who was killed by the police."

Henry was on top of the duvet instead of underneath.

"I couldn't sleep," he said, as if reading her mind.

Olivay sat up and immediately heard the wailing, the name-calling, the begging and screaming about how the man she loved did not deserve to die, and then the shouting in response that he should have kept his fucking mouth shut and so should she.

People are capable of doing all kinds of things, Olivay. The "why" doesn't even matter.

But the *why* was everything, Will. The why was all there was.

"It reminds me of the Creek Spirits in Africa. Their cries at night."

She was surprised to hear him mention Africa. "You mean ghosts?"

"No. Real people who drowned and then came back to life to haunt the living."

"Wait. Like, for real? This is something you believe?"

"It doesn't matter what I believe."

Olivay rested her head on the pillow and drew a deep breath. "She's quiet now. The woman."

"Her husband was killed before her eyes."

"So was mine," she said.

Henry kissed her on the forehead the way Will had done so many times in the dark when she couldn't sleep.

"Do you think you can sleep now?" she asked.

Henry lifted the duvet over his legs.

"I'm not saying you have to," she said.

"I want to," he said.

"I'm wide awake."

"Me, too."

"I want to go on the roof."

"For what?"

"To see the city. To see the fires in the dark."

Maybe Henry had resigned himself to this being as good a plan as any. He didn't say. He just wrapped Olivay's robe around her and carried her up the stairs to the roof garden.

It wasn't as if she'd been stuck inside for weeks, but it felt so good, like escaping, like breaking free after years of confinement.

The eastern sky glowed orange where flames ravaged the hills, and rising above it was a solid haze the winds were trying to clear, but there was always more smoke to fill its place. She didn't say it out loud, but the sight was beautiful, like a kingdom of lights on a distant shore, and she thought how like an illusion Los Angeles was in so many ways, and here again, even as it had become as true a reality as she would ever see.

"Nero," she said.

"Nero," he replied, and wrapped his arm around her shoulder, "was a terrible person."

"I know."

It was impossible to comprehend this strange optimism she felt in the face of so much devastation, imagining the Griffith Observatory destroyed. Its only purpose had been to allow a glimpse into what was surely the purer existence of the universe. Olivay remained quiet and could feel Henry in the same place, of the same quiet mind.

"I think I can sleep now," she finally said, and Henry told her he thought he could, too, and he carried her all the way back to her bed, where they wormed toward each other's arms and slept.

The next thing she knew the sun was breaking through her lids and a fresh chaos was erupting in the street, sirens screaming past the windows, men and women shouting; it was difficult to parse it all out as helicopters thumped again overhead.

Olivay scrambled from beneath the duvet and into the sharp morning light. "Shit. I bent my knee." She bit her lip to temper the pain. "I cracked the scab, son of a bitch."

Henry was already out on the balcony yelling back at her that police cars were gathering up the block, and that the water main had been stopped, and now two ambulances had arrived.

"What happened? Can you see?" Her voice was hoarse, her mouth dry and tacky, her entire body swollen and sore from the heat and the thorny, rough scabs covering her, but she was on the verge of tears with her knee.

"Can you please get me some water?" She was surprised at how quickly the pain could flare up. "And some codeine?"

She had forgotten Henry was wearing Will's clothes, and seeing him clearly in the sunlight startled her.

"You've only got two left."

"I know that. I *know!*"

The electricity had returned. The TV blared loudly into the room. "Can you please turn it down?" Olivay asked.

"Two hands, Olivay," he said like a husband, and then he handed her a pill and water and the ice pack for her knee, and quickly turned down the volume on the TV, without once meeting the scowl she was offering in return.

The mayor of Los Angeles was holding a news conference. His eyes were sunken and ringed in dark, violet puffs, his face as pale as the cream-colored tie around his neck. He spoke from a tight corner of his mouth, like a man trying to contain his fury.

"I would like the citizens of Los Angeles, and the country, and the world, to know we are doing everything in our power, including receiving all levels of help from federal agencies, to combat what has happened and continues to happen to our great city. I will start by saying that the lockdown on the Westside is still in effect. And the evacuations set forth are also still in place. We do not yet have exact numbers of casualties, but I *can* confirm that it will be somewhere in the upper hundreds, if not close to one thousand."

The press stirred and shouted their questions, and the deputy at the mayor's side raised a hand and told them to please quiet down.

"A thousand?" Olivay said.

"Yes," Henry whispered.

"I am pleased with the efficiency of law enforcement and the community working together to handle the extreme conditions of the evacuations on the Eastside. This has been an extremely difficult task, as you can imagine, and I could not be prouder of my city."

Then the mayor pointed directly into the camera. "This next announcement is *extremely* important, so listen closely. We have several people of interest we are actively trying to locate. A sketch will be released to the public within the next hour. We have good reason to believe that at least one or more of these persons may still be within the twelve-block radius of the two explosions on the Westside, and it is for this reason that the lockdown is to remain in place. If you do not want to be arrested, stay indoors. This is not a suggestion. This is an order for anyone living within the grid that all the stations have been sharing with the public and will continue to share."

Reporters shouted inaudible questions. The mayor addressed only one that was heard above the others—whether the suspects were male or female.

"I can't answer that right now. Everyone will find out in just a few minutes. We are obviously dealing with some very dangerous individuals here. Most likely more than one person is involved. This is a complicated and far-reaching investigation, and we ask for your patience in apprehending those responsible, and for returning our beloved city back to the lively, wonderful, and creative bastion the world knows it to be."

Another flash of cameras, a flurry of voices shouting over each other.

"And let me say this. If you or someone you know is harboring this individual, you need to understand this is a *very* serious offense. Just as the president has said, if you are harboring a terrorist, *you* are a terrorist. And that goes for nations who allow these people to train within their borders, and in turn allow them to execute more skillfully their dangerous and deadly attacks within ours. We will not tolerate aiding and abetting in any form."

"So they think it's someone foreign, then?" Olivay said. "It seems to be what he's getting at."

Henry remained frozen to the screen.

The ice was a huge relief on her knee. The codeine on an empty stomach was already taking effect, if not making her a little queasy.

"I want to remind you that the 911 phone lines are over-whelmed right now. Do not call if you do not have an immediate emergency. A new line has been set up to take your calls if you have information regarding these attacks. It is being shown now on the bottom of your screen. The FBI and supporting forces will judge what is pertinent. Go with your gut. Sometimes the smallest tip will turn out to be the one that makes all the difference."

Henry had his back to Olivay as he sat on the edge of the bed, running his hands through his hair. He opened his notebook on his thigh and began writing. He stopped and turned his head slightly to the left, which, according to her mother, was where new information was stored, meaning he was trying to figure something out that he didn't yet have an answer to. He sat his hand on top of his head, and then he dropped it to his knee and drummed his fingers in a way that Olivay did not know how to read.

"Did you notice how the mayor never gave away the gender of these people of interest?" Olivay asked. "Why do you think that is?"

"They don't want the press to run off in a blitz of speculation either way."

"But come on. Do you think a woman is involved?"

"Why not?"

"Because dudes are the ones set on destruction. The only time a woman joins in is if she's a suicide bomber or something, and only then because some guy talked her into it. Am I right?"

Henry shrugged and tapped his pen on the page.

"And no one has said a thing about a suicide bomber," she said.

"No one has said much of anything at all."

"Do you think the Santa Anas were part of this guy's plan?" she asked. "The mayor didn't mention it, not directly. Do you think they were the thing that just pushed them over the edge?"

"No."

"Why not?" she asked, thinking how she'd woken up yesterday morning feeling like someone else, or in any case, more like herself compared to the person she'd been waking up as for too long, and all week long she'd been feeling odd, on the verge of inexplicable change.

Henry turned toward her. "People don't wake up one day and decide to become terrorists. This much I *do* know. It's gradual, taking place over years. A growing need to be part of something bigger and, at least in their own minds, right. But yes, to be honest, I think the winds were part of the plan."

"I think it's a few lone wolves. No one is claiming responsibility. Some loner or two, desperate for connection, or rather to have attention drawn to their cause."

Henry glanced at his notebook as if what they were discussing was also contained in there. "What would make you think of all that?"

"Will."

Henry appeared confused.

"You know, the old investigative journalist creed about not assuming the obvious. That the truth could be hidden anywhere you aren't looking. So if everyone else is going for the usual suspects, I'm thinking, what about loners with a different agenda? Eco-terrorists, or those tech nerds?"

Henry turned back, nodded once.

Olivay tilted her head against the headboard and looked up at the ceiling. She could get used to being drugged. It was just so . . . pleasant.

"But you know what I mean," she said, her words floating off, carrying on the conversation even as she sensed it was already done. "Some plot hatched by a desperate man or two, and however sick their thinking, they've done it. They've got the entire world's attention. Everyone in the universe is tuned into this now, watching and worrying, the entire *human race* desperate to make sense of it all. To catch them when no one appears to have any idea what it was they were even after. Everyone is at the mercy of their need."

"Wow."

"What?"

"You seem to have it all figured out with a little too much psychological detail." He turned his back to her and shook his head in a quick little spurt, as if to rid it of her nonsense.

What a strange reaction. She stared at his head, trying hard to discern just exactly what was going on inside. She didn't know him well enough to recognize the nuance or subtext of his intentions. Still, it carried a jab.

"Yes," Olivay said. "I think I *do* have it all figured out."

The newsroom crew was now recapping everything the mayor had said. The LA MARATHON TERROR banner had been replaced by one that simply read LA TERROR. It shimmered red, white, and blue, and just above it, a chyron read: BREAKING NEWS: FBI TO RELEASE SKETCH OF PERSONS OF INTEREST IN LOS ANGELES TERROR ATTACK.

Henry leaned in.

A reporter was warning that what they were about to show was disturbing footage sent in by viewers and may not be suitable for everyone.

The pandemonium of visuals made Olivay dizzy for seconds at a time.

She pressed the quilt into her eyes, took a breath, and when she looked again she saw a man covered in flames on a sidewalk. A cop was beating the fire from his back and legs with his police jacket, striking the man all over, the white POLICE letters melting through the blaze until the man was no longer moving on the ground, just the char of smoke rising off him, and the officer turned and gripped his own knees as if he were about to be sick on the sidewalk.

The camera zipped away quickly as if the person filming only now understood what he'd seen.

"Henry," Olivay said.

He didn't answer.

"Henry," she said, and seconds later felt his arm slipping around her shoulders.

The reporter returned with an enormous sigh to tell viewers that cab drivers around the Los Angeles area, as well as San Diego and as far north as San Francisco, had been attacked inside their cabs. Men pulled from their vehicles and beaten in the streets. "This is more disturbing footage," she warned.

"Turn it off," Olivay said. "Please."

But before Henry could reach the remote, an elderly man with bright, white hair and dark skin was being yanked from a green cab in downtown Los Angeles. He was thrown to the street by several men, black and white, who stomped viciously across his chest and head.

Henry jammed his finger into the remote and tossed it on to the floor so hard the battery popped free. "Sorry," he said, and then he sat on the edge of the bed away from her with his elbows on his knees, his hands holding up his head.

Twice he looked as if he were going to get up and changed his mind. He appeared helpless, confused, unable to make a decision.

"The entire world is watching this," Olivay said. "Whoever did this must be so pleased, having us prove their point for them. They want us to look like animals."

And then it appeared from his back that Henry had begun to cry.

Olivay opened her mouth to speak. But she had nothing to say. Whatever words she'd been about to offer had turned to smoke in her mouth, and when Henry finally turned and crawled up next to her, she leaned her head into his shoulder and he stroked her hair exactly as she needed him to, exactly as she knew he would.

TWENTY-NINE

WHERE WAS SHE?

    Nearly everyone in the village gathered to hear Henry's cries for help, and the more people who stopped what they were doing the tighter the panic squeezed in Henry's chest. No one had seen her. Sweat trailed the sides of his face, and they told him he looked like the Creek Spirits, the ones who had drowned and come back to haunt the living. They said he was too white and too swift, and he needed to catch his breath so that the blood they knew was pumping inside him could return to the places it needed to go.

    Henry ran like a man trapped between invisible walls, back and forth from the village to the school, from the school to her house, from her house to his, and still he could not find her.

    When he saw two young girls playing near the road, he feared for them for the first time since he'd resolved himself to their way of living nearly two years before. Their distended bellies and wounds and lack of vaccinations caused him to suddenly cry out, "Why wasn't someone paying attention!"

    He charged up and down the footpath calling out for Genevieve, then returned to the two village police officers to tell them something he had forgotten to mention before, how she was supposed to meet him early at the school.

    "For what purpose?" one of them asked.

"Because I asked her to."

"And why is that?"

"I had something to ask her there. It was going to be a surprise."

Hours later, and still he kept saying how she was supposed to meet him, how he had something to ask, until it began to sound as if planning to meet him was the reason she'd gone missing, and he needed to stop saying it. The temperature must have been 110 degrees and still morning, but he raced around in the sun as if aiming for a heat stroke, spouting off like a madman, until a village councilman took him aside and told him to stop, just stop, and try really hard to think.

Henry had endured painful infections in his eyes, the side effects of anti-malaria medication, which had given him night terrors that seemed to change the fundamental function of his brain. He had endured the heat and constant diarrhea and become accustomed to thinking and dreaming in French to the point of forgetting words and concepts in English. He was no longer the man he'd been when they first met, when Genevieve first said his name and it sounded like "ornery," and after that it continued to make him laugh without fail, like a joke he was hearing for the first time, a nickname she had unwittingly given him.

"I love you, ornery," she said one day.

"And I love you naked," he said but she didn't get it and he had to explain, and then she understood and laughed through a kiss, a giggle and a snort, but right afterward they made love with a tenderness that became the pattern between them, a benevolent affection that never grew old. Whether this was due to the weight of the heat or some kind of reprieve from the hostile environment, or whether it was simply who they were with one another, Henry would never be sure, but that day, after they made love, Genevieve said, *"I love you ornery and naked,"* and neither of them laughed because their affection was now a sudden and serious thing they'd felt protective of, and did not want to have ruined or taken away or lost by any means. They held still, and then Genevieve stroked his hair and Henry rested his head against her breast and felt forever changed.

THIRTY

OLIVAY COULD NOT ERASE THE GROTESQUE IMAGES from her mind. They slid one over the other like transparencies projected behind her eyes. Will's head appeared there, too, just a hint, just a corner, but of course she would recognize it anywhere.

Was euphoria one of the side effects of codeine?

Her head pinged around like wind chimes when she rose off the bed.

"Wait," Henry said. "Where are you going? Don't get up."

Olivay held her leg stiff as a plank as she crossed the room. The pain wasn't gone, not completely.

"Let me help," he said, as she opened the kitchen cupboards. "I got it," she said, even as gravity was working against her, the weight of heat and swollen tissue causing her kneecap to pulse with every awkward move.

"If you're hungry—"

"I *got* it," she said, and this time he let her be.

She found the crackers, and behind those several boxes of spaghetti, and behind those a tin of lemon wafers she had no memory of buying, and she realized it must have been Will who'd bought them. She examined the box. The expiration date had passed just days ago, which meant it would have been one of the last things he purchased before he died. Lemon wafers. Why lemon wafers? Maybe Daphne liked lemon wafers. Maybe Will liked them and Daphne brought them over. It was impossible to fully know another human being.

She sat at the table and elevated her leg on the empty chair.

Calculating, inventorying, even now, a habit she could not break. Wafers he'd meant to eat, the terrorist attack he'd never see.

"Do you want some lemon wafers?" Olivay asked, and set the tin on the table.

Henry opened the plastic seal and Olivay imagined what the world would be like if everyone knew ahead of time what was coming. She saw Will at the checkout stand with wafers, the clerk taking his money and then telling him how those wafers would actually be eaten by another man in his kitchen nearly a year later, a man who would have already slept with his wife. *And you sir, will be dead.*

She started to laugh behind her hand.

Henry snapped a wafer in half and placed it on his tongue like a sacrament. He was watching her in a way she didn't quite like.

"I think you need to eat," he said, sliding the tin of wafers toward her. "I'm making some coffee now, if you don't mind."

"Not at all. Make yourself at home."

Henry boiled water for the French press.

"All right," she said. "Let's try this again. Who do you think is responsible for this?"

Henry looked over, but then seemed to be studying her knee. The gauze had hardened with brown blood, and next to that a fresh patch of bright red seeped through.

Henry came closer. "Someone with problems," he said.

"*Okay.*"

"Can I take another look at that knee?"

"We all have problems," she said, thinking of the man who had killed Will, wondering as she so often did, how he lived with himself, how he could have watched her life play out in the media, her suffering born into entertainment, and all of it thanks to him. Had someone paid him to kill Will—maybe someone he'd investigated for the paper? The police insisted they'd exhausted every possible lead in that direction. Was it nothing more than a freak accident, then? Either way, what was the first thing the rider did every day when he woke? Did he still ride a motorcycle? Did someone love him? Did they know what he had done? Did they forgive him? Did they force him to do everything they asked by threatening to turn him in?

"You need a fresh bandage," Henry said. "You really need stiches."

"It's fine."

"I'd like to take another look. I'm worried about infection."

"I'm not."

"I could go tell someone you need a doctor."

"Don't be ridiculous."

"Then let me make you a splint."

"Who do you think it was?"

He turned back to the stove, shut the water down and poured it into the press and lowered the lid.

"Hard to say," he said, now heading into the bathroom. "Enemies have a way of mutating. Al Qaeda is a singular group one day that splits off into five the next, and those five become new groups the day after that. There's no shortage of organized people who hate other people. No shortage of people willing to kill for a cause."

The kitchen smelled like coffee. How normal it all seemed. She could get used to him making coffee for her every morning. Having someone to talk to. Sleep with. She was ready for it. She thought she was.

"But who do you *think*?" she called to him in the bathroom.

"Why do you keep asking?"

"Because I *know* you have an opinion. I've never met a journalist without one."

"Ha!" Henry said, coming back into the room with the safety kit. "Then you would know that it's exactly as Will said: As a journalist, my mind is trained not to go for the obvious, so I really can't say without further investigation."

"Can't or won't?"

Henry didn't answer.

Olivay crossed her arms and let her head fall to the side. "Sure. Whatever. Will also used to say that sometimes it didn't make a difference, because sometimes the answer really was the obvious answer."

THIRTY-ONE

"*SHE ONLY HAD TWO MORE WEEKS,*" *HENRY SAID, AS IF SAYING it enough times might bring her back, might change the mind of the person who had taken her away—and from the start he was sure someone had taken her away. "She was brilliant. IS brilliant," he corrected himself and everyone stared at him, giving looks to one another that he could feel when his back was turned. She wasn't dead. Not yet. Not when he first started saying how brilliant she was.*

Henry was the first to notice boot prints swiped clean where they would have first veered off the path, but only for several feet before they appeared again. The sun struck just right and lit the way through the trees, until it was clear that two people had trampled off into the bush. The smaller prints circled out around the boots, as if she were shoved and pulled closer repeatedly.

Four hours after Genevieve would have walked up and kissed Henry hello, four hours after he would have asked what she thought about marriage, Henry understood with footprints in the sand that nothing he had ever thought or hoped before even mattered. His worst fear buckled through his body, imprinting a terror that would never lift away, a searing brand that would never quite heal. And yet he ran and he hoped for what he already knew was impossible, hoping, too, that the man who took her was still with her so he could massacre him inch by inch with fingers and teeth and fists.

Henry would never forget the sun on the loose and hasty mound of dirt, a mound that did nothing to hide the body underneath. And then the swirling eddy of flies Henry fought through as he gouged into the sand, growling and screaming for strength, until he was able to latch his arms under hers and yank and yank and yank until her upper body pulled free, exciting the flies even more, and Henry shouted and swatted and cried out for one ounce of mercy to let her be.

Later he would think of the brochures they were given and the quote from John F. Kennedy: "The Peace Corps is designed to promote world peace and friendship and shall be made available to interested countries and areas where men and women of the United States qualified for service abroad are willing to serve, under conditions of hardship if necessary, to help the peoples of such countries and areas in meeting their needs for trained manpower."

Conditions of hardship if necessary, he thought, or maybe he screamed that, too, as her bruised and broken forearms slumped in jangled sections above her head on the ground. Her bloody, twisted wrists wilted in the sand.

Her eyes were open and coated in sand the color of her skin so that the lids at first glance appeared closed. The end of her black headdress had been stuffed in her mouth, which bulged and bled like the vulgar ends of birth. If not for Genevieve's blue dress and white skin, Henry would not have been able to tell who lay before him.

Her skull had been smashed so many times she was nothing but a creature now, contorted and covered in soil-crusted blood, like black-scabbed tumors on her head and face.

How had this happened? Her body crushed by what? To guess was to imagine what she had gone through. The butt of a rifle? The tip of a boot? A hard and vengeful fist?

He would come to know what he never wanted to hear. That the soldier had raped her twice in the first hour. But she was still breathing then. Still alive, most likely still aware. No more than two hundred feet off the beaten path, hidden in her final moments by trees and broken brush in a shallow grave prepared for her the night before.

THIRTY-TWO

A LOUD BANGING ON MRS. HIGHTOWER'S DOOR ACROSS the hall startled them both, and Henry peered through the peephole. "It's a cop," he said. "Mrs. Hightower just let him in."

"I suppose we're next," Olivay said, but Henry was already scooping water into a bowl from the pot on the stove and taking it with him into the bathroom.

When he came out his hair was damp and combed off of his face. It appeared shorter this way, and she couldn't help noticing how much it changed the way he looked, in the same way the shape of her own face shifted when she pulled her hair into a twist on top of her head.

Olivay went in after him, brushed her teeth, and refastened her hair at the base of her neck. She slipped into her robe and fastened it tightly around her waist.

The second she hobbled from the bathroom the fierce pounding started on the door.

"LAPD!" a man yelled, but Henry was already opening it.

"Officer," he said, and the cop walked in without being asked.

He appeared slightly younger than Olivay and Henry, mid-twenties perhaps, short, and his brassy red hair seemed to have undergone a very recent cut. His pants were tucked into high-laced black boots, and the tips were damp, as if he'd been walking through a bit of water.

He'd rattled off his name so quickly that Olivay hadn't understood, and suddenly he was all the way inside the apartment, leaving faint traces of footprints, like tire treads, across the clean floor, stopping only when he got a closer look at Olivay.

"Oh," he said to Olivay. "I didn't realize . . . we've actually met before. I'm Officer Pendleton. I was on the call when your husband had the accident." He glanced sideways at Henry, his expression shifting from sympathy to assessment.

"I don't remember you," Olivay said, even though she vaguely did.

"I wouldn't think that you would."

"What can we help you with?" Henry asked.

"Do you live here?" he asked Henry.

"No," Olivay said. "He doesn't."

"Is there anyone here beside yourselves?" Pendleton asked.

"No," she said. "What's going on?"

"Just a safety sweep," he said. "For your own protection." He turned to Henry. "You mind if I ask for some ID?"

"How does checking his ID make anyone safe?" Olivay asked.

"Just trying to account for everyone, ma'am," he said.

If there was anything she hated, it was being called ma'am.

"I don't mind," Henry said, but Olivay could see that wasn't true. She was sure his body didn't normally move with such stiffness across a room. His right hand didn't often curl into a fist.

He pulled his wallet from his backpack near the door and handed over his driver's license. Olivay wouldn't mind having a look at that herself. Had Will made her paranoid? Did she think everyone was a bit of a liar at heart? Still, she wouldn't mind seeing his age and address, his name in official government print.

Pendleton checked the license and then Henry's face, and then the license. "Just visiting?" he asked.

Henry nodded.

"You look a little different in your photo."

"My hair was shorter then. I actually think I look the same. Well, with a shave."

"Did you spend the night?" Pendleton asked.

"That's none of your business," Olivay said.

"Let me put it another way. What time did you arrive here?"

"Well, I actually left. And then came back. I mean, I came over two nights ago, left yesterday morning, and then I came back."

She could see what the cop was thinking. She knew exactly what he was going to say.

"Where did you go?"

"Levine's."

Pendleton's head shot up. "It's in pretty bad shape."

"I saw," Henry said.

"Did you? How's that?"

"Off the balcony," Olivay said. "There's a clear view of it above the trees."

"What time did you return from there?" Pendleton asked.

Henry looked to Olivay. "I don't know what time it was, not exactly."

"You must have some idea. Don't you have a job you need to get to?" Pendleton seemed to be copying something down from Henry's license onto a small notepad.

"I guess it was around thirty minutes or so before the first bomb went off," Henry said. "Whenever that was."

Pendleton looked up. He handed the license back. "Thirty minutes."

"That's right."

"That sound right to you, ma'am?" He kept his eyes on Henry. "He returned here about thirty minutes before the first bomb exploded?"

"If you're referring to me, then yes, that sounds about right."

"Must have been hard to cut across the marathon crowd packed on the sidewalks. All those barricades down there. How'd you get around those?"

"The cross street just beyond it. I don't know what it's called. The police were letting people through in groups when the coast was clear."

"Is that right?"

"Why are you asking me? Ask your colleagues."

"You're not telling me how to do my job are you, Mr. Bearden?"

"Of course not."

"Didn't think so."

So Bearden really was his name. At least according to his license.

Pendleton wrote something more, and Olivay and Henry shared a look.

"Did either of you notice anything suspicious before the bombings?" Pendleton asked. "Especially you, Mr. Bearden, seeing how you were out there walking around."

"I was at Levine's."

"All by yourself?"

"Yes."

"You just left her here behind and went and got breakfast at—what time did you say?"

"I had work to do. It was—I don't know what time it was. I already said that. A little less than two hours before I came back."

"What do you mean about whether we've seen anything suspicious?" Olivay asked. "Like what?"

"Anything at all. The presence of someone you've never seen before. Anyone standing around, looking nervous, behaving strangely?"

"You mean like this guy?" Olivay gestured to Henry. "Leaving after spending the night, showing up again unannounced nearly two hours later? Thirty minutes before the bombs went off?"

She'd meant it as a joke, she thought she had, but now that it was out of her mouth she could see how flat it had fallen on everyone's ears. How inappropriate it was. Pendleton narrowed his eyes.

Henry had gone a little pale.

"Is this a joke?" Pendleton asked.

"A failed one, clearly," Olivay said.

"Pardon me?"

"Nothing," she said. "Listen, I still get a little, I don't know . . . just everything." She waved a hand through the air. "It's a bit too much for one lifetime, you know what I mean?" She bit her fingernail, trying to hide behind her own outburst, her unexpected use of the widow defense. "Thirty minutes before. Yes. That's right."

"Nearly two hours to pick something up from down the block?" Pendleton said.

"I was working. I told you. I hadn't planned on coming back. I went ahead and had breakfast at Levine's and was working on my laptop. At the last minute I decided to return."

"I see," Pendleton said. "You two have a fight?"

Olivay laughed, once, sharply.

Henry didn't answer.

"Nearly two hours. You sure you didn't see anyone odd hanging around?"

"I don't think so," Henry said. "But I wasn't paying attention. What exactly do you mean by odd?"

"Someone with a backpack, maybe. Someone sweating the way people do when they're nervous."

Olivay glanced at Henry's backpack several feet away on the floor. "It's hot as hell out there," she said. "Everyone's sweating." His hair had in fact been damp around the temples when he returned. But it would be. He'd taken the stairs. She hadn't heard the elevator.

Pendleton paused, taking them both in. "What happened to your knee?" he asked Olivay.

"I fell on broken glass," Olivay said.

"Looks bad," he said, glancing around the room and then up to the busted-out windows covered in sheets. He studied the sheet-covered pile of debris in the corner.

"I was about to change her bandage when you knocked," Henry said.

Pendleton didn't seem to care about that. He was studying the windows again. And then the pile. "Did some of that stuff fly in here from outside?"

"Yes," Henry said.

"Handlebars," Olivay said. "And a stop sign. All kinds of stuff."

"Don't touch it. Someone will be up here to collect it."

"Have they caught anyone yet?" Olivay asked.

"I can't answer that, ma'am."

"Look," she said. "The least you can do is give us some peace of mind, assuming you've got something that'll bring some."

He hesitated, looking back and forth between Olivay and Henry. "I sympathize. I'm afraid I've got nothing at the moment."

"Nothing you can tell, or nothing you're allowed to tell?"

He slipped the notepad into the breast pocket of his shirt, and then pulled out a card and handed it to Olivay. "If you see anything or hear anything."

"Our phones don't work," Henry said.

"Everyone is doing everything they can to get this mess under control as quickly as possible."

"And what if we see something before our phones work?" Olivay asked.

"Feel free to come to the door and flag one of us down."

"I thought we were supposed to stay inside," she said.

"The front door, I said. Not beyond." His sarcasm fit his pasty, boyish face. "And so yes, under the circumstances, ma'am, if you have information that has to do with what's happened here, I personally give you permission to open the front door and tell a police officer."

Olivay and Henry exchanged a smirk behind Pendleton's back when he reached for the door. Then Olivay raised her hand and pretended to shoot Pendleton with her finger. Henry's eyes widened.

"What about the press?" Henry asked, as if to distract Pendleton from catching Olivay in the act. "Are we allowed on the street?"

"We?"

"I work for the *Tribune*."

Pendleton placed his hands on his hips. She knew what he was thinking. She knew he was connecting dots that didn't exist, making assumptions the way a good cop should never do, believing just like that that Henry was an opportunist, that he'd swept in to console his coworker's widow. That maybe he'd once been Will's best friend.

Pendleton scratched his eyebrow with his thumb, a half-cocked look of amusement on his face. "A reporter then. A man who pays close attention to detail."

"Generally speaking," Henry said.

"And you didn't see a thing?"

"No. I don't believe I did. It was chaotic with the marathon. There were people everywhere. I probably had my head down most of the time just trying to move through the crowd to get back here."

"Probably," Pendleton said, looking a bit irritated now. "You understand what a lockdown is, Mr. Bearden. Right now even the press will have to obey the law."

"*Even* the press?" Olivay asked. "Are they usually the ones breaking the law?"

Pendleton sighed and rested his hand on the holster of his gun.

"What about the fires?" Henry asked, shooting her a sharp look. "Are they getting them under control?"

"That's Land Management and Forest Service, so I can't say for sure, but I understand firefighters are coming in from all over the country. At least they have the advantage of fighting it from the air. We don't have that luxury over here."

Surely luxury wasn't the right word. "Okay," Olivay said. "Thanks for coming in to check on us."

Pendleton looked as if he were about to clarify that he wasn't there for that purpose but instead he pursed his lips, nodded, and said, "Thanks for obliging."

Henry walked him to the door.

As soon as he was gone Olivay said, "He's suspicious of you."

Henry clenched his jaw, as if thinking her "joke" certainly didn't help matters, and she knew it hadn't but couldn't seem to help herself. What had she been trying to prove, to smooth over, to make better by making everyone as uncomfortable as she was?

He fastened the deadbolt, and without looking her in the eye again, picked up the safety kit.

THIRTY-THREE

A SOLDIER'S THROAT WAS SLIT AT NOON THE DAY AFTER Genevieve was killed. Slashed right there on the road used by everyone in the village—noon, when it was as hectic as a small village could be, with men and women and children shuffling in all directions at once, and no one saw a thing.

The soldier, seen by two boys the day before with Genevieve, was having tea in the village at noon. The soldier who had been the last person to see her alive—the one she'd been talking to, walking with, just before—was having tea at the stand beneath the mango tree. The street was crowded with children, white Toyotas rumbling past. Women were traveling back and forth from the market with their hands full.

The same two boys who had seen the soldier talking to Genevieve came to Henry on the night of her death to tell him they had heard the soldier bragging about what he had done to the French woman. Raped her twice. Beaten and broken the neck of the colonizer. How he had dug her grave the night before. Everything the soldier was telling the others made them laugh.

At noon, the soldier dropped dead at the foot of the stool he'd been sitting on, his throat slit so severely that the skin on the back of his neck was all that kept his head from rolling away. The soldier alive and drinking tea one minute—according to the tea maker—drinking from his copper cup, and then the soldier was instantly dead.

No one saw the first slump, the dangling, the blood spewing and clumping in the dirt. No one saw how the trail of blood had continued for at least a hundred feet, dripping from the hands of the killer, a man carrying a bloody machete down the middle of the road, a man whom no one saw.

Like the Creek Spirits. Blending in to perform their devilry, slipping out before others became aware.

"He was there with my cup in his hand," the tea maker said. "And when I turned from boiling more tea over the fire, he was simply and irretrievably dead."

No one saw anything except the dead man and his flies. This was the only indisputable fact that the witnesses, if one could call them witnesses, had to share.

In the collective silence, Henry questioned if he were somehow living inside his own imagination. He had wanted to kill the soldier after what the boys had told him, of course he did, but had he actually gone through with it? Was the memory of meeting the tea maker's eyes when Henry looked up with the blade in his hand real or imagined? Was the feel of a bloody machete, the weight of the soldier collapsing against Henry's calves and shoes, blood pumping and spewing like a water hose into the sand, real or imagined?

Did the soldier, seated and enjoying his tea, really smirk at Henry when he walked by moments before the soldier's death?

Pink scratches on the man's dark face had been visible from twenty feet away. Impossible not to see them, scratches from Genevieve's delicate fingers, the same fingers she had used to trace Henry's jaw before a kiss.

The machete had come from the back of a truck whose driver had stopped to buy goat meat across from the tea maker. Hadn't it? The machete, right there within Henry's reach.

Divine intervention.

Imagination.

Creek Spirits.

Henry.

Maybe wanting to kill a man as badly as Henry had wanted to kill this one had caused his mind to play tricks, to substitute himself in place of the real killer in order to gain control, to stop himself from feeling helpless. He had never known such helplessness.

The sound skin makes as it tears apart is not as quiet as one would think.

How did he know this?

How did he get those scratches on his wrist across the artery where his own blood continued to pulse so warmly, so safely, seeing him into another day?

THIRTY-FOUR

OLIVAY TOSSED PENDLETON'S CARD ONTO THE TABLE. "Did you hear me?"

"Of course he was suspicious of me," Henry said. "He was just doing his job."

Olivay watched him take a deep breath and run his hand through his hair, pushing it from his face as he glanced toward the door.

"And now I'm doing mine," he said, holding up the kit. "On the floor." He was like a coach demanding push-ups. "Let's change that bandage."

"Speaking of assholes," she said, but she was smiling when she said it, and Henry appeared to take it as a joke. She slowly lowered herself down, surprised he hadn't offered to help, and watched as he sat crossed-legged and lifted her thigh across his lap, gripping her ankle a little harder than she thought necessary.

Having a cop in the apartment had unsettled them both. She'd noticed right away, before she'd even made the crack about Henry behaving suspiciously. Her own reasons for feeling ill at ease were obvious—memories of Will, the week after his death when the police followed up with their obligatory, invasive questions. *We want to make sure it was nothing more than a hit-and-run accident. Did your husband know anyone who rode a motorcycle? Did he have any enemies? Is it possible he could have been having an affair?*

"Hold still," Henry said.

"I am," she assured him.

But what reasons did Henry have for clenching his jaw, for making a fist?

"Is Daphne married?" she asked.

Henry frowned as he unraveled the bloody gauze from her knee. "No. Not that I know of. Why do you ask?"

"What about a boyfriend?"

"I don't know."

"Ouch." She grimaced, as the gauze pulled at the scab.

"Try to relax." The final threads stuck inside the clump of scab, and suddenly a corner lifted from the bone.

"Ow, ow, *ow*!"

Fresh blood dribbled from all sides.

"Sorry." Henry held the scab in place with his finger while peeling away the remainder of sticky gauze. A foamy string of white pus released with it.

"I was afraid of that," Henry said.

Olivay squeezed her eyes shut.

His hands shifted around her legs, and then a soft towel slipped beneath her knee. She heard him unscrewing the bottle of peroxide and the small plastic lid clicking against the concrete floor. She opened one eye.

He held the peroxide at an angle above her knee, and then he saw her and stopped. "Close your eyes," he said, and she did.

A cold splash and then a scorching burn. Olivay jerked backward, but Henry had set the bottle down and gripped her leg so quickly and with such force that his fingers hurt nearly as badly as the peroxide in the open wound.

"Son of a bitch!" she yelled, eyes wide-open, palms flat against the floor near her hips.

"I'm almost done," he said, loosening his grip, blowing cool air on her knee, and then dabbing the bloody foam with the towel. His pink handprint still showed in her thigh.

"Was that really necessary?" she asked, trying to catch a breath.

"Yes."

"You could've warned me."

"I tried."

"How?"

"I told you to close your eyes."

"That's not a warning. That's *not* a warning!"

He applied a gooey antibiotic cream, and her breath jumped again and again as if she were stepping into a freezing cold lake.

"Give it a second," he said. "It's got a numbing agent that should help a little with the pain."

Her heart continued to bang around her bony chest as he picked up the magazine with the ranch house and cactus garden and rolled it into a sturdy cylinder. His hands were quick and agile with the duct tape he used to hold it in place, and when he was done the splint had the look and heft of a handmade billy club.

He wedged it behind her knee with slightly more force than seemed called for. He tore the tape with his teeth and bound it above and below her knee.

"A little rough," she said.

"But not too rough," he said.

"No," she said, and he slid her leg from his lap to the floor. An energy buzzed through his hands as he returned the medicine and gauze to the kit—a heat, a fierce animal vibration seemed to be coming off his skin, and Olivay couldn't move beneath the force of it. Her palms remained glued to the floor.

Henry wasn't shy about holding her gaze. He radiated with the calculated, intoxicated look of a man aroused as he crawled up next to her, untied her robe, and peeled it away from the front of her. They were face-to-face, so close her breasts grazed his shirt through the nightgown, Will's shirt, the faded face of Peter Frampton across his chest. He flattened his hands down on top of hers, pressed until the full weight of his upper body anchored her in place.

The longer he waited to kiss her, the more inflamed she became. Flurries of pleasure and rage stirring sex and memories, rumors roiling around her head, even as she tried to push them away.

He kissed her slowly and a trace of Will's scent from the shirt wafted toward her.

Her breath came in maddening sweeps. A vicious little something rising up inside, and she could feel it rising in him, too.

"Everyone thinks they've lived through something worse than the next person," she said. "But it's all relative to your own pain."

He sunk his teeth into her shoulder where the nightgown had slid off.

She flinched and jerked, but only slightly.

"You make me want to bite you," he murmured.

"You make me want to slap you," she said.

Henry kissed her again, long and slow, she could feel him holding back, caught inside some kind of deliberate restraint.

He bit harder the second time.

She slapped him in the face, and the crack of it aroused her even more.

Did your husband know anyone who might have wanted to do him harm?

Besides me? she'd wanted to say, for wishing him dead and alive at once.

Henry wrenched her robe away, her nightgown up and off her body so quickly her arms hung above her head as if she were surrendering naked to the police.

He gazed at her breasts at the same time Olivay slipped her hand inside the elastic waist of Will's pajamas, feeling every bit of Henry in her hand.

His mouth fell open in pleasure. "You're like a goddamn wasps' nest," he said.

"Fuck you," she said inside their kiss, and he gripped her arm, his thumb pressing and pressing, hard enough to sting her like broken glass, and Olivay said nothing as he shoved her flat onto the floor, pinning her hands above her head.

This was exactly what she wanted. Exactly what she needed, and deserved.

Henry crawled on top of her, careful of her knee, and now too careful in the way he kissed her lips, her cheek, her throat, until Olivay whispered *Please*, and it was like the crack of a gun at a starting line, the revolver lifted from its pretty box and fired into the room.

THIRTY-FIVE

GENEVIEVE HAD A DELICATE, SMALL-BONED FRAME, AND yet her singing voice had been husky—deep and rich as Nina Simone's, whose songs Genevieve had loved to sing. They passed by the ears like velvety ribbons on the wind. Enough of the poetry, Henry told himself, but that was back when Genevieve was still alive. To hear her sing was to die a little in the face of it. He'd thought that, too. Die in the face of it. How stupid he was.

She came to teach young women to sing while she had the chance, and she'd said so that first day, having no idea what her words would eventually mean. An idealist, a romantic, who'd come to give instruction at the renowned Perouix School of Music before her other life began back in France where a career had been put on hold. She came to give the young girls something they would not otherwise have, the same way her uncle and vocal coach had taken her in and made her understand the gift she possessed, how easy it all came to her, and what a sin it would be to withhold such a thing from the world. "Listen to their pretty voices rising up with confidence," Genevieve had said in her thick French accent the first hour Henry had met her, and how happy she was, even when she had just come through the anti-malaria terror and had swarms of giant flying cockroaches greeting her in the shower.

The students' voices were nothing compared to hers.

"It's a cold and it's a broken Hallelujah," she sang, and Henry stepped back as if having been pummeled in the chest, his breath coming up short, a terrible love no matter where he turned, and he didn't even know, at first, which he loved more, the sound of her voice or the young woman to whom it belonged.

The soldier had shoved her headdress in her mouth. Henry had yanked it free, his thoughts racing everywhere at once. Had she died of suffocation with it so deeply wedged in her throat? What was the last thing she said? Was it ornery? Was it please?

He was convinced that she had been screaming his name in the same moment he had been stifling his grin, waiting for her on the concrete half-wall, feeling smug and nervous in his tidy shirt, his hands shaky with excitement. A twenty-three-year-old French woman in love with a twenty-five-year-old American. This was where their story would begin. Henry would ask her with nothing more than a paper tab he had pulled from a bottle for a ring. He knew she was going to say yes.

Hours before the soldier was murdered, Henry staggered through the murk and blur to make sure Genevieve's directive was being followed. She had written down exactly what to do in the event that something should happen. All volunteers had to fill out such a form. Genevieve would have signed her name with the knowledge that she fully understood the risks.

Who believed such a thing could really happen? The headmaster's face was swollen from tears and anger, and even then Henry felt like shoving her to the ground for being so careless with a document that Genevieve had once held in her hand, placed her signature upon, placed her trust in—that someone would send her home to her uncle if it came to that. By the time the headmaster unearthed the paperwork, Genevieve was on her way to be cremated. Henry had to speak to her *uncle in French, which he found impossible to do once the man began to weep, and Henry handed the phone to the headmaster, rubbed his ear, but could not the get the sound of the man's cries out of his head, cries that had taken over mind on the village road around noon.*

Genevieve would return in the form of ashes. There had been no choice. The heat of Africa held no mercy for the dead. Genevieve was already severely decomposed by the time Henry had found her.

He had kept her favorite blue scarf for himself.

The rest he gathered from her room—mp3 player, novels and biographies her uncle had sent from Paris, her copper cup and hard plastic plate—all returned to the duffel bag she had carried with her all the way from home.

THIRTY-SIX

OLIVAY HAD PLANNED TO CLOSE HER EYES FOR JUST A moment, but instead dozed off in front of the television and fell into a busy dream filled with hundreds of small details, which made it feel as if the dream had gone on for years. A chemical dream, no doubt. Children everywhere, and they were exhausting her, keeping her awake with their crying at night, their dirty hands pulling at her clothes throughout the day, snotty noses glistening, fevers spreading from one to the other, and finally to her, and she was sick, deathly sick, and there was no one around to take care of her.

She sat up in a blur of ghost children, feeling thorny, feeling guilty for the way she'd handled them.

The first thing that came to her was that something had changed.

She didn't see Henry. Was that it? She didn't think that was it. She called out to him, but could see he wasn't there, or in the bathroom, its door standing wide open. His backpack wasn't anyplace she could see.

She pressed both palms into her forehead in a lame attempt to ward off a headache. After a moment, she reached for her laptop and saw that she had been asleep for an hour. She opened the screen at the same moment Henry walked through the door.

"Hey," he said, slightly out of breath but smiling, and she could see the traces of what they had done with one another in his face.

Olivay reached for him, a huge grin spreading across her own face, and Henry entwined his fingers into hers and kissed her on the lips.

"Where'd you go?" she asked. "Has the lockdown been lifted?"

"Not yet," he said, releasing her and crossing the room to the table where his laptop sat. "But Wi-Fi is coming through now. So are the phone lines." His clicking fingers on a keyboard was a sound she associated with Will.

"The Internet's working up here?" she asked, signing on to her computer.

"The neighbors said it was, but I don't see your network showing up."

"What about your phone?"

"It came on just long enough for me to call my family and tell them I'm fine."

"That must be why you seem so cheery," she said.

"Cheery?" His smile was happiness personified.

It was only now that she noticed a pie tin on the table. Mrs. Hightower. "A pie?"

"Oh, right. Your neighbor. I saw her in the hall. She handed it to me. Insisted."

"Did she?" Olivay must have really been out not to hear any of this. "What kind of pie?"

"Marionberry?"

"Oh, god. Have you tried it?"

"I was waiting for you."

"You didn't have to do that."

"*Manners*, my mother would say."

"Yeah. Mine, too. Will you cut us each a piece?" Olivay was suddenly starving.

Henry was up, grabbing utensils and plates. He seemed to know where everything was, moving through the kitchen with ease. The closet door near the bathroom stood slightly ajar. In the rear of it lay Will's messenger bag, bloodstains and all, and inside of that his broken laptop and everything else listed on the police report.

She hadn't noticed the closet door open before she fell asleep.

"Were you looking for something in there?" she asked, pointing to the closet.

Henry glanced across the room. "The wireless modem. It took me awhile to find it. I tried resetting it. I guess I didn't close the door tight enough and the wind sucked it open."

Olivay nodded.

"Do open closets bother you?" he asked, and closed it.

She couldn't quite tell if he was poking fun or not. "Not really," she said.

He handed her a slice of messy purple pie and a cloth napkin from one of the lower kitchen drawers. "Like a summer picnic," he said.

"Thank you."

The network was showing up on her computer, so she wasn't sure why he couldn't see it. But she didn't say anything. Something was off here. Something had changed, and she was caught off guard.

She ate slowly, aware of the feel of her body, the place on her shoulder where Henry had sunk his teeth, the bruise on her side from his arm crashing into her when he had lunged and thrown her to the bed yesterday.

She took a huge bite and wiped her mouth clean.

"I'm just not seeing it," he said.

"So you called your parents?" she asked as she started to log onto the Internet. "I didn't hear you talking."

"I did," he said. He'd gotten up and now his head was ducking inside the refrigerator. "And they had done exactly as I said with the map and calculations. My mother told me that they didn't want to hurt my feelings, but they weren't really worried until the fires started."

"Oh," she said. "Good. That's good."

Henry opened the freezer.

Olivay was suddenly online. The connection was slow, but her mind was quick, spinning through what felt like hundreds of thoughts at once, and she vowed to keep her mouth shut, not blurt things she'd rather not say, like how she was wondering about Will and how different this whole thing would have played out if she had been here with him instead of Henry. And then, without warning, she missed Will's irreverent humor, his freckled nose, the way he was so willing to say he was sorry, and how she'd so often believed him, and believed him still, because people were not so easily defined, he would not have been lying to her every time, and she wanted to say that right now to anyone who would listen. A small tear slipped from her eye and she wondered at her own sudden sadness, such a strange contrast to Henry's joy, and she thought she was just a little too wobbly in her thinking, not really making sense, but mostly it was just a feeling of loss, of the truth that she'd once had a husband who had been meant for growing old with, and he should have been here with her now, and he wasn't, and they should have gone through all of this together, and they weren't.

Henry removed the pizza box, took out a slice, and started eating. He held up what was left in his hand and she shook her head no.

"So that's what one eats after pie?" she said.

Henry nearly choked.

"More pie?" Olivay said.

When their laughter had played out, the room grew silent again. Olivay searched for the news.

"Tell me your three favorite foods," she said.

"Why?"

"I'm curious."

"That's an odd curiosity."

"You can tell a lot about a person by the answers," she said.

"Why three?"

"Why not three?"

He held up his free hand and started counting with his thumb. "Plum jelly on a biscuit."

"Is that *a food*?"

"It's something my father makes really well. I had it for breakfast a lot as a kid."

"Okay. Fine. What else?"

"D'affinois cheese. I can eat it like candy." He gave her a look as if to ask if that one passed the test.

She tilted her head a bit right, a bit left. "Okay."

"And figs."

"Who *are* you?"

Henry smiled, then grimaced, then smiled again.

"You're a small French rabbit," Olivay said. "It's like you were raised by *The Little Prince* on that funny little planet of his."

Henry took another bite, nodding his head with a small smile as if considering the truth in what she'd said.

"As a matter of fact," he finally said. "That book is one of my favorites. One of my *three* favorites, if we're still playing the game."

"Why doesn't that surprise me?" she said, and she could feel the smile freeze on her face as she glanced at the computer.

ARE THESE THE MEN? WITNESSES DESCRIBE POTENTIAL TERRORISTS.

"Don't you want to know the other two?" Henry asked, his head back inside the refrigerator.

The sketches quickly unfolded, and now facing her across the screen were the renderings of four men, side by side with written descriptions underneath each one. Police sketches were always terrible, the faces somewhat misshapen, the proportions an odd mix of shapes, as if a chin were taken from one person and placed on another, and the same with the eyes and nose. Nothing ever quite matched enough to create a human being who appeared the way one might actually appear in real life. Sketches looked like sketches, and these were no different. Except for one. That one on the end really threw her.

The wavy hair shoved beneath a baseball cap, an unshaven face, sport-style sunglasses covering the eyes. "He appeared to be just over six feet tall," the caption beneath him read. "Caucasian. Early thirties."

Henry said something else.

The way he'd grabbed his backpack after the first bomb. His knife. His lack of panic, or any true emotion until the fires, which she hadn't understood. The two hours he spent away from her apartment, only to return before the explosions. The unease he felt with the cop. A self-confessed liar who did not even use his real name.

Henry spoke again.

"What's that?" Olivay asked, but she was studying the shape of the face, touching the screen, running her finger along the edge of his jaw, the curve of his lips. "What did you say?" she called out, but when she looked up Henry was right there on the other side of her screen, smiling down at her, his face directly above the sketch.

"The other books," he said. "Don't you want to know what they are?"

THIRTY-SEVEN

NOT ONE PERSON IN THE VILLAGE WOULD SPEAK OF THE soldier's murder. Whatever had been seen, whatever was known appeared to have been erased by the heat of the sun, by the wind and sand and desert air. Whatever had happened was replaced by myth and dreams rushing in like water filling a dry riverbed.

Had Henry been anywhere near the village road that day, or was he still hours into lying on his back on the cot in his room watching cockroaches and flies zip through the heat above him?

Then an answer came without warning. Everyone began speaking at once. Chatter crackled through the air like flint.

Henry's neighbors yanked him from his cot, going on about the two-way radio in the church, and how Vera, in particular, wanted him out of there. "Now!" everyone shouted in English, not French, not Sango, nothing but broken and desperate English so that they might reach him in a place where their words were sure to be understood.

"In! In!" they cried, wedging him into the back of a white Toyota truck, shoving him across its bed between irrigation supplies and sacks of millet.

They sped away just like that, quickly and with nothing for him to sit on, and his tailbone bruised if not cracked after three hours of thumping against the metal. He only understood that this might explain the stiff burn the next day when he found himself wandering the sidewalks of a bustling, modern country whose language he did not speak.

But before that, when he first crawled from the truck and into the small airport, he held his backpack tight against his chest as if he were holding a baby, or a doll. He checked several times to see that Genevieve's scarf was still coiled up inside.

What if the wrong soldier had been killed?

What if someone else had been waiting for her on that path after the soldier walked away? What if the boys who'd said they heard him bragging about what he'd done to Genevieve were telling their own wild story?

There were no witnesses, and now the only man who might have known was dead.

Vera would later find a way to send Henry an email, telling him how the truck that carried him away from one end of the village had escaped only minutes before a jeep arrived on the other, carrying a CAR officer on a rampage to find out how the nephew of his childhood friend, a soldier this commander was responsible for, had been murdered by a civilian. An American citizen. Such a thing could not be true.

No one in the village could tell the officer what had happened. No one knew where the American had gone. They insisted the Creek Spirits had been up to their mischief again.

In the airport, Henry nodded and gave the woman behind the counter his passport and credit card and she put him on the first international flight, leaving within minutes—to Frankfurt, Germany, a place he'd never been. His backpack was all he had. It contained Genevieve's scarf, of this he was sure. When he looked a fifth time he saw it also contained two dirty shirts, a second pair of jeans, and the notebook on which Genevieve had doodled JE T'AIME *on the cover. The clothes he wore belonged to someone else.*

THIRTY-EIGHT

SHE WASN'T INTERESTED IN THE OTHER BOOKS. THIS would not stand. She would prove them wrong. *Henry* himself would prove them wrong.

She closed her laptop. "Pose for me," she said.

"Now?" he asked.

"Why not?"

"There's just a lot going on."

Stall him, was all she could think. It wasn't possible. What had happened between them. What was happening still. It could not be him in that sketch.

"Is it anything you can fix?" she said.

"What do you mean?"

"Does watching it all unfold make a difference?"

"It could. They're about to release a sketch of the suspects."

"People of interest," she said.

"Does it matter?"

"No. And that's kind of the point. When was the last time a news story changed your life? I mean, really changed it in some life or death way over the long term? We get so worked up every time, and then we forget until the next thing comes along, over and over—we're like a nation with amnesia, panicking anew at everything that comes along"

"Olivay," he said in a loud voice. "Are you all right?"

"And who can say what will happen to us when this is all over? When you are no longer sitting in my apartment all day. When you have to go back to work, and I have to—move on to—whatever I'm moving on to. I'd like to have this portrait of you sitting here."

"Okay. All right. But I'd like to see who these people are."

"They'll find them, Henry. You know they will. What are we going to gain by watching and worrying like this? The door is locked. We're safe in here. Like the Dalai Lama says, if a problem is fixable, if we can do something about it, then there is no need to worry. And if it's not fixable, then there is no help in worrying."

"And now you're quoting the Dalai Lama?"

"Will you pose for me?"

Henry sat across from her in Will's lounger, the one she'd forbid him from sitting in the day before. He sipped his coffee. "Nude?" he asked. Maybe it was a joke. Maybe not.

Olivay opened her sketchbook and readied her pencil. "No. Stay like that, with your cup in your hand. Relaxed. Like a man without a care."

Henry nestled his shoulders back.

It was possible that his body was the most beautiful of any man she'd ever seen, certainly of any man she'd ever slept with.

"Did anyone ever tell you how beautiful you are?" she said.

"Beautiful? I don't know about beautiful."

"Yes," she said, coaxing her pencil across the page. Rendering his likeness on the page itself felt like a sensual act. "I can't find a better way to say it."

Henry leaned his head back and watched her draw. "Well, that makes two of us."

Olivay smiled without looking up.

Henry crossed and uncrossed his legs. "Am I okay?" he asked.

"Better than okay." It wasn't as if she had to force her smile. An endless supply seemed to have formed inside her, one at the ready any time she looked up to see him.

Whoever had described this "person of interest" to the sketch artist had managed to capture the shape of Henry's jawline exactly. It was fairly prominent and perhaps not easily forgotten, and she was capturing it now in the very same way. But surely the witness was someone who'd had time to look at him for longer than a fleeting second. Someone in Levine's? Someone who recognized he wasn't a regular? But then the sunglasses and hat.

"I could try the TV again," Henry said.

It was all just a misunderstanding.

"I'd rather you stayed right there," she said. "Quietly."

"Sassy," he said.

"Yes."

Maybe it was Mrs. Hightower, whom Olivay had insisted he check on. She had spoken to Henry more than once, and face-to-face. The neighbors in the hallway had, too. And the cop, Pendleton, of course, though Henry's hair had been pushed back, his photo looking different than the way he looked now.

If you are harboring a terrorist, *you* are a terrorist.

"You really could use a haircut," Olivay said, filling in the wisps and waves of his locks.

Will had always appreciated her sense of vision, her ability to predict many steps ahead, *like the way you visualize two-by-fours and studs into roofs and walls and doors.* She always beat him at chess, visualizing five steps to his two. Checkers, forget about it. *Don't play her. She will destroy you!*

If she had told him to go to work earlier, he would have trusted her that it was time to leave, and leaving would have meant strolling past the corner before the motorcycle plowed through, and she would have never been left behind to count and count and count all the steps that she had missed that would lead to an alternate reality.

She sighed.

"What is it?" he asked.

"I like this. Drawing you."

Henry started to grin.

"Will never liked to be drawn."

The air stiffened.

"Why was that?" Henry asked.

"He said he had trouble sitting still. But my guess is that he didn't like me staring at him for too long. It unnerved him. You know, the eyes being the door to the soul, and all that. Suddenly it all makes sense."

Henry's expression shifted into mild unease.

"It's all right, Henry. Go back to being happy. It makes for a much more textured portrait. It makes you come alive."

"I was just thinking how in Africa people believe the likeness of their bodies causes something of the soul to escape."

And here she had thought he was thinking of Will betraying her.

She carefully shaped his fingers and hands, the ball of his knee, and back up again to the hair, those wisps were so beautiful, so soft in her fingers, so easy to grip and pull.

"What do *you* believe? Do we have a soul? Is there a God?" She laughed. She wasn't being serious. He must have known that.

And yet she could see him considering, taking his time to answer. "I don't know. I think the best I can think of comes from a line in a song."

"Some philosopher you are. A song?"

"'God is a concept by which we measure our pain.'"

Olivay couldn't help smiling, thinking of her mother. "My mother was a huge Beatles fan, and by proxy, a Lennon, McCartney,

Harrison, and Starr fan. 'I don't believe in Kennedy, I don't believe in Goethe'—that one, right? 'I just believe in me. Yoko and me.'"

"That's the one."

Henry caught her eye and held her there the same way he'd done when he introduced himself to her in Levine's.

"Thank you," he said.

"For what?"

"For changing everything."

"That's my line," she said, and neither shied away from the other.

"You really could use a haircut," she said.

"No kidding."

"I can cut it," she said, and began drawing him again. "I used to cut Will's."

She could hear him draw a breath.

"I have some razors, too. If you want to shave."

"Yes. I do. Thank you."

A clear likeness to Henry began to take shape on the page. "I can do it all for you, there, in the lounger—a cut and a shave. You can lay your head back and pretend you're at the barber."

"Do you miss him?" Henry asked.

Olivay's pencil slipped in her hand. She glanced up.

"Not much. Not anymore. But sometimes it still surprises me. Sneaks up in a wave. One passed over a little while ago, when you were eating pizza."

"When you asked me about my three favorite foods?"

"Yes."

"That was something you used to say to one another?"

"Yes."

"I saw it in your face."

"I think it's going to be harder and harder to hide things from each other. Don't you?"

Henry nodded. "Why did you ask me that? What did it mean to you, to the two of you?"

"It was just a little way of keeping tabs on who we were or becoming, tabs on each other, too." Olivay laughed. "I guess I wasn't very good at playing the game."

"Yeah. Well. You can't blame yourself for what other people do."

"Do you blame Genevieve for whatever she did?"

"Genevieve is dead, Olivay."

Olivay felt a sickening cave in her chest. She rested her hands on the sketch, covering Henry's face as if to shield it from the conversation. "I'm so sorry."

"It's all right."

"What happened?"

"She was murdered."

"*Oh.*"

"In CAR"

"God, Henry."

He shook his head at the floor.

"I'm sorry I brought it up like this," she said. "You didn't have to tell me, not in this way."

"I realize that. You're not forcing it out of me. I wanted to tell you."

"So, then . . ." She set aside the drawing. "What happened? Was the person ever caught?"

"Yes. He was."

Olivay hesitated. "I guess that's a relief. In its own way?"

Henry clenched his jaw as if biting at a sharp, quick pain.

The pipes beneath the sink began to clang and strain, and water suddenly spurt from the faucet that Mrs. Hightower apparently hadn't shut all the way off.

"Back on," Henry said.

"I'm probably wrong about what I said," Olivay added. "I wouldn't know if it's a relief or not. Obviously. All I can do is imagine."

He nodded.

"So that's all. That's all I wanted to say. If you want to say more—"

"I know who hit Will," he said, glancing down, kneading his thumb across his wrist.

THIRTY-NINE

THE FLIGHT OVER THE MEDITERRANEAN SEA SEEMED TO have taken days and no time at all. Henry was suspended into nothing, without time or country, no way in which to grab hold of one reality over another. He was nowhere and everywhere at once.

He looked down, sure he'd eaten already, but there sat a meal on a tray. Lasagna. His hands trembled around the soft white roll that came with it. It did not resemble anything meant for his mouth. A spongy toy, an artificial mushroom. The roar of the plane was so loud, so constant, he wasn't used to such noise, and yet whispers sifted between the seats, and children's cries echoed above them. Was it morning or night? The shades had all been drawn for a movie.

The clothes he had on were not his own. Yes, yes, he'd noticed that already. He remembered now that Vera had dressed him in her husband's clothes, switching out his own. Why had she done that?

Henry studied his hand in front of his face and wondered if he should assume it belonged to him just because it was there. Oh, he was not thinking clearly. He understood this, and dropped his hand into the lasagna, and the red sauce splattered on his arm and shirt and he shoved it away, and he shouted and shouted and shouted and crashed into the aisle, and the next thing he knew he was on the floor just outside of the cockpit where flight attendants were wiping the sweat from his forehead, another swiping the stains from his clothes.

"Are you sick?" they asked.

"No," he said.

"We are trying to find a doctor on the plane," someone said.

He didn't need a doctor. He knew exactly what was wrong with him. He knew exactly what he had done.

He wished there were someone in the world he could say this to. Someone who understood without him saying.

A priest? A cop? A psychiatrist?

His brother, George, whom he hadn't seen in a decade, hadn't heard from in at least six months. His brother, whose emails were culled from a brilliant mind, even as they often made no sense, nothing more than the ramblings of a man who was not well, little George a different kind of child, more feelings than thoughts, a nervous system too raw for this world, too sensitive to others' pain. "I want to go home," George used to say, but no one ever knew where that was.

"We're already home, George," Henry would say when he found his brother alone and in tears. "What can I do to help?"

The flight attendants allowed Henry to remain curled on the floor away from view of the passengers, allowed him to weep all the way to Germany until just before they landed, and even then they helped him up into a seat reserved for one of them so that no one could see his wet and twisted face, no one could judge his behavior, and this simple kindness felt so extraordinary, so completely undeserved.

FORTY

WHEN HENRY LEANED FORWARD TO SPEAK TO HER, OLIVAY leaned back against the headboard.

He seemed to notice, and hesitated before continuing. "Calls would come in to the *Tribune* and we were supposed to pass them on to the police. This kind of thing happens all the time, witnesses contacting the media instead of the cops, people wanting their own story covered just as much if not more than the one they're calling about. But because the story was local and got so huge, after the videos broke, and because Will had worked for the paper, we were all constantly fielding these calls."

Olivay glanced at the sketch. It was mostly finished. She didn't dare pick it up with her sweaty hands and smear the lead, and for some reason it was Daphne she thought of now, Daphne listening to callers describe the scene of her lover being killed. She imagined her own name, *Olivay,* floating into Daphne's ears day after day, sitting at the same desk where Will had told her Olivay was onto them. The same desk she cried over for months when he died.

"Here's the thing. I answered several calls from a kid who told me he was the son of a cop. He was sixteen years old, and he claimed to have done it himself."

"Really," Olivay said. "A sixteen-year-old."

"I thought it was a prank. At first, I did. He sounded like he'd barely gone through a voice change. But that was actually what made me start to take him seriously. I could hear a tremble in his voice."

"What did he say?"

"That he couldn't go to the cops. That if he told his father, it would just get covered up, and the boy didn't want that. He also didn't want his dad to have to carry around the secret, too. He knew he would hate him for it in the end."

"Sounds elaborate," Olivay said.

"He's a smart kid," Henry said. "He gave me his cell and told me I could call him and talk to him more if I didn't believe him. Eventually he gave me his address."

"Wow, Henry. So you're like, his friend?"

"He lives about eight blocks from here."

Olivay sat straighter now. "Wait. Did you go to the police with this? Please tell me you've gone to the police."

"Just hear me out."

"Henry."

"No, listen. It's important. If you want to go to the police with this I won't stop you. It's your right and I wouldn't blame you if you did."

"Blame me? What on earth? Blame *me*?"

"He's a kid who snuck off on his brother's motorcycle. He has no license and no one knew he'd taken it. His brother goes to UCLA and was in class when it happened, and both of his parents were at work."

Olivay shook her head, her eyes never straying from his. She threw up her hands and let them fall beside her. "How do you know any of this is even true? That he didn't just make it all up?"

"I'll get to that. Just . . . Too much of it started making sense. This kid, his name is Luke. He said there was no one he could tell without them trying to protect him. He'd never gone to church but thought about walking into St. Mary's and pretending he was Catholic just so he could confess to someone. But even then, he knew that priests keep everything confidential. It wasn't enough for him."

"This is ridiculous, Henry. What did you do, take him under your wing? Make a little brother out of him? A confidant?"

"Yes."

Olivay slapped her hands down onto the bed. "Why would you do that?"

"Because over time I gained his trust, and he started to tell me more and more about his life and I couldn't help but see him as a good kid who had made a stupid, average mistake that resulted in something so inconceivably horrific and out of control that he would be punished for the rest of his life. And for what?"

"Oh, I don't know. How about for *killing* a man!"

"It's not as simple as that."

"I really can't believe what I'm hearing. This is crazy, Henry. So you just let him go? Just like that? What the hell are you telling me?"

"Give me a little credit, would you? There's a lot more to it than that."

Olivay crossed her arms. "Great. Let me pop some popcorn. This is quite the show. You're full of twists and turns, you know that? Like nothing I've ever seen."

Henry wiped his mouth with the back of his hand as if clearing his lip of sweat. He wasn't happy with her. She didn't care in the least.

"He's just a kid with his whole life ahead of him. He did a dumb thing by taking the bike out for a spin, but come on, Olivay. If the world were fair, he would have put it back under his parents' carport that morning and no one would have been the wiser. Maybe

I'm wrong here. Okay? Maybe I'm not seeing it all clearly. I've got a little brother of my own. Maybe that makes me biased. But god-damn. I just don't believe that sneaking a motorcycle out for a spin makes that kid a killer. It shouldn't equal spending the rest of his life with real killers behind bars. How would that help anyone? How would that help *you* to have him there? The only thing it would do is destroy him and his family. That's it."

"That's not it! What about me? What about how I feel?"

"About what?"

"About never knowing who it was? What about all the fear I've lived with because of it? All the media attention because of it? It has ruined *my* life, Henry. You're acting like my life doesn't count at all."

"Will dying is what ruined your life."

"My God. Shut up. You can shut up now. I don't want to hear anything else."

"I'm sorry this is hard on you, but I won't shut up."

"Just leave me alone."

"I'll think about it."

But she was off again, unable to let it go. "You make it sound like it was Will's own fault, like he died on purpose. Like he shouldn't have been in the way of this innocent kid!"

"That's not at all what I meant."

"Who cares what you meant? This kid killed my husband." *Husband.* Like a shield she could hold up to Henry for protection. Husband. Something solid. Defined. A commitment she had made to someone else for a lifetime.

"Does it make a difference to you now?" Henry asked.

"I don't even know if what you're telling me is true! How do you even know for sure that he did it? How do you know he's not some deranged boy looking for a mentor, a Big Brother to hang out with after school?"

"I'm sure, Olivay."

"How?"

"He told me he saw his father walking around the motorcycle in the carport the evening after it happened. He stepped back to look at, kneeled down to examine the fenders, ran his fingers along the tires, that kind of thing."

"And?"

"It was a used bike to begin with, scratches and dents all over the place. Nothing obvious about the accident stood out after Luke rinsed it off and wiped it down."

"You mean Will's brains weren't marring the tires when he had a good look?"

"I understand that this can't be easy for you."

"You have no idea." Olivay shook her head at the closet that contained Will's messenger bag, Will's blood.

"Yes, actually, I do."

Her head shot back. "You said he was *caught*. The person who killed Genevieve was *caught*."

"It doesn't really matter in the end. Knowing isn't going to bring her back. And it isn't going to bring Will back either."

"Where is your *proof* that it was this kid, Henry?"

"The first thing I did was look him up on social media. I followed all of his posts going back over an entire year. He was a normal kid. There was nothing other than jokes with friends and stuff about video games and teachers and a few girls here and there. One or two posts about his brother or his parents, the fact that his dad was a cop, which the other boys liked to tease him about. But as soon as Will was killed, everything changed. His posts became less frequent, a bit darker. He went from looking like a normally groomed teenage boy, to a long-haired, greasy recluse."

"That's conjecture. All teenagers change like that. Become dark and moody. I changed like that for a time, and I'm sure you did, too."

"But the timing of it fit. That's the first thing."

"What's the second?"

"I snuck into his yard and examined the bike myself."

Olivay narrowed her eyes.

"I know someone who works as an assistant in a forensic lab. He gave me a small kit to do a couple of swabs. I told him I was doing a story on evidence left at a crime scene and that I would quote him in it if he helped me out. People love seeing their name in the paper."

"Not always."

"In general they do. Anyway, I swabbed underneath the front fender in several different spots, and then I swabbed along the edges of the rims."

"And?"

"It came back positive for human blood."

Olivay recoiled at the word, at the vision of her husband's blood spattered on this kid's motorcycle. A kid. A goddamn kid.

She dropped her head in her hand, allowing herself to imagine, the terror and confusion he must have felt. She knew Henry was right about everything, but this did nothing to calm the fury, the fact that he had killed Will. She glanced at the sketch, stopping herself from ripping it to pieces.

"Does he know you did all that?" she asked.

"No. I didn't see any reason to tell him."

"But you saw some reason to tell me?"

"I thought it would bring you some relief."

"*Relief?* Are you fucking kidding me?" She threw her hands in the air and let them fall. "Relief!"

"You said so yourself, living with the unknown, the fear of who it might have been, wondering about the motive, worrying about him still being out there."

"He's still out there, Henry."

"He's a kid. A harmless kid. It was a terrible accident. And now that you know, you also understand that you have nothing to worry about. This wasn't some killer. It was just a kid on what was supposed to be a joyride through the neighborhood."

She couldn't think straight.

"It's only my opinion, Olivay, but I don't see how a mistake of this kind deserves the horrific variety of punishment that this boy and his family would face. As it stands, he's already living in a state of constant mental anguish. He inflicts it on himself every day, and if that's not its own kind of prison, its own kind of punishment, I don't know what is. He'll never be free of it. You know that. Not completely."

"What are you saying? Life isn't fair? Because I've pretty much got that one figured out."

"I could have broken the story, Olivay. I could have written it and brought the paper and myself all kinds of notoriety. But I didn't. And I won't. No one knows about any of this except me, and now you."

"What am I supposed to say? *Thank you?* I appreciate you sacrificing your big story for me?"

"No. You don't have to say anything. I just thought you deserved to know."

"Sure, Henry. Okay." She looked at the sketch, then him, then the sketch. "And what if I *want* you to write it? What if I told you I would feel better having it out there for everyone to read?"

"I wouldn't believe you."

"Are you under the impression that you know me so well?"

"I am."

Olivay winced. She didn't know whether to be intimidated or completely and utterly relieved.

FORTY-ONE

SOMETIMES WHEN HE'D THRUST HIS HANDS INTO THE DARK soil, he'd see flashes of Genevieve beneath him. It wasn't as if he didn't understand that turnips and carrots were the real objects in his hands, he wasn't so far out of his mind that he believed it was anything other than vegetables he was yanking free of the earth, and yet he saw Genevieve's arms as he reared back at the sight of her face, her body whole again. Most times it was beautiful to see, though never quite alive, she was never quite dead either, and it was not unpleasant to look at her this way, as if she were lost in a deep and peaceful sleep in his hands.

Other times were different. The visions came without warning in the middle of the field that smelled of manure and green growing things in the sharp Bavarian air, and he would see Genevieve's face as it really had been the day he found her, and he would drop to his knees, let his head fall forward, and bawl without making much of a sound.

The first weeks were like this.

The farmer didn't seem to mind.

Henry guessed that most people who came to do work that paid little more than free meals were desperate, running away from something, and had come there to push their bodies to the limit so their minds wouldn't have to work so hard, so they could survive another day without the effort it took to navigate whatever had once been their previous lives.

Few words were exchanged between Henry and the farmer, and of those most were hand gestures and guesswork. The man's only language was a dialect of German called Swabian, and it was so far removed from anything Henry might have understood, and yet it never seemed to matter. The continued silence appeared to suit them both.

The nights were different.

The soldier's throat, the machete in Henry's hand. He didn't know if his cries escaped the thick stone walls of his attic room in the dark. Sometimes the thrashing in his sleep was so violent, he would wake shivering on the cool pine floor without any memory of how he got there. After that, he would crawl back into the sweat-soaked featherbed and try to sleep before the rooster crowed at the first hint of sun.

After a month, he felt suited to the work, the quiet, the pleasant sun and lack of intrusions, but by then the harvest was over.

He understood, days later, that the farmer was telling him he had to leave. But it wasn't until he grabbed the back of Henry's shirt and pulled him from the barren soil that Henry fully understood what was happening. He had gone on digging when there was nothing left to give.

"Wie ein Geist," the man kept saying in the dark and chilly air, and Henry understood that he was calling him a ghost. The ground had quickly become moist after the sun went down, and the smell of the surrounding pines crossed the fields and made Henry think of Christmas mornings with George and his parents—every year someplace different, so that it was impossible to savor any kind of tradition with the menu always changing, the weather never the same, the smells and customs a revolving door leading to something unknown.

"Auf Wiedersehen," the farmer said the following morning, goodbye the only word Henry had understood as he set off on foot toward the train station.

London because they spoke English. It was almost as simple as that.

And because he knew someone there, a man named Tony, who, as children, Henry and George had befriended in Australia. They'd kept in touch over the years, nothing deep, nothing too binding, more curiosity than anything else, but Henry knew Tony was working as a diver in the water show in the Windsor Safari Park. As soon as he got in touch, Tony offered him a place to stay. Tony had recently heard from George, and Henry felt instantly connected.

"He's an odd duck, isn't he?" Tony said. "Heart of gold, but you know. You know, right?"

Yes, Henry knew. The obsessions he'd latched onto at MIT, his fixation on free sourcing information, BitTorrent protocols, bandwidth throttling, net neutrality, all things Henry had never heard of at the time.

"Everything we think we know about the world comes from Los Angeles," George had written in his last email to Henry. "And none of it is real. Movies, television, a world portrayed in ways it doesn't actually exist, an illusion for the sake of money, a fucking crime is what it is. Mind-numbing the masses. This is the real totalitarianism, Henry. A select few deciding for the majority. Only it's on a worldwide scale and people don't even know they're being controlled. You understand that, right?"

"You think I'm being controlled by forces bigger than me?" Henry wrote, but of course George never answered him directly with another email.

Henry would eventually find himself in Los Angeles for this very reason—because everything known about the world started there. Because the idea, the philosophy of a reality as nothing more than an illusion seemed to define Henry's life. Because Henry wanted to be near his brother, even as his brother continued to elude and confound him on the best of days.

But those days in London—if ever he were to feel the full weight of loneliness and grief, it was on those sidewalks and in that rain, carrying his backpack everywhere he went, Genevieve's blue scarf always there on his back. Sometimes he would take it out and wrap it around his neck when he stopped for coffee, and dare himself not to cry as he imagined her there with him.

These dares would lead his attention away from himself to the stories of others, overhearing the concerns they shared with each other, stuffing their worried mouths with what always struck Henry as an endless supply of food.

Now that he understood the language around him, now that Sango was no longer stopping him from understanding exactly what was going on around him at all times, now that the silence of the Bavarian hills was behind him, Henry finally absorbed without effort what everyone was saying, and yet he did not understand what they meant. With every passing day, he fought off the yearnings to return to a world of ignorance and silence. A world where he didn't know everything he knew.

Relationships, work, money—everyone wanting desperately to get these things right, everyone failing in spite of how hard they appeared to try.

"I don't know what to do with her."

"I think I'm going to be fired."

"I think she's leaving me."

"I'm going to leave her, but I don't know how."

"I'm no longer happy in that place."

"How am I going to pay my rent?"

"Stop. Just stop. Why do you always bring that up? Are you trying to punish me? Yes, you are. You love it when I suffer."

As far as he could tell, the only people who seemed to be happy were small children humming to themselves, wandering between tables and chairs, an act which unnerved their parents who, in turn, tried everything to temper their enthusiasm and get them to sit quietly. Henry thought of the children in Africa with distended bellies and flies around their eyes and their beautiful grins, and he did not have an answer for anyone about what to do about anything, and these were the thoughts running through his head first thing every morning as he listened to the cries of peacocks, and if he was lucky, a lion's roar like a cyclone wiping everything clean.

FORTY-TWO

IT WAS LIKE AN ELASTIC BAND WINDING THROUGH HER brain, pulling tighter and tighter, growing thinner and weaker with every word Henry spoke.

"You're right," he said.

So taut, Olivay burrowed her fingers into her temples to see if that might loosen things up. Don't say another word, she thought, holding the top of her head as if it were a hat about to fly off in the wind. I cannot bear to hear you speak.

"I really could use a shave and a haircut."

And just like that, like a tiny silver mallet to her head, a ping, a snap broke something free.

"I'm happy to do it," she said. She squeezed her arms as if to see if they were real. Of course they were real. What was wrong with her?

She'd already taken the last codeine. There were other pills, and she would get to those in a minute, but she had to admit that the codeine had been so nice.

She placed the scissors on the counter next to the trendy kit she'd bought for Will from a specialty shop in London full of turn-of-the-century remake gadgets for men. A horsehair brush and soap, straight razor, and a cotton cloth for steaming the face afterward. A unicycle and a pair of oxfords had been used as window dressing in the store.

Henry had scooted the lounger to the sink so that his head could lean back while Olivay shampooed his hair. "Are you sure, are you sure?" he kept asking.

"Yes, I'm sure, I'm sure." She stood with her leg propped on a chair as if she were doing ballet.

There was a lot going on here.

"Just relax," she said, and Henry wormed his neck into the rolled towel on the edge of the sink. Olivay held her fingers beneath the running faucet. "There," she said. "It's good now."

"I trust you," Henry said, and when he said it, he didn't smile. He closed his eyes.

She held the spray nozzle against his hair and rolled it around until she had thoroughly soaked the strands. She set it back and massaged a dollop of shampoo into his hair until the suds began to form and her fingers glided slowly into the same round rhythm, and Henry's lips parted with contentment, and Olivay's breathing heightened and she had to stop herself from leaning in for a kiss.

His perfect skull in her hands, the easy pleasure of his wet hair, the warm, foaming suds. She massaged his temples and the crown and all along the base of his head.

Henry's chest rose and fell in easy waves. He was drifting off in her hands. The lather grew so thick it made gentle slapping sounds when she lifted her hands a little too far from his hair.

She could get used to all of this. She was sure he could, too.

She switched the water from the spigot to the sprayer. His eyes opened, and when he looked at her he smiled.

That face. Beatific, innocent-looking. Even upside down, when he didn't exactly look like himself.

Olivay slowly rinsed the suds down the drain. It was mesmerizing to watch the bubbles swirling, the white foam, like being hypnotized into a tender, altered state, and she recalled a song her mother used to play at the piano. *All of life contained right there, Olivay,* she said. *How can you reject it so easily? Relationships with anyone, with the world itself, are always give and take. Always some kind of compromise.* Olivay pointed out that her mother had never been married, and wasn't it easy to believe such a thing when the only "person" she had to compromise with was actually a cat?

No. Not this cat, her mother said. Oskar was long gone by then and some drab tabby named Angelika had taken his place while Olivay was in college. *She's a stubborn little hellion.*

Henry's lids sprung open and he snatched her wrist.

She realized she'd been humming, and now she stopped. "What?" she said, dropping the nozzle in the sink. "What did I do?"

He blinked several times, and then he opened his fist and let her go.

She hadn't done anything. Of course she hadn't. Calamities might be piling up inside her, but she hadn't shown it. She didn't think she had, and now she wished she could take back the question. She held her arm away from him, against her chest.

"Nothing," he said. "Sorry," he said, and he seemed to be searching her face. She, too, was upside down from where he was looking, and maybe this was why he didn't seem to recognize her so clearly. "I must have fallen asleep," he said, and laid his fists in an X across his chest like a dead man.

When the suds drained completely away she wrapped a towel around his head and rubbed his hair gently. He opened his eyes and rolled them up to see her, his dark irises watching, and then he smiled strangely, as if remembering that he didn't need to be afraid. That there was nothing to worry about. That it was only Olivay he was looking at, after all.

FORTY-THREE

NO ONE SPOKE TO HENRY IN PUBLIC, NOT DIRECTLY, AND *not even Tony all that much in private once he got a good look at Henry, at the hollow stare Henry surely must have been carrying around in his skull, and Henry knew Tony must be thinking how he was a lot like his brother now, and there wasn't anything Henry could say or do against it. Other times he wondered if he had become invisible, if he really was a ghost, and it would startle him into palpating his forearm, his wrist. He would cup his own jaw and remember how Genevieve had touched him there, and he would think that this was what it was to be alive and dead at once. He had arrived in purgatory, a particular ring of hell, and for all he knew, this was where he had come to stay.*

All those snippets of conversation continued to sift into his ears.

Sometimes he hunched over his notebook with a pen in hand as if he were writing something down, but he was really just concentrating, puzzling out what was being said around him, because not much of it seemed to make sense. The same complaints and worries. The same pat answers, as if everyone were living inside the same spinning eddy, watching the same problems and solutions swirl by day after day and all they could do was repeat them to each other. And then one afternoon, it finally struck Henry that the meaning behind what was being said was found in the power of the thing that was never said.

The answer to nearly everything turned out to be one thing: the absence of love.

It was why so many people acted out in the way they did.

It was why so many withdrew, fought tears, and became angry.

It was why no one could ever seem to let things go.

He imagined himself through the eyes of others—a stranger in tattered clothes with a strange accent—neither American nor French, certainly not British—scribbling things in a notebook, glancing up with a small smile every now and then as if wanting to speak, and he'd wish for permission to whisper the strange declarations from his notebook into their ears, but of course that permission never came.

It was with George in mind that Henry began to write longer pieces. George, the strange surveyor of communication, the one absorbed with codes and data, information streams that made no sense to Henry, aside from the bigger idea of expression and knowledge being shared from one person to the next.

Henry started with the Perouix School of Music, a place bursting at the seams with love, and then Genevieve working as a vocal teacher there, and he found that he could write and write well, so well, in fact, that this very first piece, written in French, was sold to Le Monde.

No one knew that what he'd written was different from what had actually happened in the CAR, that it simply mirrored the official story of the Peace Corps about a tragic attack, a young teacher killed by an unknown stranger, someone who was never caught. There had been no mention of a soldier's death, and anyway, Vera had let him know that a small inquiry had been made and the only answer those interviewed had ever given was "the Creek Spirits and their mischief." He understood this was not what they believed. He understood they were protecting him, and he missed the village and Vera and his students and speaking French, and he missed the rawness of his daily life, the pure and fundamental happiness he had shared with Genevieve.

So he wrote about the girls' choir being trained by an up-and-coming French singer named Genevieve Bonnet, a beautiful young woman who had coaxed their talents out of them with her own ethereal voice. He wrote about the chorus echoing across the vast blue sky, filtering through the trees and into the village, where some said they could still hear it long after the girls had finished singing and were sitting at their desks studying English.

He wrote about Genevieve's tragic death, this selfless young woman who had changed so many lives before leaving behind her own. He wrote that he had known her in passing and she had always been kind. He included the night of her high fever and the way Vera had saved her life, erasing himself from this scene and all others. Ornery no longer existed if there was no one but him to tell the story.

He developed a compulsion for jotting down small sentences on scraps of paper he carried in his pockets. Later, when he slipped his hand among the lint and pence to the papery edges, he'd remember what he'd scribbled that day and remembering felt a lot like someone reading it to him out loud, a voice so calm and sure, right there at his ear, like teaching George to read, the way his brother would repeat the words back to Henry and the joy they felt at the knowledge, the mastery taking place. Words in his pocket like a coded message, and he missed his brother George, missed the boys they used to be.

Over time he was overcome with sudden spikes of panic or rage, and he would reach for a kernel of wisdom in his pocket and they calmed him, these pieces of seemingly random advice turning out to be exactly what he was looking for. Of course, this was how con men worked. He knew that. Psychics. Palm readers. He knew he was conning himself with the laws of probability. With laws of reliability. With universal truths.

He was conning himself with peacocks and lions in the morning.

George had always loved those laws, using science to prove that everyone was connected to everyone else, that given the right equation, birds and lizards and a single cell from a baby's strand of hair were all woven from the same source. The "underground" he called it, where everything and everyone met up.

This was exactly how Henry felt the day he came upon a quote by Walt Whitman on a postcard in a coffee shop. Genevieve had loved Walt Whitman. Was there a law of probability that Henry would find such a thing in London?

Happiness, not in another place but this place . . . not for another hour, but this hour.

He copied it down and put it in his pocket. An American poet loved by Genevieve in a coffee shop 3,500 miles away from the East Coast of the United States where Whitman began—his words suddenly appearing in a storefront Henry had chosen as a shelter from the rain.

What were the odds?

There was a number to this, a calculation George might have given him if the two were still close, if George would just email back when Henry reached out to him.

FORTY-FOUR

THE LONDON SCISSORS WERE STILL SO SHARP. AND WHAT a pleasing sound they made as Olivay snipped through Henry's hair. Like a whisper, like someone too small and shy to say the thing he really wanted to say.

Snip.

Snip.

Like sharpening knives.

"There's still a lovely golden blond underneath," she said.

"Hm," he said.

"That's unusual."

"Is it?"

"And a little gray, too."

"I'm aware."

"You know the famous architect, Gaudi?"

"Of course," Henry said without opening his eyes. "The cathedral in Barcelona that looks like a bad dream, like the world is melting."

"That's one way to look at it."

"What about him?" Henry asked, his face still resting in a state of bliss as she pulled with the comb, clipping the scissors in a constant flow of rhythm around his head.

"He once said that nature didn't present us with anything in monochrome. That the contrast of color was the source of life itself."

Henry didn't open his eyes, didn't have much to say about that, she guessed, and she didn't need for him to say anything anyway. She saw color all the time in places other people seemed to miss it. But she'd never seen that cathedral. She'd always wanted to, always planned on it, and now? She was talking to herself as if she'd never get another chance.

Henry had begun to remind her of Oskar. Not because of their conversation in Levine's, but because the cat was the only living creature she had ever tamed, ever owned, ever loved without condition.

She cut around Henry's ears, so close to the flesh, and the hair fell in quiet lumps at her foot.

"What if a building were more like a nest?" she asked. She wasn't the first to pose the question, but really, what if? "You know, made from materials we could find out there right now on the street and put to use. A structure that wouldn't last longer than was needed, wouldn't leave a trace of anything behind when it was gone."

"Africa," Henry said, dreamily. "I've lived exactly that way, in a home made of clay and straw."

"Oh, yes, of course. You *did*. You actually did." She found this exhilarating for reasons she didn't quite understand, didn't try to understand.

Henry was drifting again beneath her fingers.

"Don't fall asleep, Henry. We still need to put this razor to use."

FORTY-FIVE

ORGANIC FARMING, GERMANY'S INNOVATIVE SPIRIT AND social formalities, their gratuitous use of cream and potatoes in nearly every dish, London's tea shops and specialty shops and clever sense of humor, the water show in the Safari Park and the large, inexplicable crowds they could still bring in—Henry wrote about it all. Travel writing. Feel-good stories. Essays based on pleasure and based on truth.

'Based on' was always the ticket.

Editors for magazines and newspapers loved articles that were: a) well-written, and b) easy to fact check. Henry never lied about what he put on the page. No one ever asked what, if anything, he might have been leaving out. He had a way of making it all sound complete.

He wrote stories in French for France and Montreal, he wrote others in English for the London and Dublin papers. By then he had returned to the United States, where he was getting the most work he'd seen so far, when he decided to settle in a place he'd never lived before, in a place he was convinced he would never like, never be happy in, which was what he deserved, a place where he could never get too comfortable. He zipped his motorcycle between cars on the freeways during rush hour, raging at drivers, engaging them in shouting matches, which they could never hear behind his bulky helmet, and sometimes he would smack the back of a car just to frighten the driver. They had no idea what he was capable of, and he enjoyed the look of terror on their faces. For a time he really did.

FORTY-SIX

AS AN ARCHITECT OLIVAY KNEW A LOT ABOUT LAND-
scaping, and by turns, growing things. She'd once read how wild-
fires had a way of destroying all the death and decay across forest
beds, how they could wipe out diseased plants and toxic insects
and invasive species in a way nothing else could, and how it was, in
fact, a necessary means to allow some nutrients to be released into
the soil so that new growth could take place. And what about that
Ponderosa Pine, with its fire-activated seed that actually required
burning for germination to take place?

What a funny thing *that* was.

She was thinking about the transformation of such things when
she slid the straight razor down Henry's foamy white cheek. What
a terrible scratchy sound it made as it sliced away the stubble. Like
fire crackling through branches.

"Hold still," she said. "Hold very, very still."

She didn't need to remind him. He lay back beneath the razor
in her hand as stiff as a dead man, or a live one surrendering his
future to her hands.

Either way.

She dipped the blade around in a warm bowl of water. She scraped from top to bottom again. And again. "Now pull your lip tightly over your teeth," she said. "I don't want to cut your beautiful mouth."

But she thought about it, how easy to commit one false move, or a calculated one just right to open his skin. There was definitely something wrong with her.

"Lean your head way back," she said. "That Adam's apple is a bit pointy. It just might be a challenge."

Henry said nothing. It was as if he'd fallen asleep.

She was so close to his face, and she wondered if he could feel her breath against the cool, smooth skin left behind by the razor. Could he see how hard it was for her not to kiss his creamy-soft skin with every row of whiskers she removed?

Ah, Henry. You are such a beauty. How careful she was with him. Not one nick.

"Look at that," she said. "We both survived."

Henry opened his eyes.

"I'm just going to throw a hot towel on your face for a moment and then we're through."

Still he said nothing, as if resigned to whatever she said, whatever she wanted, and anyway, now the cloth was steaming over his face so he couldn't say much even if he'd wanted to.

Olivay peeled it off like a magician unveiling a trick. "Voilà!" she said, which was, of course, French.

Henry sat up.

"Look at yourself," she said, holding up a hand mirror for him to take. "The transformation is astounding."

And it was. The haircut seemed to have taken years off his life. The shave perhaps even more.

"Wow," Henry said, holding his jaw, turning his face side to side.

For all the pain she was in, an excitement coursed through her. She was going to get to the bottom of everything. She had told him she never wanted to feel helpless again, hadn't she? A person could only take so much. It was good to know one's limits.

Henry swiped his hand down his smooth cheeks. "I look like I did as a boy," he said, and his face changed to that look of sorrow again, the return of his melancholy mood.

The pain in her leg was building, and she thought that this must be what it feels like to walk across hot coals, fire shooting from one's feet to the hip. The pus in her knee that Henry had tried to clean out earlier, well it was infected now, she was sure of it, but just how badly was yet to be seen.

She hated self-pity, and she thought about what Henry had said earlier, the way his parents' enthusiasm had filled him with dread, that whole forced optimism, all that manufactured safety. Her own mother had done the same with her, hadn't she? Practicing this kind of soul-crushing mentality, practicing a lie, living in denial that life was more complicated than what everyone would allow for. No one seemed to be saying what was really going on inside their own heads, and yet Olivay would guess that everyone at one time or another was thinking the exact same thing. Why wasn't sadness a legitimate and worthy feeling, when everyone had it? What about confusion, loneliness and distress? What was the point of living a lie?

"Wow," Henry said again, and Olivay excused herself to the bathroom.

Once inside, she shut the door and removed two sleeping pills she'd been prescribed back when Will was still alive and she used to get insomnia.

She ground the pills beneath the blue cosmetic bottle on the sink, ground it harder and harder, thinking of how peacefully Will used to sleep, how he'd never had any trouble at all once his head hit the pillow, as if his thoughts had been as innocent as hers, his life as honest as hers, and she ground and ground until she reached a nice, pulverized powder, which she swept off into her palm and into the pocket of her robe.

"How about a drink?" she said, coming out of the bathroom. "I think we should celebrate."

"I still can't find your network on here." He was on his computer.

Jesus. She had forgotten all about it. Thank goodness for the consistent trouble with technology.

"Who cares?" she said. "Let's have a drink."

"What are we celebrating?"

"Being alive."

He glanced up.

"Which is more than we can say for a lot of people, including the two people we used to love." She turned her back to him as she stood at the sink. "Do you like bourbon?"

"Sure."

"My beautiful coup glasses were broken in the blast, so you'll have to settle for something plain out of the cupboard."

Henry started to turn the TV on.

"No!" Olivay said. "Please don't. I just want, I just need to have this time with you right now if you don't mind, without the outside world interfering. Please. Just give us a few minutes without it."

Henry slowly lowered the remote. He nodded once, but she could see his look of concern.

"I can't get over how different you look," she said. "You sure clean up nice."

"I thought you liked my scruffy look."

"I did. I do. I like it all, Henry."

Henry started to get up. "Can I help you with any of that?"

"No, no. Please sit. I want this to be a normal moment between us. I'll be done in one second. Just relax. My only regret is that I don't have a mint sprig."

"What are you making?"

"A Kentucky Corpse Reviver."

"Jesus."

"You're in for a treat."

Olivay eyed his backpack. Always with him. Did he think she hadn't noticed?

She slid the container of sugar toward her, opened the lid and then turned just enough to hide that she was reaching into her pocket against the counter, pinching what she could of the powder and then pretending to reach into the sugar container before sprinkling what was between her fingers into the glass on the left. *Left, left, left,* sprinkling like sugar, and then she sprinkled real sugar on top of it and stirred briskly and everything dissolved as easily as she'd hoped. Then she finished preparing her own drink, sprinkling the sugar with her right hand. *Right, right, right.*

"All right, Henry. Here we go." She held the left glass in her left hand and Henry crossed the room to take it.

"Cheers," she said, clinking his glass with her own. "Bottoms up."

Olivay leaned over and turned music on from the sound system.

Henry drank. And drank. Olivay, too, though slower, of course, more a pretense than anything else.

Joni Mitchell shuffled onto play and Olivay was hit with a terrible, visceral sadness, remembering her mother at the piano, telling her how she loved the way her front room faced west, where the day ended, and that she could easily live out her entire life in that one room, and then went on to do mostly that, without complaint. Maybe this was why Olivay had felt so comfortable in a loft apartment—or used to feel, anyway—an entire life in one place, the closeness it had, or was supposed to have. Now Olivay pictured adjoining rooms and long hallways and doors that could shut and separate, close people off from each other, and she knew that if she lived another day that this was what she wanted.

"Whew," Henry said. "This stuff is potent. What did you put in here?"

"Bourbon, Curacao, a little lemon."

"Terrific."

"Some sleeping pills from the bathroom."

Henry laughed.

No one could call her a liar.

For a while they remained quiet, listening to the music, and then Henry moved toward the bed. Just before he sat down he glanced at her, understanding now that she wasn't joking, a knowledge that filled his arms and legs with a leaden feeling she knew too well, and everything about what was happening to him crossed his face before he collapsed on the bed with her name leaking from his lips.

She grabbed hold of his backpack. He wasn't even all the way out yet. He lifted a hand as if to stop her, or maybe to ask for help. Maybe he only wanted an explanation.

"I'm sorry, Henry. But it'll be all right. You haven't slept in days. You could use a rest."

His backpack contained his wallet, two small notebooks, three black pens, and one larger-sized and very tattered notebook with JE T'AIME written across the front. Loose papers and envelopes were shoved in between the pages of the larger one. She emptied everything out and set it aside, but when she lifted the backpack up it was still so heavy.

She slipped her hand down along the inside seams until she felt a bulky lump of some kind behind the vinyl and she peeled apart the Velcro strip of a pocket to set the bulky thing free. A tattered blue scarf had been wrapped around it, and Olivay knew what was inside the minute she felt the hard, cold metal. She was not expecting that. She made sure not to grab hold of it anywhere near the trigger, and lifted it out by the short barrel. A revolver. Just like the one she'd imagined in a box on her mantel. Instead of it being wrapped in blue velvet it was wrapped in blue cotton.

"Henry," she whispered. Adrenaline was taking over, her thoughts running circles through her mind.

She didn't feel so bad now about tying his wrists and ankles to the wooden legs of the bed. In fact, she further secured the binding with duct tape. Who knew how strong he was? Who knew how angry he could get when provoked?

FORTY-SEVEN

HENRY WAS NAKED AND CHILLED AND SPOOKED BY THE *dark and the river he could not see, only feel, rushing chest-deep against him. He didn't understand where he was, not at first, only that he needed to tread water before he could reach the bank. His bare feet sucked into the muddy riverbed as if it were a living thing forcing him to take root where he stood, while the current coursed against him, plunging him to his knees and he choked on silt and the waste of things he could not name.*

He understood now that he'd returned to the Central African Republic. They'd been expecting him, too, and this was why he'd gone into the river—to erase his footprints, his scent—to eliminate every last trace of himself.

He remembered Olivay and called out to her, but of course she couldn't hear him on the other side of the world, and what did it matter when his voice never made a sound? He remembered now, filled with a sickening panic, that she was no safer than he.

"Home?" they had said the day they shoved him into the back of the truck. "The place you come from. Home? HOME!" He did not understand where they were sending him. He had lived all over the world by

then. He would have barely understood the meaning of the word under the best of circumstances.

But that first night in Olivay's bed, the very first place that felt like . . . "Oh come on," *Jerry was saying to him now, berating him.* "Don't paint it with such sentimental bullshit. You think a guy in his underwear having coffee in the morning wants to read that shit first thing with his eggs?" *But it did, Jerry. It felt like home.*

"Can you hear me, Olivay?"

He was dizzy. He was sick and stumbling, smothering inside a gauzy web from which he could not escape, and he was begging to go back to the way he'd felt when he walked out of Levine's with her, his heart banging lopsidedly, filled with self-condemnation but exhilaration, too, thumping so off balance that he'd pressed against his chest with his open hand.

And now he slipped through in an opening in time, to waking that first night while she slept, to pacing the length of her windows in the dark, knitting strings of their conversation through in his mind, trying to understand how one act wove into the next, the consequence of one thing leading to another and another, walking around while his heart toppled onto his spleen, stirring waves of nausea, a swirling thrill broken only by the text from George, asking in the middle of the night to meet Henry for breakfast. Meet me at Levine's, *he'd said. I promise to be there this time. Three days in a row he'd promised but never showed for the first two, never appeared, thank God, the morning Henry sat down with Olivay.*

"Leave her alone," *Jerry had said.* "She's been through enough. Give her a goddamn break."

Olivay's life usurped by the public was no fault of Henry's. Her story's absorption into the collective consciousness was not his doing. He hadn't contributed to it, not even engaging others in conversation about her, except to ask Jerry what he thought about inviting her to coffee,

just a kindly invitation. "*Did you actually just use the word 'kindly'?*"
Jerry replied before walking away.

"*I have a plan, Henry,*" *George said at the coffee shop.* "*I need to
share it with you.*" *He pecked his dirty fingernails onto the table.* "*I
need you to understand.*"

*Just one coffee with Olivay. But then, by some miracle, Henry had
ended up in her bed, and he'd worried in those first hours that he'd
somehow taken advantage of her, forced her to do something she wasn't
ready to do. He couldn't have read her so completely wrong, could he?
She seemed to want him in the same way he wanted her. And yet he
couldn't get past the truth that her trauma was more recent than his.
Maybe he should have shown some kind of restraint. Should he have
been more careful with her? Or did he do the very thing she needed most?*

Olivay.

Olivay.

*Jesus Christ. What was the main idea here, the lede? The who,
what, when, where, and how? Henry couldn't keep his thoughts
straight. He needed to get out of this river. He was choking. He was
trying to answer Jerry's voice in his head—*"*So what's your story here,
kid? When are you going to get to the point?*"

FORTY-EIGHT

WHEN SHE OPENED THE LARGER NOTEBOOK, SEVERAL loose pages slipped out, and she laid them in a row on the floor where she could get a clear look at a set of very skilled drawings of flames, colored with orange, yellow, and red pencils. The trees and hillsides were engulfed, the charred homes among them smothered in smoke.

Olivay glanced up at the bed. A little light-headed, she held her forehead and rocked slightly, forward and back, whispering to herself like a madwoman. She would not jump to conclusions. There was an explanation here, it's just . . . She rocked and rocked. She hadn't expected something so . . . obviously incriminating to have to explain away.

Maybe someone had given these drawings to Henry. But if so, had he told the police? If not, why?

They weren't his.

They couldn't be his.

Maybe they could.

"Shit, shit, shit." What the hell *was* this stuff? Henry's eyelids were fluttering, his lips, too, but he was out. Deeply, deeply out. It would be at least eight hours before she could get an answer.

The pages looked old and used, lined with creases, the edges softened from being moved around, perhaps inside Henry's backpack, as they had surely been when the bombs went off, and when he secured it over his shoulders, and every time he took it with him to check for Wi-Fi outside.

Maybe Henry had known what was coming, but wasn't actually part of it. Will had been privy to details about crimes that even the cops didn't know, and cops knew things the courts didn't know. Journalists were like priests and doctors and lawyers, with a duty to protect confessions and sources, and in turn protect themselves. That didn't make them complicit to the crimes, did it? There were laws, there were limits, but in the end it was subjective. It came down to someone's judgment.

If you harbor a terrorist, *you* are a terrorist.

She examined the revolver in her open palm, turned it over and studied the other side, struck again by the heft of it. She held it up, taking extreme care to keep her fingers outside the trigger guard. She pointed it around the room at nothing, then at the Egg Chair in the corner, at Henry, at her own temple.

"POW," she said, and gently placed it on the floor.

She flipped the drawings over. The backs were covered with large, loopy phrases, writing that didn't look like it would belong to Henry, least not in a normal mental state. It appeared to have been written in a strange kind of code, some letters in caps, the rest lowercase, and several of the sentences spiraled down the page like a helix.

JEt fuel in the bombS—hiLLsides ignite more quickly, and harder to extinguish, especially with winds.

The illusion of stars, STARS. The Griffith Observatory. The Hollywood sign. What do you really see?

Olivay dropped the pages, unsure of what she'd held in her hands. The capital letters didn't seem to spell out anything of sense.

They seemed to be the ramblings of a madman. Henry? A split personality thing? "Goddamn it. I'm going to need you to wake up." Had he written this stuff to himself?

She managed to come to her feet in spite of her knee. What she needed right now was to pace. It would help her think. Running would be even better—long and hard, up the hills the way she used to when Will was alive, when she was so angry at him she couldn't stand to be in the same apartment—but Olivay wasn't going anywhere. She could hardly cross the room.

She made it to the wall, sweating, panting. She pressed her forehead against it, tapping lightly to get the answers flowing, but it didn't help the tiny fractures in her heart, the little openings busting to pieces. Henry, this stranger who had swept into her life without warning, Henry who had changed everything.

She needed to get this right.

And yet, she couldn't get past this nagging idea that the cause of his shaky hands, the thing that had him jumping up at the news about the fires, wasn't fear or frustration, but a different kind of adrenaline rush, a dizzy awareness that comes with seeing one's hard work finally set in motion. From blueprint to move-in, so to speak. It wasn't a journalist's reaction. She didn't think he'd be so suddenly troubled by hearing more bad news. Journalists were used to bad news. Bad news was all there ever was.

A knock on her door halted the spiraling inside her head.

Olivay turned to Henry, his mouth now slack in sleep. She hobbled over to him and pulled the duvet over the side of the bed to cover the twine and tape that bound him there.

Another knock at the door, and Olivay limped against the pain, and the knock came again just before she peered through the peephole at Mrs. Hightower.

She opened the door just a foot.

"Oh! Hello dear. You're up. Are you all right in there?"

"Of course," she whispered, her finger held to her lips. "I'm fine. We're fine. Just resting. Henry is completely out." She jerked her thumb toward the bed, but when Mrs. Hightower tried to see around the edge of the door, Olivay didn't allow it to budge.

"About that, about your friend there—"

"He's exhausted. So am I, of course. But you, you're looking fine through all of this. And the water is back on, the electricity. Thank goodness."

"Is he . . . tell me, dear, how long have you been seeing one another? I haven't noticed him coming around before yesterday."

"Well, you know how I am . . . discreet, because of, well, of course you know. But he and I have, it's been a while, some weeks already. I'll let you in on a little secret."

Mrs. Hightower leaned in with wide eyes.

"He's a journalist, too. A colleague of Will's."

She drew her head slightly back and covered her mouth before dropping it. "So that's how you know one another then?"

Olivay nodded. "But nothing ever . . . I mean, we never, you know . . . while Will was still alive."

"Oh, really, you needn't tell me everything."

"I just thought you might be thinking . . ."

"Certainly not. Just thinking of your welfare."

"And I appreciate that."

"Did you see the sketches?" Mrs. Hightower asked.

"Yes, I did. We did."

"He resembles . . ."

"Oh, yes, we noticed that, too! Where do they get these artists? Those renderings are so generic. They never really look like the criminals in the end, aside from skin color. But yes, we had a good laugh about that one guy looking similar to Henry. Is that what you mean?"

Mrs. Hightower laughed quietly and shook her head as if embarrassed. "Oh, dear, just, well, never you mind. Go get some rest with your beau. If you need anything, don't hesitate." She pet Olivay's shoulder and apologized for bothering her. "Everyone is a bit riled, you understand. Naturally, with the fires and evacuations, everything so unexpected and terrible. I apologize."

Olivay took her hand. "I appreciate you looking out for me. Always. Thank you. It's late. You should get some rest yourself. My guess is it'll all be over by tomorrow."

FORTY-NINE

*THEY WOULD BE COMING FOR HIM, IF THEY WEREN'T
already. Of this he was certain.*

*It was impossible to see in the black of night, but he knew they
needed to kill him. They were going to kill him. "You have every right,"
he said. He knew too much. He'd known, and yet, he'd stopped no one
from doing anything—except that soldier, a man Henry had no right
to stop, not like that, no proof at all, nothing but the stories of boys, and
that greedy, knowing smirk on the soldier's face as Henry walked past,
and then the wicked satisfaction of having killed him, as if that alone
meant justice had been served, how it rushed through Henry when he
slit the man's throat, a conqueror's satisfaction—that was him, that
was Henry, pleased with himself on a level that wasn't even human.*

*The Creek Spirits roiled like worms in his gut, in his throat,
squeezing off his air.*

FIFTY

HENRY STARTED MAKING STRANGE NOISES, A STRING OF whimpering moans. His throat jerked upward as if caught in a series of small convulsions. Convulsions? Not exactly. What was he doing? Olivay worried he may be trying to vomit in his sleep. But then he calmed again, his chest rising and falling softly.

She glanced down at her open computer on the floor next to her. She'd been reading—

a) How to shoot a revolver. Because, who knew?

b) About Genevieve. Her last name was Bonnet, and *her killer was never found*. Henry had lied to her about this. Why would he lie?

c) Henry's articles on Climate Change and Net Neutrality. He was a really good writer. He knew a lot about a lot of things. He also wrote in French for *Le Monde* in France and *La Presse* in Montreal; the articles were there with his byline, though she couldn't read them.

She learned these things by going through his backpack:

a) He wrote strange sentences on small scraps of paper. Philosophical notes, it seemed, *happiness, not in another place . . .* Were they his writings or copied from someone else?

b) He'd been keeping close tabs on the fire, as well as the timeline of everything that happened yesterday morning, and so when Pendleton had asked specifics about what time Henry did what, Henry faked the whole bit about not knowing exactly. It was all there in his notebook. *Levine's, 9:06, waiting in the second booth on the right. Was quiet a minute ago but now filling up. Eleven customers and counting.*

c) *Saw Olivay two days in a row. Still no sign of George.*

George? He hadn't mentioned anything about meeting his brother.

d) The thing he told her about the kid and the motorcycle, that boy Luke. It appeared to be true. He'd kept track of their conversations, had added up all the facts. This line from the kid, "I don't know how to live now," was circled repeatedly in black pen.

And now Henry was making noises again, grunting and gurgling, his head lolling to the side. It had been an hour since he'd fallen asleep. Was it two? His throat was doing that funny thing again.

"Shit, shit, shit." He really was trying to throw up. She needed to roll him over before he choked to death, but when she pulled at the twine and duct tape on his wrist to undo the knots, it wouldn't come loose.

"Henry!" she yelled, as his throat jerked again, and without thinking she jumped off the bed and ran toward the cupboard for the pot he had grabbed for her earlier, only she couldn't run, of course she couldn't, and fell to the floor and smacked her knee.

If the neighbors never heard her cry before, they surely heard her now. She screamed and kicked the kitchen chair over with her good leg. She flung his backpack across the room and screamed again. She screamed between catching her breath as she squirmed to the counter and pulled herself up, every curse word she'd ever known flying from her mouth as she grabbed a bowl from the counter and hopped across the room back to Henry, who appeared to be gasping for air.

She held his head sideways off the pillow, lifted it at an angle, and Henry let loose a stream of yellow bile into the bowl. It smelled like chemicals, like the pills and alcohol. He threw up several more times, and began to cough. His eyes slowly opened and closed.

She hopped to the bathroom, cursing again, and retrieved a wet washcloth, which she used to wipe his face, the sweat now forming on his forehead. She sat with him, asking him to wake up, asking him questions about the stuff in his backpack as if he might understand, and who was to say he couldn't in whatever state he was lost to.

The vomiting had cleared his body of some of the sleeping pills. An hour later he was trying to sit up, and when he did his hands, of course, didn't come up with the rest of him, and he fell back, his eyes widening at the sight of being bound. He sunk into the mattress and stared at her like he was staring at someone he had never seen before in his life.

"You lied to me, Henry," Olivay said.

He squinted so hard his eyes nearly closed. She had turned on all the lights.

Henry pulled at his feet and wrists once more.

"What is all of this?" She held up his notebook and the drawings. "How are you involved in what's happened, Henry? What have you done?"

She picked up the revolver. "And for fuck's sake, Henry."

He began to pull at his wrists, hard. He was furious now, and no matter how she tried to calm him he wouldn't stop flailing, and he began to scream at her to let him up, so she stuffed his mouth with the first thing handy, the blue scarf from his backpack.

"Now. Please." Olivay scooted slightly away. "Let's just calm down."

He was quiet after that. He nodded *okay*. He had gotten the hang of what was happening here.

She held the revolver again. "Okay. What is this, Henry? It really needs to be addressed, don't you think?"

Of course he couldn't answer with the scarf in his mouth.

She lay the gun down on the floor and picked up her laptop, and she could see how shaky her hands were and she tried to steady them, tried to show she was in control when she turned her computer so Henry could see the screen. "The police sketch," she said. "But even then, I wasn't sure. You know how bad those renderings are."

Henry stared. He wasn't even trying to speak.

"I didn't find any hat or sunglasses in your backpack, but then again, you kept taking it with you every time you went out. I did find these drawings, though." She held them up, and his face turned hard, his eyes appeared to well up. "I remembered how jumpy you got when the news reported the fires breaking out. So, tell me. What is all this stuff? What in God's name have you done?"

FIFTY-ONE

WHAT HAD HE DONE?

He growled and shook his head for her to remove the scarf from his mouth, and she did, slowly, timidly, as if she were afraid.

"Olivay," he whispered, his head sinking into the pillow, eyes closed. Where to begin? "Please put the gun away, Olivay," he said. "It's dangerous."

She laughed. "Said the man carrying it around in his backpack."

"It doesn't belong to me," he said, and then he stopped before explaining that he'd stolen it months ago from George's apartment, and that he knew now that George was responsible for the attacks, that George had played some role in it with several other people. He didn't tell her how much he and George looked alike, how close in age they were—Catholic twins, people said—how close they once had been. He didn't tell her, couldn't tell her, that he hadn't seen George since the day he stole the gun and the drawings from his brother's apartment, not until George asked to meet at Levine's. Henry couldn't bring himself to say that he brought the gun with him to Levine's to protect himself against his brother, while at once charged with the need

to protect George, too. He didn't tell her because he had no way of knowing where it was all headed, and he needed to protect her, too.

"Have you gone to the police?" Henry asked.

"Not yet," she said. "But I can't speak for the neighbors."

FIFTY-TWO

THEY HAD ALL DONE THEIR BAD THINGS, HADN'T THEY?
Will, Henry, and of course, Olivay—sending Will out the door to
his death, and the way she had slowly stopped missing him, her
own husband, their *Camelot* of a life. And now she didn't think
she would ever forgive him for betraying her, even as he lay dead in
the ground, she was sure she was going to hold that grudge, be just
that petty because it was all she had left against him, against the
way he'd tried to shame her for accusing him, the way he'd tried to
make her think her suspicions were petty, and therefore so was she.
It was almost funny now. Almost. And here she had fallen in love
overnight with a man who was somehow involved in something
beyond atrocious. She had tied him up in her apartment. She was
holding his gun.

"God help us both," she said.

"Please put it away."

Of all the people in the world, he had fished her out. And then
the world reset, just like the lion's roar.

"I need you to tell me everything," she said.

"Untie me," he said.

"Not until you tell me."

The ringing in her ears came back to fill the quiet. She sat up straight, turned her head side to side. The quiet was too extreme. Olivay didn't think she'd heard the absence of noise in just this way since living in that apartment. And two of the windows were out, no less. What was causing such an eerie silence?

She felt a little sick with herself, trembling with all kinds of pain. She needed his confession. She needed to know that what she'd felt for him, what she was feeling even now, didn't make her a horrible person. She began to cry, and slid off the bed and walked around the room through her grunts and seething tears, walking and crying, riddled with pain. Henry called out to her, but she covered her ears against the sound of his voice, everything feeling so finite now, this room like a box where all of eternity was about to play out.

FIFTY-THREE

*"I NEED YOU TO DO SOMETHING FOR ME, OLIVAY. I NEED YOU
to believe me when I tell you that I am not responsible for what's happened, but that I know who is."*

She spun around to face him.

*"I need you to understand that I didn't quite believe him at first, I
didn't want to believe him, and so I didn't try to stop him, and I will
have to live with that for the rest of my life."*

"Why?" she asked.

"What do you mean?"

*"Why do you need this from me?" she asked, but of course she knew
why, of course she did, it was all there in her face, in her eyes, in the
way she had touched him, been with him, in the way she was pleading
with him now to give her some kind of peace.*

*If only he had peace to offer her. If only she could offer him the
same. But people like them didn't go on to live peaceful lives. They did
the best they could with what was left.*

"That's not the whole story," she said. "That's not your whole story."

"You're right. It's not."

"Oh, Christ, Henry."

"I've done something awful. Something unspeakable. But it has nothing to do with today."

"Did you kill her?"

"Who?"

"Genevieve."

"Jesus, Olivay. No. Of course I didn't kill her."

"Well, whoever did was never found. You lied to me, Henry. You've lied to me so many times. And the thing is, you didn't need to. You understand that, right? You could have told me everything from the start."

"I didn't kill her, Olivay. I swear to you. It wasn't me."

He watched as she peered through the windows, down the street, and into the back alleyway. If they were coming for him—and he believed it was only a matter of time; if not Pendleton, then a call from Mrs. Hightower to the hotline would surely send someone on their way—and they would enter through the back door of the building and this was where Olivay continued to check, thinking as he thought, feeling what he felt.

"I believe you," she said.

"Untie me."

FIFTY-FOUR

ABOVE OLIVAY'S DESK HUNG A QUOTE FROM THE Norwegian architect Sverre Fehn:

Each material has its own shadow. The shadow of stone is not the same as that of a brittle autumn leaf.

She stood next to it, running her fingers across it when she looked out into the dark alley and she saw what she had been expecting to see for hours. A team of men slipping into the building.

FIFTY-FIVE

HENRY HAD SO MUCH TO TELL HER. HE WOULD GET TO IT all, to the village at noon, and he would spare no detail, he wouldn't stop until he'd told her everything.

He had felt the consequence of everything, would continue to feel it for the rest of his life, however long that turned out to be.

And what of it? What now? Like Luke after his brother's motorcycle had flown out of his control, after he'd ended Will's life—how would Henry live now, forever associated with his brother, the terrorist? How would he make a living now? Jerry would be forced to let him go. Who would hire him? Strangers would threaten to kill him. Where could he live in the world after this and ever feel safe again?

And Olivay. What about Olivay?

FIFTY-SIX

SHUSH, SHUSH, SHUSH. SHE UNTIED HIM AND ASKED HIM
to stay right there on the bed next to her and he said he would. He
had not seen her slip the revolver beneath the duvet. She didn't
think he had.

They lay on their backs, holding hands.

She recalled, as a child, sitting beneath the blue rays of a beach
umbrella against the sun and how it had turned her arms the same
blue as the ocean, as if the color alone had cooled her from the heat.

The most beautiful things in the world were the most useless.
Peacocks and lilies, for instance.

She had turned the intercom on so that any sound in the hall
would be magnified, and now she could hear the soft squeak of their
boots on the other side of the door, the creak of their equipment
as they readied themselves, prepared to bust the door wide open,
and take Henry, and perhaps her, too, for keeping him safe. If you
harbor a terrorist . . .

FIFTY-SEVEN

THEY'D BOTH LOST EVERYONE THEY'D EVER CARED ABOUT.
A dangerous place from which to connect to someone new.
But he loved her. How he loved Olivay.

FIFTY-EIGHT

THEY'D BOTH LOST EVERYONE THEY'D EVER CARED ABOUT.
A dangerous place from which to connect to someone new.
But she loved him. How she loved Henry.

FIFTY-NINE

TIMING.

Her mother's insistence that the whole of life could be contained in a song—listen to the rise and fall, the violence and forgiveness, the suspense in tension, not knowing how it could end, and therein lies the beauty, and there the two of them lay on their backs, Olivay and Henry, holding hands like Pompeii lovers, though they were not dead, not yet, just quiet and staring at the cracked white ceiling, while Olivay clutched the piece of paper from Henry's backpack in her free hand, the hand near the revolver, near the paper that read, *Happiness, not in another place but this place . . . not for another hour, but this hour*, and the ink blurred from her sweat until the words were no longer clear when she opened her palm to read them, but she'd known what it said and she closed the paper back inside, and they held hands and looked forward, looked upward, looked to where one could see the other, and they understood without question that each was the other's entire world.

Acknowledgments

First and foremost, a huge thank you to my agent Larry Kirshbaum for his friendship and counsel no matter where I find myself in the world. What a wonderfully strange and fortuitous meeting of the minds we have.

Thank you, Terry Goodman, Jodi Warshaw, David Downing, Jessica Poore, Gabriella Van den Heuvel, Jacque Ben-Zekry, and Dennelle Catlett for such tremendous support of my work and me, several years running now.

And thank you my fellow writers, early readers, dear friends, and new acquaintances. I am honored by your willingness to read my initial, problematic drafts, and/or answer my random questions, and support me in various ways this past year. Stephanie Bane, Tabitha Blankenbiller, Sean Davis, Lindy Dekoven, Sharon Harrigan, Adrianne Kalfopoulou, Chrissy Leavell, Amalia Melis, Sheila Redling, Nancy Rommelmann (you deserve a medal, my dear, dancing friend), Leigh Rourks, and Major John Gilbert USMC, retired, who answered my questions about terrorist attacks. If I messed up it's my fault, not yours. Same goes for you, Stephanie Bane, for your time and generous advice on the Peace Corps and Africa, and for helping to guide my way through unknown territory. Any discrepancies or false notes are solely due to me.

I am grateful for the support of Kathie Hightower and Vera Wildauer, whose generosity toward so many writers is humbling and tireless, and whose generosity and kindness toward me and this particular novel in the 11th hour have forever earned my gratitude.

A huge thank you to Pauline Brown for being such a steadfast reader and supporter, for telling so many others about my books, and without whom I may have never heard the name of her sister, *Olivay*.

Thank you, Holly Lorincz, for jumping in at the last minute to save the day. What a wonderful surprise to have found you again.

Thank you Andrew, Dylan, Kelley, Liam, Lou, Biggie, and in memory of Bunch, who was still around when I began this novel. What a funny, wildly creative, and inspiring family you are. Thank you Dad, Mom, and Tom for the constant encouragement and laughter, and for recommending my books to everyone you meet.

I would like to thank the people of Boston and those who were affected by the Boston Marathon bombings. My heart was with you that day, and always, in peace.

And finally I want to thank my students, old and new, whose eagerness and love of the written word keep the conversation going, keep the art alive, and inspire in me ever-changing ways to get it right.

About the Author

Deborah Reed's novel, *Things We Set on Fire*, sold over one hundred thousand copies in the first six months, while *Carry Yourself Back to Me* was a Best Book of 2011 Amazon Editors Pick. She wrote the bestselling thriller, *A Small Fortune*, and its sequel, *Fortune's Deadly Descent*, under her pen name Audrey Braun. Several of her novels have been translated or are forthcoming in German. Her nonfiction has appeared in publications such as the *Literarian, MORE*, and *Poets & Writers*. She holds a master's degree in fine arts in creative writing, and teaches at the UCLA Extension Writing Program. She is also codirector of the Black Forest Writing Seminar at the University of Freiburg in Germany. She resides in Los Angeles.